D1038584

SUZI CLUE

THE PROM QUEEN CURSE

MICHELLE KEHM

DUTTON CHILDREN'S BOOKS

DUTTON CHILDREN'S BOOKS | A division of Penguin Young Readers Group

Published by the Penguin Group | Penguin Group (USA) Inc., 375 Hudson Street, New York, New York 10014, U.S.A. | Penguin Group (Canada), 90 Eglinton Avenue East, Suite 700, Toronto, Ontario M4P 2Y3, Canada (a division of Pearson Penguin Canada Inc.) | Penguin Books Ltd, 80 Strand, London WC2R 0RL, England | Penguin Ireland, 25 St Stephen's Green, Dublin 2, Ireland (a division of Penguin Books Ltd) | Penguin Group (Australia), 250 Camberwell Road, Camberwell, Victoria 3124, Australia (a division of Pearson Australia Group Pty Ltd) | Penguin Books India Pvt Ltd, 11 Community Centre, Panchsheel Park, New Delhi - 110 017, India | Penguin Group (NZ), 67 Apollo Drive, Rosedale, North Shore 0632, New Zealand (a division of Pearson New Zealand Ltd.) | Penguin Books (South Africa) (Pty) Ltd, 24 Sturdee Avenue, Rosebank, Johannesburg 2196, South Africa | Penguin Books Ltd, Registered Offices: 80 Strand, London WC2R 0RL, England

CIP data is available.

Published in the United States by Dutton Children's Books,
a division of Penguin Young Readers Group
345 Hudson Street, New York, New York 10014
www.penguin.com/youngreaders

Designed by Heather Wood

Printed in USA | First Edition

ISBN 978-0-525-47953-6 | 10 9 8 7 6 5 4 3 2 1

for the tomato lady

SUZI CLUE
THE PROM QUEEN CURSE

Mountain High Prom Night, Circa 1988

Prologue

Kathryn had never been happier in her whole life. She had a hot boyfriend (he looked just like that dreamy Rob Lowe from St. Elmo's Fire, so who cared if he flunked senior year), a totally rad bod (thanks to Jane Fonda and her awesome workout tapes), the perfectly ratted Madonna 'do, and she had just been accepted on a sports scholarship to UCLA. She couldn't wait to get out of her boring Seattle suburb where it rained 360 days a year and all the guys sported flannel shirts and stringy mullets although the George Michael big-hair look was très today. No, Kathryn had bigger plans on her horizon, like sunshine, palm trees, and salty surfers galore.

But tonight Kathryn was happy to be exactly where she was. Tonight was the night she was to be named Mountain High's prom queen, 1988! She couldn't believe it. Well, that's not entirely true. She could believe it a little. After all, she was sooo popular at school. She was perfectly fake 'n baked, blond, and tore through the school parking lot in her convertible '88 Volkswagen Rabbit (graduation gift from the folks). Plus, she was the school's varsity volleyball star to boot. Success and good looks were totally her bag.

But all her fabulous fortune aside, Kathryn did have one small problem—and it was named Porsche Pettibone.

Porsche was Kathryn's only viable competition for the crown tonight. Like Kathryn, Porsche was blond, popular, and gorgeous, but Porsche had the one thing Kathryn didn't have—a set of killer pom-poms. While Kathryn racked up blue ribbons, Porsche racked up brownie points for looking oh so cute in her cheerleading uniform. Kathryn knew the whole school loved her for her peppy school spirit and performance on the court—but everybody flat-out worshipped Porsche. She was the school's sweetheart sundae with a cherry on top, and everybody wanted a spoon.

But if Kathryn's dad had taught her anything in her eighteen years, he had taught her to succeed. How else would she have racked up the mantel full of first-place trophies for almost every sport under the sun? First and foremost, Kathryn was a winner, a blue-ribbon-only type of gal, and she was treating the prom queen ceremony tonight as she would any other competition—she was going to defeat the enemy.

So, wearing Vaseline on her teeth and a smile from ear to ear, Kathryn was standing tall, proud, and confident, up onstage in front of the whole school, in her electric-blue Jessica McClintock dress and high-heeled Candies, while the sounds of her favorite song, Duran Duran's "Save a Prayer," bounced off the gym walls and swirled around her head. The whole scene was a little surreal, Kathryn thought, her being up onstage in a beautiful dress with the music and spotlights and the crown just moments away. She felt like Princess Diana must have on the day of her wedding. It was almost too much!

The prom queen court was down to the last two girls—Kathryn and Porsche, of course. After thanking the last three contestants and hustling them offstage (losers . . . Kathryn smiled to herself), the school principal, Ms. Stern, stepped back up to the microphone and the music died down.

This was it. The big moment. Kathryn was oh so ready. That crown was oh so hers.

Just then, Porsche's boyfriend, Mr. Macho Quarterback, walked up to Ms. Stern and handed her a gorgeous bouquet of red roses, a sparkily pink rhinestone crown—and one single white envelope. The envelope. Kathryn's eyes were locked on target.

But suddenly some idiot turned the spotlight on high, and Kathryn lost all sight of the envelope, the victory bouquet, and even the school sweetheart standing next to her. Kathryn was completely blinded. All she could see was the dull gray hair on the back of Ms. Stern's head; the crowd, and the rest of the gym were swallowed in darkness. Kathryn found herself suddenly disorientated by her blindness, the unforgiving heat of the lights, the tightness of her dress, and the overbearing smell of Porsche's Love's Baby Soft perfume, but she kept it all together— like a pro. She just wished Ms. Stern would read the damn envelope already and get this over with.

Suddenly something soft touched Kathryn's left fingertips, and she realized with a jerk that Porsche had reached out with a delicate porcelain hand and grabbed Kathryn's bigger, rougher, athletic hand. Porsche moved a step closer to Kathryn and smiled up at her, and Kathryn noticed that Porsche was wearing blue mascara to accent her eyes. Kathryn smiled back, and on impulse, gave Porsche's hand a little squeeze of acknowledgment, albeit she did it just a little too hard.

Just then, as Kathryn was (still) staring down into Porsche's deep blue eyes, Porsche suddenly broke her grasp and flung her hands up to her face. She was shaking, really shaking, and Kathryn just thought that Porsche couldn't handle the stress of the moment any longer. Then Porsche's eyes started bugging out of her head in a most unflattering way, and she started to cry, really cry. It's okay, Kathryn thought as she comforted Porsche mentally. It's nothing personal, I'm just a natural-born winner, she smiled smugly to herself.

But then Kathryn noticed that Porsche was holding the bouquet of red roses, the victory roses, up to her perfectly upturned little nose and her boyfriend the quarterback was placing the pink tiara on Porsche's angelic blond locks. Wait a minute, Kathryn thought, I thought the roses and the tiara were for the winner, not the runner-up. Hey, what the hell is going on here?

Kathryn felt a sudden chill in the air as she realized that the heat of the spotlight had gone down on her tanned, strapless shoulders and risen on Porsche in all her delicate, porcelain, pristine glory.

And that night at the prom, up onstage and under the spotlight, as Porsche held her bodacious bouquet of red roses, her sparkily tiara glistening like a halo atop her perfectly blond locks, Mountain High's newest prom queen (read: not Kathryn) gave her acceptance speech as tears of joy streaked blue mascara down her rosy cheeks. It was only when Kathryn felt the warm sting of tears on her own cheeks that she realized she, too, was crying. But unlike Porsche, and all the other prom queens crowned across America that same night, Kathryn's tears weren't out of joy, excitement, or undiluted happiness.

Kathryn cried out of stone-cold anger.

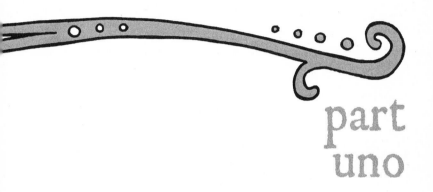

part
uno

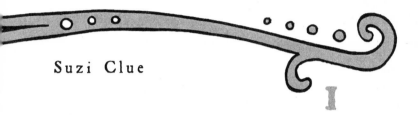

Suzi Clue

"Suzi Clue, ma chérie, your eyes are like pools of light, your skin like snow, your hair like . . . a luscious pink cupcake . . . and your lips, oh, your lips are like a sweet candy that I just have to taste . . . if I may . . ."

Suzi was in heaven. Xavier's French accent could make a soup-can label sound like poetry. She was immune to the chill of the spring day and the wet grass seeping through the picnic blanket and into her bright pink overalls. Heck, Suzi didn't even feel the painful little pink blisters on her fingers from her new drumsticks.

All she could feel was Xavier Fontaine's soft lips on hers.

Xavier Fontaine. His name alone was dreamy enough to melt Suzi into a little pool of goo. He was French. He wore cool European clothes. He had a sexy accent. He was the hottie exchange student every cheerleader at school was shaking her pom-poms for this year, and here he was kissing her, Suzi Clue! Freshman nobody. Little miss indie girl. Suzi tried her hardest to be different from the swarms of perky, tan girls with creamy blond highlights who ruled her school—and she had succeeded. Most of the boys at school walked by her with hardly a glance. But considering most of the boys at Mountain High were frat boys in training, she didn't want much to do with them anyway. Well, except for one. And here they were, together at long last, totally making out on the grassy bank of the Seine River in Paris. And we're not talking Paris, Texas!

Xavier and Suzi had awoken that wonderful Parisian morning, walked to a cute little café for croissants and coffee (the best coffee Suzi had ever tasted and she was from Seattle), toured the Pompidou and the Louvre museums (Xavier knew so much about art), and now they were picnicking on a soft grassy knoll, enjoying French cheese, bread, and of course, kisses.

"Thank you so much, my darling, for coming to Paris to visit my parents. I so much wanted them to meet you," Xavier said as he reached out, adjusted Suzi's beret, and looked deeply into her eyes. "Of course they love you. Almost as much as I do."

Suzi just died. She really was in heaven.

"But why me, Xavier, when you could have any girl at school?" she asked coyly.

"Because you are different, *ma chérie*," Xavier whispered in a French drawl. "Wonderfully different. I love the colors you put in your hair, your clothes, your sophistication, your worldly flair. You are more like a Frenchwoman than any girl at Mountain High. You would fit in here very, very well."

Suzi silently agreed, smiled at Xavier, and looked around at the fabulousness of her surroundings. She had never been to Paris before, and she had certainly never been kissed like this before. Everything was happening so fast, so perfectly, and she loved it.

Suzi turned to face Xavier, suddenly more turned on than ever before. She reached out to cradle his face, admiring how his dark brown eyebrows contrasted with her powder-blue nail polish, and started making out with him big-time.

They lay down together on the blanket, rolled over onto the cheese, and held on to each other like a last breath. Xavier was stroking Suzi's hair and it felt so, so good. She was pulling him in as close as she could, she couldn't get enough of his lips. This was it, this was the moment she had been waiting for her whole life . . . God, Suzi loved France . . .

I'm Slim Shady, yes, I'm the real Shady all the other Slim Shadys are just imitating . . .

Suzi looked up from her make-out session with Xavier. Where was that annoying music coming from? Eminem was so not France and this was so not the moment . . .

So will the real Slim Shady please stand up, please stand up, please stand up . . .

Suzi looked around at the tourist boats, the sun reflecting off the Seine, the birds, the buildings . . . she looked at Xavier's sexy eyes and hands and lips . . . and then, just like that, her French bubble burst.

On instinct, she reached out and slapped at the snooze button. It was 7:30 A.M. Monday morning. A school morning. In Seattle, Washington. Seven thousand miles from Paris.

"It's seven-thirty, sweetheart," Suzi's mom said a moment later as she lightly knocked on her daughter's door.

"'Kay, mom," Suzi said. She rolled over with a grunt and looked outside her window at another gray rainy May day. This was so not cool. Only fifteen more minutes of sleep and maybe she would have gone all the way with the sexiest man to ever roam the halls of boring Mountain High. Well, that idea made her a tad nervous, but at least she would have seen more museums and drunk red wine with lunch. The French were so cool about that stuff.

Suzi kicked off her comforter and put her feet on her bedroom floor. A black guitar pick stuck to the bottom of her right foot, probably her best friend Jett's, and Suzi played with it between her toes for a few minutes as she contemplated the day before her. She had a Spanish vocab quiz, which she was pretty sure she'd ace, she had to meet with her Spanish teacher, Ms. Picante, about her being a teacher's assistant, and she had some kind of an assembly during fourth period that she could probably ditch and ride her bike to her favorite sushi joint for a quick lunch.

No problem, Suzi thought to herself as she procrastinated getting up a moment longer and let her gaze linger around her room. Posters of some of her favorite rock icons were taped to her walls. The Ramones standing outside CBGB in New York City, Death Cab for Cutie looking cute as a button, and Sleater-Kinney looking fierce in a forest (drummer Janet Weiss was Suzi's personal inspiration).

Suzi's shoes were lined up against her wall, everything from Converse to Chinese slippers, and her CDs were strewn about the room. Dog-eared mysteries lined her bedroom bookshelves and were stacked two feet high on her nightstand. Her latest knitting project, a pair of black arm warmers, lay on top. Suzi couldn't wait to wear them with her zebra tee and her hot pink skinny jeans. They were going to look so awesome—but speaking of clothes, it was high time Suzi put some on.

"Elvis," she said, looking over at her black Lab, who cracked one eye when Suzi mentioned her name. "I think this gray day needs a splash of color, don't you?"

She picked out a fuchsia sweatshirt that she had cut the neck out of. She paired it with a black tee to hide her bra straps (so tacky), a clean pair of black Levi's, and her favorite, scuffed-up pink cowboy boots. She topped it all off with a black beret.

Very cool, in a Frenchy eighties sort of way.

Suzi was thinking about how perfectly her boots were going to match the pink streak she had put in her naturally jet-black bangs this weekend, when all of a sudden it hit her like a brick.

Oh. My. Gosh.

The assembly today at school. It was the preprom assembly. The prom was this week. It was prom week.

With a precious five minutes left until her mom would make the rounds again, Suzi sank back into bed, beret and all, pulled the comforter over her head, and stared into the darkness.

It was going to be a very long week.

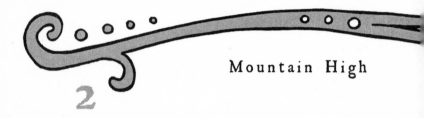

Mountain High

2

"Oh my gosh. I am so excited! Aren't you just so excited? I am going to look so hot, Chet is going to crap his Calvins!" These were the first words Suzi heard as she entered Mountain High. They came from the lips of head cheerleader Gigi Greene, who was standing by her locker with her posse of cheerleaders and other beautiful girls with big boobs, white teeth, and perfect hair. But Gigi was the Queen Bee. Tall, skinny, and blond. Fake blond, of course, but a good fake blond, even Suzi had to admit.

"Don't you know it, Gee!" Gigi's best friend and cheerleading partner in crime, Kitty Sui, said to Gigi. Kitty was drop-dead gorgeous, with long, glossy black hair that Suzi would've killed for, and flawless skin. Kitty was Gigi's right-hand gal, and they shared everything—clothes, boyfriends, even the same cup at keg parties. Needless to say, Kitty and Gigi had been best friends for almost two whole years.

"He's going to want to take a big bite out of you," Kitty said as she fake-bit Gigi in the neck like a vampire. Gigi and the gang giggled. "No, serious," she continued, "do you know which dress you're going to wear yet, the red one or the white one?"

"Well, the red one is racy and sexy, and the white one is pure and virginal," Gigi said. She said "racy and red" with a spicy rolling r and "pure and virginal" in a little whisper as she looked up, supposedly at a halo that wasn't there.

"So considering my plans for after the dance," Gigi continued, "I guess I'll go for the r-r-racy r-r-red . . ."

All the girls erupted in fits of high-pitched laughter.

This whole time, Suzi was trying to make her way through the crowd to her locker. Unfortunately for her, Suzi's locker was right next to Gigi's.

Suzi rolled her eyes, put on a polite smile, and managed to squeeze through the mass of miniskirts and hair spray. She opened her locker and kept to herself, but she couldn't block out the girls' conversation. It was like a car crash, her curiosity was too strong.

"We should rent a limo and get everyone in there and have champagne as we drive around," Gigi was saying. "Yes! Let's get a Hummer limo!"

"A Hummer! Definitely!" Parker Peets chimed in as she pulled her long blond hair back into a quick ponytail. Parker was another one of Gigi's best friends. She was the school's tennis star and as wicked on the court as she was off. Rumor had it that Parker ate her Wheaties, and boyfriends, for breakfast.

"But no champagne for me, man, or coach will—" Parker continued.

"My dad can get us a Hummer," a girl named Trixie Topp interrupted. Everyone stopped talking and looked at her uncomfortably. Trixie was cute, in a very suburban sort of way. She always hung out with the A-list girls, and they let her for the most part because her dad was loaded. Trixie could always pay for a cab ride home, a shoulder-tap tip, or a round of skinny vanilla lattes with whip. But Trixie's closet was full of khakis and plain cotton tees (expensive ones, mind you, but boring), and her studious, Goody Two-shoes taste didn't really mesh with the other girls' sexy miniskirts, low-cut cashmere sweaters, and high-heeled boots. But Trixie had her daddy in her back khaki pocket and his Visa in her pink Coach clutch, and that was her ticket to ride the popular crowd. Or rather, for them to ride her.

"Yeah," Trixie continued, her voice high and promising. "My dad knows somebody who owns a limo service, so I'm sure he can help us out and get a good—"

"Do it then," Gigi snapped. "We're running out of time, so just make sure it seats six."

"Six?" Trixie asked, swallowing her gum. "But what about me and my—"

"Oh, yeah. I forgot about you," Gigi said. "Make it eight. I guess," she snapped.

Trixie nodded and, her moment of glory over, sank back into the circle.

Suzi slammed her locker shut and started making her way back into the open space of the hallway when she heard her name.

"Hey, Suzi Clue." It was Gigi Greene. Talking to her. Which wasn't that uncommon, they weren't enemies or anything, and their lockers were right by each other.

"Hey, Gigi," Suzi said.

"I like your bangs. *Très* cool," Gigi said.

"Thanks. I did them myself," Suzi responded, still moving through the crowd. Must. Keep. Moving.

"So what do you use on them, like food dye or cherry juice or something?" Gigi asked. The girls laughed a little, not sure if it was meant to be a joke. Better laugh and play it safe.

Suzi just furrowed her black brows at Gigi, contemplating the statement. Suzi took her hair color very, very seriously.

"No, really," Gigi continued. "I use lemons on my hair, and carrot juice sometimes if I want a strawberry-blond tint, so I was just wondering."

"Panic Attack. Cupcake Pink. It matches my boots," Suzi said, as she finally broke free of the crowd.

And with that, the girls did erupt in laughter, and Suzi was sure they were laughing at her, not with her. Except for Gigi. She seemed genuinely interested for a moment.

Suzi flipped her shoulder-length black shag and just kept putting one pink cowboy boot in front of the other. She knew she had better fashion sense than all those girls combined. Besides, Suzi wanted to get some coffee in the cafeteria before first period.

If she couldn't have France, well, at least she could have French drip.

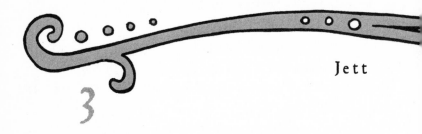

3

Jett

"Hey, girl, *bonjour*," said a voice from behind Suzi.

Suzi was standing in line for her desperately needed cup of coffee, and the voice was from Jett Black, guitar player, future photographer, and Suzi's best friend.

"I prayed this weekend for the first time in years," Jett continued, her voice dry and cynical. "Prayed this cursed school would burn to ashes. But God, like everybody else at this school, apparently doesn't listen to a word I say."

Suzi loved Jett's cynicism. She could always trust Jett to tell it like it was, straight up, even in the most awkward of circumstances. That blunt honesty, and a mutual love for fashion, art, music, and Asian food, are what had kept Suzi and Jett best friends since the third grade.

"God, Jett," Suzi said as she swung around to face Jett, cup of joe in hand. "Puh-lease. Not this morning. I just had a full week's dose of the bimbo squad, before I even had caffeine."

"The BGs?" Jett asked, using one of the two girls' many secret code names. BGs was short for "Bimbo Girls." "God, Suz, why don't you just move your locker. Step away."

Suzi and Jett found a table and sat down. Suzi used her napkin to give the table a quick wipe.

"No, it's not too bad really," Suzi said. "It's just when they're all there together . . . hovering . . . screaming . . . it's just crazy insane." Suzi put her hand on her forehead and screamed in a high voice, "Chet! Zack! Tom! Dick! Harry!"

Jett giggled. She loved this girl.

"Want some coffee?" Suzi offered.

"No thanks. I'm on a triple breve cappuccino buzz," Jett replied, slumping in her chair and picking at her red nail polish.

"God, don't I know it. Just give me a caffeine IV," Suzi said, exasperated. "I was up until two in the morning. Reading a real juicy one. A lovers' spat, one of them ends up dead, literally with a knife in his back, but both of them had other lovers, and those lovers also had lovers! It's crazy. I have absolutely no idea how this one's going to end."

Jett interrupted. "It's the chick. It's always the chick."

"You never know. That's what makes it a good mystery, my good woman," Suzi said, reaching into her messenger bag and grabbing a bag of hot wasabi peas and popping two in her mouth. She held out the bag to Jett.

"Well, you would know, considering you read like a different mystery book every week," Jett said, waving the peas away. "But I still say it's the chick."

The girls sat in silence for a few minutes and perused the cafeteria. So much to see this Monday morning. A senior guy practically had his tongue down his girlfriend's throat; a table of BG wannabes was sitting quietly and trying to act bitchy and pretentious. And then there was the popular section at the back of the cafeteria. That section was particularly abuzz with energy and enthusiasm this morning, probably because of prom week. The thought made Suzi want to regurgitate her coffee all over the table. But then she remembered something.

"Oh. My. Gosh. I had the most amazing dream last night," Suzi said.

"Was I in it?" Jett asked, joking.

Suzi lightly slapped her friend's sleeve. Jett was wearing a wicked black motorcycle jacket with fringe on the sleeves, and Suzi's slap sounded harder than it actually was. Just then, a beam of sunlight shot into the cafeteria, making Jett's naturally curly, bright red hair almost impossible to look at without sunglasses. On Suzi's suggestion, Jett had chopped it into a supercool urban 'do that was half *Bride of Frankenstein*, half hip-hop video vixen.

"I was in Paris . . ." Suzi continued, once the sunbeam sank back into the clouds.

"With Mr. Fry, no doubt!" Jett interrupted, perking up a bit. Mr. Fry was another one of the girls' code words. It was code for the hot and crispy Mr. French Fontaine.

"Oh, man. It was sooo hot," Suzi said. "No, correction. He is sooo hot. How can anybody be so hot?"

"Yeah," Jett agreed. "That accent of his is pretty cool. And his clothes rock. Those Euro boys are just so much more in touch with themselves. Not like these no-necks who either want to bench-press you or feel you up."

Just then Chet Charleston, football hero, beer-pong king, and Gigi Greene's boy toy, walked by Suzi and Jett's table on his way to the back of the cafeteria. Chet looked down at Suzi and gave her his "someday if you're lucky" smile.

"Or both," Suzi mumbled, and both girls burst out laughing. For no particular reason other than they could.

The warning bell for first period rang out long and loud. Plastic lids were placed on paper coffee cups, bagels were shoved either into mouths or book bags, and lunch plans were made. Suzi and Jett walked out together, the cafeteria slowly emptied, and so began prom week at Mountain High.

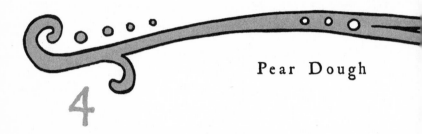

Pear Dough

4

Oh. My. Gosh. There he is, there he is, there he is, there he is . . .

Shut up! Suzi silently screamed to the inside of her head. *Just shut up!*

But Suzi couldn't shut her brain up. In the second row over from the window in Ms. Picante's third-period Spanish class was Xavier Fontaine's seat. And, her brain was flashing over and over like a cheap neon sign: There. He. Is.

Xavier was talking to the viciously gorgeous Kitty Sui. Kitty sat one desk in front of him, and Suzi was constantly trying not to notice how, all through class, Kitty would flip her long black hair behind her so that it pooled all over Xavier's desk. Suzi was sure it was on purpose, but she didn't think the two were an item. At least she hoped not. The thought made her stomach sink.

Kitty was now twisted around in her chair, her shiny hair draping over her left shoulder, talking to Xavier. When Suzi walked in and saw him sitting there in his light blue button-down with his sexy messy hair and violet eyes, her eyes hit the floor on reflex. But not before the damage was done. Suzi's and Xavier's eyes had locked for half a moment, no doubt about it. Suzi could hear Kitty gabbing on to Xavier about how excited she was to go to the prom and what she was going to wear. Suzi kept her eyes glued to her boots, but she swore she could feel Xavier's eyes following her to her seat and lingering on her as she sat down, crossed her legs, and pulled out a book. What a rush!

"And my dad said I could stay out all night!" Kitty continued. "Isn't it just rad? I'm even going to French-braid my hair and, hey! Are French braids from France?" Kitty asked. Suzi wanted to vomit. Kitty was a senior, but she acted like such a freshman sometimes.

Kitty was doing all the talking and so far Xavier hadn't muttered a single word. Suzi fought the urge to look over her shoulder at him. How embarrassing would it be if she turned around and he was staring point-blank into Kitty's brown eyes, dumbstruck into silence by her drop-dead gorgeousness? She would look like such the idiot.

"*Buenos días*, class!" Ms. Picante said as she stormed into the room. Suzi snapped out of her mental meandering. God, she needed more coffee.

"Vocab test today," Ms. Picante continued in an ominous voice. She put her laptop down on her desk, hung her red knit shawl on the back of her chair, and smiled brightly at the class. "Are you all ready to show me what you know about the preterit tense?"

The class mumbled in unison. Suzi could hear Kitty say, "Don't you just hate tests, Xavier?"

"*Silencio!* Take one and pass them back, *por favor*," Ms. Picante said, smiling as she handed a stack of tests to the first person in each row. Ms. Picante was the youngest and feistiest teacher at Mountain High. That's why Suzi liked her.

Suzi grabbed the tests from the guy in front of her, took one, and turned around to pass them behind her. When she looked back, she couldn't help but sneak a peek at Xavier. He was furrowing his brows as he stared at his papers intently. Suzi loved the way he tapped his pencil's eraser against his pouty, voluptuous lips. So hot.

"You'll have the whole period to finish this test," Ms. Picante continued. "If you get stuck on a question, come to my desk. I won't give you the answer, but I might help you figure it out yourself." She gave a little wink, sat down, and the class got to it.

Suzi was cruising. She had studied last night and knew almost all the answers. Just then, somebody's chair moved and broke the room's silence. Suzi could feel Xavier displace the air as he passed her left shoulder, and she got a little whiff of musky lavender soap. She inhaled the moment, slowly, deeply, and the hairs on the back of her neck suddenly felt prickly.

Xavier walked up to Ms. Picante's desk, bent over, and started whispering. Apparently he didn't understand a question. The Spanish test was written in English, and neither was his first language after all.

Suzi kept her head down, but her eyes were on Xavier. His mannerisms were so . . . feminine? Soft? Expressive? Hell, they were just hot!

Xavier and Ms. Picante finished talking, and Xavier started walking back to his desk. Suzi looked down and pretended to be deep in thought about question number nine.

Bam! Xavier knocked into Suzi's left elbow, and because Suzi was a lefty, her pencil fell out of her hand and onto the floor at Xavier's feet. Xavier had nice shoes, by the way. Not sneakers, but real shoes. Like loafers.

"Pear dough," Xavier said quietly, with emphasis on the word *dough*. He bent down to pick up Suzi's pencil.

"Hmm?" was all Suzi could manage. *There he is there he is there he is . . .*

"Pear dough," Xavier repeated. He held out Suzi's pencil and looked sincerely into her big blue eyes.

"You're pardoned," was all Suzi managed to squeak out. Her mind was reeling. She attempted a weak smile and, not knowing what else to do, looked back down at her test. She heard Xavier sit down behind her.

Suzi didn't even think about erasing the long, squiggly line on her paper where what was supposed to be the last *o* in the word *rojo* had taken flight when Xavier bumped her. It was an unruly line on an otherwise perfectly neat test paper, but it was special. After Ms. Picante had graded the tests, Suzi would take this paper home and put it in her top dresser drawer, where she kept all of her extra-special stuff. She would cherish that precious squiggly little line for the rest of her life. It marked a moment.

Gigi's surprise

Totally gross, I've put on like at least three pounds, *Gigi thought while looking at her butt in her Mountain High cheerleader skirt. Gigi was in the girls' locker room before third-period practice, and she was supposed to be getting the teams' bag of pom-poms. But she had walked past the full-length mirror by the showers, and* of course, she had to stop and admire her gorgeous self. Just for a second.

Unfortunately for Gigi, the cheerleading uniforms were in the school colors. Brown and yellow. Whoever chose Mountain High's colors should be shot, Gigi thought. Nobody looks good in brown or yellow. Brown is just so blah, and yellow makes everybody look like they have a major case of hepatitis.

Gigi gave her skirt a little flip to admire her butt one last time, then walked down into the basement to retrieve the pom-pom bag. Last year, some total losers kept on stealing the squad's pom-poms. So this year, as head cheerleader, Gigi had made an executive decision to keep the bag of precious pom-poms, the tools of their team spirit, behind locked doors, down in the gym equipment basement.

Orange parking cones, parallel bars, punching bags, wrestling mats, a stray jockstrap, (ew) . . . Gigi grabbed the nylon bag, slung it over her shoulder, and started to head back up the stairs. She hated this basement. It was dark and cold and gave her the creeps.

Gigi made it up the stairs, put the bag on the floor, and turned around to relock the basement door. That'll keep those no-spirit losers out, Gigi thought as she turned the key and then put it, and the gold chain on which it was attached, back around her neck and under her varsity cheerleading sweater. The key felt cold and powerful against the cleavage created by her Victoria's Secret lacy red push-up.

Gigi bent down and grabbed the bag, thinking how it was getting late and the squad was probably getting fussy. But something was wrong. The bag was all wiggly. Something was moving around inside it! Gigi gave out a surprised shriek and dropped the bag onto the floor. It tipped over onto its side, and out poured swarms of hungry black spiders crawling in all directions!

Gigi screamed. And screamed. Cornered, she threw herself against the basement door with all her might, the doorknob hitting her squarely in the left butt cheek. Pain rushed down her leg, but she barely noticed as swarms of spiders were running through the threads of the team's precious pom-poms, over her spankin'-new white Tretorns, and (no! no! no!) climbing up her bare legs and biting her shins, her knees, the insides of her thighs!

All Gigi could do was scream her brown and yellow sweater off.

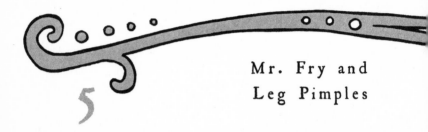

Mr. Fry and Leg Pimples

5

Fourth-period bell rang out loud and clear. Suzi closed her Spanish dictionary and smiled to herself. She was sure she had aced the Spanish quiz, it was lunchtime, and right after lunch was the prom assembly, which she had absolutely no intention of attending. She had a whole hour until her next class! Time to meet Jett in the cafeteria and sneak off to Fishi Sushi for green tea and a killer spicy tuna sashimi roll. Just then, Suzi felt the air swish by her left shoulder again as Xavier walked past her (alone, she noticed) toward the door. Suzi savored the lavender-scented moment.

"*Señorita Suzi, tengo que hablar contigo, por favor.*" The words came from her Spanish teacher, Ms. Picante. She had just told Suzi that she wanted to talk to her. "So, Suzi, are you still thinking about being a TA?" Ms. Picante asked as Suzi approached her desk.

"You bet," Suzi answered. "I love your class."

"Well, you are quite *un estudiante excepcional*," Ms. Picante continued. "But you must understand that being a TA means that you will have more work, not less."

"Oh, I understand, Ms. Picante," Suzi said. Spain someday, so it's worth it to me."

"You want to visit my home country of Espa asked, her attention obviously perked.

"Oh, yeah. I want to go everywhere and s Suzi said, feeling that Ms. Picante was more like a friend than a teacher. "I want to go to Europe, Africa, and Asia."

Ms. Picante was listening to Suzi intently and nodding her head in approval. "You have much curiosity in what the world has to offer, Suzi Clue," she finally said. "And I do need an assistant starting next week. But you see, I have *un problema*."

"Problem?" Suzi repeated.

"Yes, *chica*. You see, there is one other student who also wants to TA for me, and I'm thinking that he might also learn much from the experience," Ms. Picante continued.

"Okay," Suzi said, shrugging. Bummer. She'd really wanted this TA thing.

"His name is Xavier Fontaine," Ms. Picante continued. "Do you know him?"

After her meeting with Ms. Picante, Suzi practically floated into the cafeteria.

"Hey, girl, what's the news?" Jett asked suspiciously. Something was definitely up. Suzi was glowing from head to toe, and her cheeks practically matched the pink streaks in her hair.

"Ooh-la-la!" was all Suzi could manage. Jett had her motorcycle jacket on and looked like she was ready to make a sushi run. Their other best friend, Uma Ashti, was also at the table.

"Yeah, Suz. You look like you just saw Shiva herself," Uma

d, looking at Suzi and smiling excitedly. Uma had moved to Seattle five years ago from Madras, India, when her father took a job building planes at Boeing. She had thick black hair and dark brown eyes offset by a gorgeous gold nose ring.

"Yeah," Jett said, responding to Uma's observation of Suzi's bouncy entrance. "Do you realize you just . . . skipped?"

"Oh. My. Gosh. You guys won't believe this," Suzi said, trying to keep her voice down. "You know how I was thinking of TAing for Ms. Picante's class?"

Jett and Uma nodded, hanging on Suzi's every word.

"Well, it seems that someone else wants to TA the class, so Ms. Picante has decided to split the responsibilities between the two of us!"

"So?" Uma asked, applying a thick coat of clear lip gloss as she listened.

"So I will be one TA, and, drumroll please, none other than the foxy Xavier Fontaine will be the other!" Suzi beamed. "Mr. Fry and I! We'll share everything, the work, the responsibility."

"The late nights?" Uma teased. Suzi turned red, and Jett and Uma laughed.

"He's a fox." Uma nodded.

"He's a fox-a-lot," Suzi agreed, her big blue eyes sparkling.

"But why on earth would a French guy want to TA a Spanish—" Jett started to ask, but Uma interrupted her.

"Hey, guys, what's up with the BGs?" she said, looking over Suzi's shoulder and motioning toward the back of the cafeteria. "Looks like there's trouble in pom-pom paradise."

Uma was always noticing what was going on with Gigi Greene and her gang. Between the three girls, Uma was the most BGish. She was pretty in a cheerleader sort of way, with long legs, long hair, and the demeanor of an ice princess. But Uma was anything but cold. Uma was just stone-cold awesome. She actually considered herself above the Bimbo Girls. In a way, Suzi knew that the BG's antics entertained her.

Suzi turned to look. Uma was right. There was quite a commotion going on back there. Gigi Greene was completely surrounded by her followers, had black mascara running down her flushed cheeks in a most unflattering way, and was telling a very animated story. Suzi and the girls couldn't hear what she was saying, but the way Gigi was saying it, waving her arms in the air and making faces, made it seem like a pretty big deal.

"Hmm . . . I wonder what's going on?" Suzi asked slowly.

"The football team was probably busted for drinking again," Jett said drily. "Who cares? Let's go get sushi, Suz."

"Yeah, right," Suzi said, but she found it hard to tear her eyes off Gigi. She was wearing her cheerleading skirt, and Suzi could have sworn she saw red welts on Gigi's perfectly tanned and waxed legs.

"Is Gigi having an allergic reaction or something?" Suzi asked her friends.

"Yeah, it looks like she's having a major zit attack. On her legs," Uma said, giggling and throwing back her hair.

"You want sushi?" Jett asked Uma as she threw her books in her camouflage messenger bag and stood up.

"No thanks, I'm going to hang out with Li Jung," Uma said as she packed up her cell phone and lip gloss. Li Jung was Uma's main squeeze and a bona fide Mountain High hallway hottie.

"I'll pass, too," Suzi interjected, looking up at Jett who was all ready to go. Jett flashed her patented "what are you up to,

Suzi Clue?" look, even though she already knew. She had been friends with Suzi long enough to know that once Suzi's interest was piqued, there was no stopping her. Suzi always needed to figure things out and solve all mysteries big and small. It was just one of the things Jett loved about her.

"Sorry," Suzi said, giving Jett a friendly wink before she looked back over at Gigi. "But I wouldn't miss this assembly for the world."

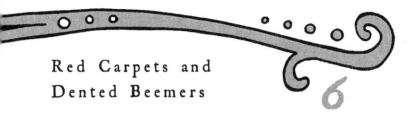

Red Carpets and
Dented Beemers

Some kids got into their cars and hit their favorite greasy drive-thrus; some kids walked three blocks to thickly forested Mountain Park to swing on the swings and make out; some kids got their contraband cigarettes out of their lockers and went out to the football bleachers. The rest of the Mountain High kids single-filed into the stuffy school gym, parked their butts on the yellow plastic bleachers, and stared down at Principal Peasey in anticipation.

Principal Peasey was standing under the basketball scoreboard, fiddling with an uncooperative microphone. He was a big, buff guy who obviously had a hard time finding clothes that fit, because everything he wore was always a smidge too tight. He also had a purple fetish. On any given day, Peasey could be seen wearing at least one item of clothing in some shade of purple: violet, lavender, grape, plum.

Suzi had managed to drag Jett into the assembly on the promise of a Stumptown run after school. (Stumptown's muddy coffee and chill atmosphere was one of the girls' favorite escapes.) The girls were sitting in the gym's nosebleed section, right where they liked it. Here Suzi could watch what the whole school was up to, and Jett could go unnoticed at a school function. Especially this school function. Jett Black at the prom assembly? Whatever would people think?

Suzi did a quick scan of the crowd and saw Xavier, sitting with who else but Kitty Sui. Xavier was talking to her, and she was smiling and looking at Xavier oh so intently. Suddenly Suzi's whole body felt heavy. Maybe they were going out after all, she thought.

"So what's the haps?" Suzi asked Jett, tearing her eyes away from Xavier and motioning to Gigi and her gang. The whole group had been abuzz since the cafeteria incident, and they showed no signs of letting up. They definitely had their lowrider thongs in a pinch.

"Dunno, Suz," Jett replied. She was less interested, but agreed that her girl Suzi was onto something.

Just then, the high shriek of microphone feedback filled the gym, piercing everyone's ears and quieting them down. Principal Peasey tapped his fingers three times on the microphone.

"Students and faculty of Mountain High, thank you for coming this afternoon," he said in his perfectly enunciated English. "As you all know, I have brought you together to discuss the Mountain High prom." On cue, the whole gym started clapping and cheering. Suzi looked over at Gigi. Gigi wasn't clapping. Instead, she was scratching her thighs as if she had a bad case of fleas.

"So," Mr. Peasey continued, "let's get on with it. First off, I'd like to introduce our prom committee captain, Sam Witherspoon. Sam may be a boy"—Mr. Peasey whispered the word *boy* as if he were saying a swearword at the dinner table—"but I'm certain that his ideas are right on. So, let's hear what Sam has in store for us!"

"Peasey sounds like a cheesy talk-show host," Jett said to Suzi, rolling her eyes. Suzi clapped along with the pack as she watched Sam make his way down from the bleachers and up to the mike. It was a little strange having a guy as prom committee captain, Suzi admitted, but she agreed with Peasey in that Sam probably had better taste than most of the girls at school. He was dressed impeccably today in perfectly distressed jeans, a purple shirt with the collar up, and brand-new Pumas. Suzi noticed that Peasey's eyes were lingering on Sam's purple shirt. How funny, she thought.

"Hi, everyone!" Sam yelled enthusiastically as he waved at the crowd. "How are we all today?"

A few of the kids clapped, but for the most part, the auditorium was quiet. Sam was a bit of a social enigma at Mountain High. Girls loved him, but guys were nervous around him. He told everyone that he had a girlfriend who went to college somewhere, but nobody really believed him. Word in the halls was that he was gay, and a lot of guys teased him for it. They called him "Samantha" and would follow him down the hallway, laughing behind his back as they imitated his bouncy walk. It was as if small-minded people had to make fun of Sam in order to prove that they were big, or to prove their own masculinity, Suzi thought. It was so unfair. Sam never did anything to hurt anyone.

"Well," Sam continued, "I have to say that I personally am soooo excited about this year's prom, it's going to be soooo fabulous! I've been flipping through fashion magazines and wandering through malls and watching music videos all in search of the perfect prom theme, and by Georgia, I think I've found it!"

Sam held one finger up in the air like he was trying to figure out which way the wind was blowing. The gym was silent in anticipation. Sam really knew how to work a room.

"And this year's prom theme will be . . ." Sam said as he brought both hands in the air and motioned to two students holding scissors and standing at opposite sides of the gym. On Sam's cue, they cut two pieces of ribbon, and a huge red banner unrolled from the ceiling like a red carpet coming down from the heavens.

"How did they get that up there?" Jett said, looking up to the rafters. Suzi was just watching the show, clearly impressed with the presentation.

The banner read GO GEISHA! PROM in Japanese-styled lettering.

"Now, that's a cool idea for a prom," Suzi said to Jett.

"Beware of the dark side, darling," was all Jett had to say. Suzi couldn't help but giggle. Jett was such a kick in the ass.

"So, *konichiwa*, people!" Sam was back at the mike again. "We're having ourselves a far-out, Far East prom night! I have my people searching high and low for Japanese lanterns, red streamers, tatami mats, and get this, we'll even have a sushi buffet!"

When Sam mentioned the sushi buffet, Jett and Suzi looked at each other and raised their brows. Maybe this prom thing wasn't so bad after all.

"So, wear a kimono, wear a Versace, I don't care, but be there. It's going to be a geisha of a time!" Sam wrapped it up by bowing deeply to the crowd, then jumping up and down a few times and waving as he (galloped?) back to the bleachers.

"I wonder who Sam's taking to the prom?" Suzi asked Jett once the clapping died down.

"Isn't that the million-dollar question?" Jett responded with a mischievous smile. Both girls looked down as an all-smiles Peasey walked in front of the mike again and prepared to speak.

"Let's hear it for Sam, people! *Konichi-wa!*" Peasey said enthusiastically. A little too enthusiastically, actually. Suzi noticed that he hadn't stopped clapping. Or smiling.

"And now, students, drumroll please . . . the question that's been on the brain of every student at Mountain High." Peasey paused as he waited for total attention. "Who will be Mountain High's next prom queen? Will it be . . . the lovely . . . Miss . . . Kitty Sui?"

Upon hearing her name, Kitty gave Xavier a little hug (gag) and gracefully walked down the bleachers in her trademark short skirt and knee-high boots, with boys following her every move. She took her place next to the principal, smiled, and waved up at the crowd. Suzi heard some guys next to her grunt in delight as Kitty's skirt hiked into dangerous territory. Kitty was what the boys so intelligently referred to as a "total babe." She looked like a model, and despite that she was only five feet three, she actually was a petite model for a local underwear retailer once. Suzi had seen the ad in the Sunday paper and thought Kitty looked great, but at school the next day, some idiots had plastered the pictures of Kitty in her skimpy red underwear all over the school. Needless to say, Kitty was horrified and didn't come to school for a whole week.

"Or maybe . . . it's Parker Peets?" Peasey continued. Jett was right. He did sound like a talk-show host, Suzi thought. Students whistled as Parker stood up from the bleachers, whipped her long blond ponytail back, and ran down and stood next to Kitty, giving her a big hug. Parker then took a step and pretended to hit a tennis ball into the crowd, and the students cheered. Parker was a BG to the bone, Suzi thought. But lately she had been seeing a sophomore at Puget University, and Suzi had overhead Gigi bitching about how Parker didn't hang out with her "besties" anymore.

Next, Principal Peasey called out Trixie Topp's name, the third nominee for the court. Trixie came down from the bleachers in her creased khakis and crisp pink polo, with her pink-ribboned ponytails swinging sharply from side to side. Watching her wave just a little too fast and smile just a little too much, Suzi felt just a little sorry for her. It seemed Trixie was always trying so hard to be something that somebody else wanted her to be.

And then it was time for the last prom queen nominee to be announced. But duh, nobody was hanging on the edge of their seats. Everybody in the gym knew who it was. It could only be one girl . . . the Queen Bee herself . . .

"Gigi Greene, come on down!" Peasey yelled while holding one arm out, motioning for Gigi to take her well-deserved place with the other three girls. The crowd went crazy, but when Suzi looked over at the BG posse, she was surprised to see that Gigi wasn't smiling from earring to earring and bouncing down the bleachers. She just sat there, scratching madly at her legs and whispering to her boyfriend, Chet, who had his arm protectively around her shoulders.

Suzi thought it was awfully strange for a girl who'd waited her whole life to be nominated for prom queen to drag her heels when her name was finally announced. But then Chet removed his arm from around her shoulders and helped Gigi to her feet. Suzi noticed that Gigi winced as she stood up, and unconsciously, Suzi winced a little, too.

"Did the Queen Bee fall off the top of the cheerleading pyramid?" Jett asked with a smirk. Suzi just shrugged. Gigi was definitely hurting, surely because of the mysterious welts on her legs. But for some reason, Suzi sensed something more was upsetting her.

Gigi pulled at her cheerleader skirt to try to cover her legs and then slowly limped down to where Kitty, Parker, and Trixie were standing at Peasey's side. But instead of falling in line and waving up at the crowd like the other three girls, Gigi pulled Mr. Peasey aside and started to talk to him in private. Suzi furrowed her brow. What was going on?

Gigi was staring up at a much-taller Peasey, slowly shaking her head and holding her hands at her sides, palms up. It looked as if she were trying to explain something she felt guilty about, as if she had dented her parents' BMW or trashed their house while they were away for the weekend. Peasey just put one arm gently on Gigi's shoulder and listened intently. Even from up in nosebleed section, Suzi could see that Gigi was crying.

After about a minute, the two stopped talking and Peasey reached out and gave Gigi a big hug. Gigi buried her head in his shoulder, and when she pulled away, Suzi could see wet mascara smeared on Peasey's otherwise impeccable lavender oxford. Peasey then walked back toward the mike, and Chet came out of nowhere, put his arm around Gigi, and slowly walked her out of the gym.

The whole scene reminded Suzi of what happened when a football player got injured during a game and his teammates walked him off the field. There was a certain sense of defeat in the silent air, as if the crowd's star player had just been injured.

Then Mr. Peasey broke the silence by clearing his throat and said the three words nobody wanted to hear.

"Gigi is out."

Together, the crowd let out a long deep sigh of disappointment.

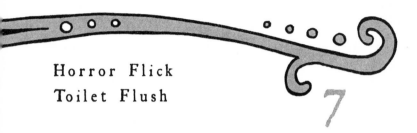

Horror Flick
Toilet Flush

7

It was almost three o'clock, and Suzi felt like it had been the longest Monday ever. Recap: The BG ambush by her locker first thing in the morning, Parker and her posse laughing at the pink streaks in her hair, her near heart attack when Xavier bumped into her in Spanish class, and seeing Xavier and Kitty together at the prom assembly. Then there was Gigi's mysterious leg welts and her even more mysterious behavior at the assembly. Gigi had backed out of the race for prom queen, a race she'd been almost sure to win.

Gigi had been talking about the prom since the first day of school. After all, Suzi's locker placement meant that she knew almost everything that went on in Gigi's life. Suzi knew what type of music Gigi wanted the prom DJ to play and what color balloons she wanted to fall from the ceiling at midnight. Suzi even knew what type of corsage Gigi wanted Chet to buy her. Gigi wanted a blue lily bedded in baby's breath. To match her eyes.

But this afternoon, something had happened to Gigi to make

her step back and throw it all away. Why? Suzi was dying to find out, but it would have to be later. Suzi had volunteered to help Ms. Picante grade a quiz after last period.

Suzi really liked Ms. Picante and would do anything to help her out. But while Suzi was sitting in the classroom, listening to a Spanish CD that Ms. Picante was playing as she graded papers, she couldn't help but feel a bit uneasy about the fact that she would soon be TAing with Xavier in that room. Now that Suzi was pretty certain that he and Kitty were an item, the whole TA thing didn't taste so sweet.

"Okay, Ms. Picante, I'm finished," Suzi said as she looked up from the stack of papers Ms. Picante had given her.

"*Bueno*, Suzi. Thank you so much," Ms. Picante responded as she picked up the quizzes.

"Do you like music from España, too?" Ms. Picante asked, motioning to the CD player sitting on her desk. "It's Dulce Diablo. She's a very close friend of mine and we—"

"Ms. Picante," Suzi interrupted. "I'm sorry, but I really have to be somewhere." She hadn't meant to interrupt Ms. Picante's story, but she had to hightail it to Stumptown. Jett and Uma were already there waiting for her. After all, Suzi owed Jett an extra-dry cappuccino for going to the assembly with her today.

"Certainly, Suzi," Ms. Picante responded gently. "You do what you must, and thank you again. I look forward to having you as my TA."

"Me, too," Suzi said, and genuinely meant it. But a touch of that same uneasiness, a pang, came back, if just for a second. She grabbed her jacket, said good-bye to Ms. Picante, and heard Dulce Diablo's voice grow faint as she walked down the hall toward the girls' bathroom.

Before Suzi hopped onto her bike and headed to Stump-town, she had a quick pit stop to make.

"Oh my God. I just don't know what to do! What the hell am I going to do?"

The voices and footsteps cut through the otherwise silent bathroom and startled Suzi, who was in the last bathroom stall. The door to the girls' bathroom had suddenly crashed open, and a group had poured in, all of them talking very fast and at the same time. Suzi didn't know how many girls were there—she couldn't see through the stall door, after all—but she recognized the voice of Gigi and her pet-on-a-leash, Kitty Sui. They didn't know Suzi was in there, and she kept quiet. She loved being a fly on the wall. Not because she was a gossip queen—she was far from that—but she liked the idea of spying. It made her feel like one of the characters in her mystery books.

"I mean, is this really happening to me?" she asked, and Suzi could hear real fear in her voice.

"C'mon, Gee," said Kitty in a soothing voice. "It might not mean anything. You said it yourself, that basement is probably infested with spiders."

Suzi quietly put her pink cowboy boots up against the back of the stall door. She didn't want her shoes to give her away. This was way too juicy.

"I know I said that, Kitty," Gigi said, sounding a little pissy. "But what about the note?"

"I know, Gee," Kitty said sweetly, consoling her friend. Suzi could hear Kitty blow out a long slow drag. "I know," she said again. "But what if the curse note is just someone's idea of a sick joke? What if someone's just messing with you?"

Curse note? What curse? Suzi thought, jumping to attention as much as she could, considering she was sitting on a toilet seat.

"This curse is so bogus," repeated a nasally voice that Suzi easily identified as Parker Peets's. "I mean, who writes a threat note on somebody's locker in pink lipstick? It's so B horror flick."

"Parker's right, Gee," Kitty said softly.

"Besides," Parker continued, "what's more believable—that you opened a bag full of spiders in a spider-infested basement? Or that there's a prom queen curse at Mountain High?" she said, putting overdramatic emphasis on the words *prom queen curse.*

"I'm in the running for prom queen, too. Do I look scared?" Parker finished.

"Listen, Parker. You aren't the one that was eaten alive by that bag of spiders. I am," Gigi spat out, and then paused abruptly. "You can't possibly understand how scared I was. Look at these bites on my legs!" Suzi could hear Gigi's sneakers squeak against the bathroom floor. She was probably twirling around to give Parker a three-dimensional view of her red, itchy leg pimples, which Suzi now realized were spider bites.

"I can't cheer like this, and I'm the head frickin' cheerleader!" Gigi spat out, her voice almost a hiss when she said "frickin'." Suzi could picture Gigi standing there in her cheerleading skirt, hip cocked, staring down her tagalong friends with her famous ice-princess glare.

"But what if Parker's right, Gee?" Suzi heard Kitty say, in a comforting, motherly tone. "Do you really want to throw away your life's dream just because of some stupid note? What would school do without you?"

"We need you on this," Parker agreed.

"You can't abandon us," Kitty quickly added.

"If Gigi's afraid of some prom queen curse, then don't give her a hard time," said a voice that Suzi didn't recognize. It was a low, raspy voice that was rough and sandpapery. "You can't possibly know how she feels," the raspy voice continued. "She's a shoo-in for prom queen. You're not."

"Who invited you into this conversation?" Kitty blurted out, sounding pissy. "Go back under your rock, freak."

"I have the same right to be here as you do, dear heart," the raspy voice countered confidently.

"Mind your own business, then," Kitty said, her voice sweet yet vicious.

"Just my luck I'd have to pee while you beeyotches were in here," the mystery voice said. Suzi heard footsteps and the sound of the door opening and closing.

"Good riddance," Kitty yelled out dramatically.

The bathroom went quiet for a beat.

"I've gotta get to practice, so later," Parker said, and Suzi listened as the bathroom emptied out. Her butt was really starting to hurt from sitting all crunched up on the toilet, but she didn't move a single inch.

"I want nothing more than to be this school's prom queen, Kitty," Suzi heard Gigi say softly, after a long period of silence. "But when I think of those spiders—"

"It's scary," Kitty interrupted.

"Damn straight it's scary," Gigi agreed. "Why would anyone want to hurt me? I mean, what have I ever done to anyone?" Suzi heard the sink faucet turn on and could smell fresh perfume being sprayed.

"Screw this. Let's go tanning," Kitty suddenly said triumphantly.

"You know I have that future alphas of Kappa Beta thing," Gigi huffed. "My mom is on me like white on rice."

"Kappas are the best, Gee! You're sooo lucky your mom can get you in—" Kitty was saying, when suddenly, she was interrupted by the thunderous sound of a toilet flushing.

In an attempt to shift her weight from one butt cheek to another, Suzi had straightened up quickly, a little too quickly, and put her right hand behind her to keep from falling off the toilet seat and onto the floor. But instead of finding the wall or even the back of the seat, Suzi's hand had hit the flusher.

Water was splashing out of the toilet and getting her shirt and jeans all wet, but even worse, she could almost feel the girls' combined laser gazes burning through the steel of the stall door and into her flesh. Crap. She had to think of something. And like right now.

"Who the hell is in there?" Gigi yelled more than asked. Suzi could see two sets of perfectly white Tretorns storm the stall door, and through the cracks in the sides of the door she saw cheerleading skirts and glossy hair galore. When Suzi didn't answer, the girls started pulling on the stall door, and it rattled on its hinges.

But then Suzi coolly unlocked the latch, opened the door, and acted surprised when she came face-to-face with the fuming cheerleader posse.

"Hey," Suzi said, a little louder than necessary. She took her headphones out of her ears and the sound of electric guitar and fast drums screamed out of the earpieces. "I didn't know anybody was in here," she said as calmly as she could. She had never been a very good liar.

Suzi motioned to the pink iPod in her jacket pocket, forced a smile, and then turned sideways and finagled her way through the pack. The girls just stood there looking angry and suspicious but they let Suzi through.

"My mom says I'm going to go deaf by the time I'm twenty," Suzi yelled over her shoulder as she made a beeline for the door. She carefully paced her steps in order to get out of there as quickly as possible without seeming rushed or scared. She knew she had to keep it cool. But it was so hard.

She could feel the girls' fiery stares burning into the back of her head the entire way.

"So what's all this about? Is Gigi running for prom queen or not? And will somebody please tell me why I'm holding a wad of wet toilet paper in my hand?"

Suzi had finally landed at Stumptown, where Jett and Uma were waiting for her, and Suzi couldn't tell if Uma's babbling was because of her BGesque genes or the supersized caramel mocha she was sucking up through a straw.

"I tell you, Uma, you really should participate in more school activities. You might just learn something," Jett joked as she licked foam off the top of her extra-dry cappuccino. Uma showed her a perfectly manicured middle finger.

"Gigi's not running for prom queen," Suzi said, ducking Jett's joke and looking over at Uma.

"Wow, that's huge. Gigi was a sure thing for prom queen this year," Uma said. Suzi could see her mind churning over all the juicy tidbits.

"And then," Suzi continued after taking a quick sip of her cinnamon soy latte, "before the stupid toilet flushed in the bathroom, Gigi was saying that the reason she dropped out is because she's afraid of some curse." Suzi lingered on the word "curse" and looked at her friends for input.

"Curse?" Uma gulped through a mouthful of mocha. "Like witchcraft, Egyptian mummies, and stuff?"

"I have no idea," Suzi said slowly, shrugging. "I heard Gigi say someone used pink lipstick to write a threat note on her locker about some curse."

"A threat note?" Uma asked, her coal-colored eyes widening.

"That explains it," Jett said.

"Explains what?" Suzi asked, leaning in closer to her friend. Jett flashed Suzi a look and calmly took a sip of her cappuccino before continuing.

"Well, I was waiting for you by your locker after school, I forgot that you were grading tests or whatever," Jett explained. "And all the baby BGs were there with paper towels, scrubbing down Gigi's locker. I just thought it was some freaky initiation thing," she said as she nonchalantly examined her chipped red nails.

"Did you see what the note said?" Suzi asked excitedly.

"I couldn't see the locker through the hair spray," Jett answered, smirking.

"I wonder what it said. I wish I could have seen it . . ." Suzi trailed off.

"So Gigi was attacked by a pom-pom bag full of spiders, that's what happened to her legs, and then someone wrote a threat note on her locker, something about a curse," Uma said softly as she put the pieces together.

"That's what I heard," Suzi said, trying to get the last cloud of foam out of her cup with her tongue. She succeeded and then put her empty cup on the table.

"Too bizarre." Uma shook her head and checked her ruby rhinestone cell for messages.

"We still on for band practice tonight?" Jett asked Suzi, clearly bored with the prom queen conversation.

"Yep," Suzi said, gathering her jacket and messenger bag. "I'll meet you there in ten," she continued. "There's something I need to check out first."

"Suz," Jett said, looking at her friend impatiently. "I know you smell a mystery here, and that you won't sleep until all your questions are answered. But is it really worth the energy? I mean, who cares about a bunch of prom queens anyway?" Jett stated the last sentence more than she asked it while twirling her finger along the insides of her cup and collecting froth on her finger.

"I happen to like the prom," Uma interjected. "Everybody's all dolled up and tipsy and flirty. Mmm . . . yummy!"

Jett gave out a disgusted sigh and flicked foam onto Uma's pink cashmere sweater. Uma shrieked.

"All mysteries are worth solving, my dear friend," Suzi said as she stood up to leave, and something in her voice told her friends exactly what they already suspected.

Suzi Clue was on the case.

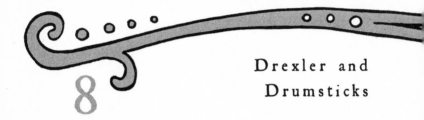

Drexler and
Drumsticks

8

It was raining like crazy and starting to get dark, but Suzi rode through the puddles like a champion, locked up her bike at the school, and ran straight to her locker. She then walked two lockers down. Gigi Greene's locker. There it was. And it was spotless. Damn.

Suzi dropped her wet messenger bag onto the floor and examined the steel door close up. She ran her fingers over the surface, over the little heart and G.G. + C.C. carved into the steel and over the rough patches of chipped yellow paint, but the alleged curse note had been cleanly wiped away. Suzi couldn't find any proof of a note written in pink lipstick, just some smeared patches of oily, sticky residue.

Discouraged, she picked up her bag and started to walk down the hall to meet Jett in the band room. The school was practically empty, except for the random club meeting and sports practice, and Suzi loved the silence. There was something oddly calming about it. She stared down at the scuffed brown tiles as she walked, deep in thought. She was sure something strange was going down at school, but she had nothing to go on except what she had overheard Gigi talking about in the bathroom, and even that didn't make much sense.

Just then, Suzi heard an all-too-familiar voice up ahead, a sexy, whispery, accented voice. She looked up from her sneakers to see Xavier talking to Parker Peets. Parker was holding her tennis racket and standing with her back to her locker, and Xavier was leaning in and talking to her very, very closely. That was weird, Suzi thought. She thought Kitty was with Xavier. Was Parker moving in on her best friend's boy? And didn't Parker have a college boyfriend anyway? Suzi was puzzled, but she snapped out of it fast. All questions melted away when she realized she had the perfect view of Xavier's gorgeous butt.

He was wearing a pair of loose-fitting, soft gray slacks (so Euro!) that cinched up and made his butt look so hot, like a soccer player's, Suzi thought. On the flip side, Parker was wearing her short, varsity tennis skirt, and the way she was leaning up against her locker made the hem ride up and show off her long legs. Suzi's stomach silently sank. She realized that she would never look like Parker; she didn't want to look like her, but still, she wanted Xavier, and if Xavier wanted girls that looked like Parker . . . It was all so confusing!

Suzi tried to look back down at the oh-so-interesting brown floor tiles before Xavier or Parker had a chance to notice her, but her reflexes were too slow. Xavier had caught her out of the corner of his eye. And he wasn't letting go.

Oh my gosh oh my gosh oh my gosh, Suzi screamed to herself as every muscle in her body froze. Thank goodness her legs had the common sense to keep walking, but Xavier was still staring right at her and she just could not tear her eyes away. She kept getting closer, and closer, and closer . . . she could almost smell his sexy, leathery lavender scent . . .

Bam! Suzi was knocked out of her love spell by running head-on into somebody. She dropped her messenger bag and books spilled out all over the floor. When she bent down to pick them up, Xavier furrowed his brow in sympathy, but then went back to talking with Parker.

Game over.

Suzi looked up to see who it was she had just slammed into, but she didn't even need to see his face to ID him. The scuffed black oxfords with untied shoelaces, brown corduroy bell-bottoms, baggy button-down shirt.

It was Drexler Penn. Aka: Drex the Hex.

"I am so sorry! Oh, man, I am so stupid!" Drex rambled as he bent down to help Suzi with her books. When he leaned over, three ink pens fell out of his front shirt pocket and rolled onto the floor.

"It's okay, Drex, it was my fault. I wasn't looking where I was going," Suzi said, trying to comfort an obviously flustered Drex. It wasn't enough that Drex had run head-on into somebody in the hall—he had run head-on into Suzi. He had sported a wicked crush on her since his family moved in next door to hers in the fifth grade. It was so painfully obvious.

Back in the fifth grade, Drex would leave flowers on Suzi's doorstep, wilted flowers picked out of people's yards in the neighborhood. In the sixth grade, he had offered to walk her to school every day, and then, when she turned him down because she wanted to walk with the girls, he offered to ride her on the back of his banana seat. She tried it once just to be nice, but she had nicked up her ankles real bad on the spokes of the back wheel, so once was enough. Then, in the seventh grade, Drex had offered to tutor Suzi in geometry. Suzi took him up on his offer—geometry was her worst enemy—but she always felt a little sorry for him at their tutoring sessions. He would come over to her house after school, her mom would give them oatmeal cookies and juice, and then they would sit at the kitchen table and Drex would stammer through his instructions on how to find the hypotenuse of a triangle or the area of a circle, the whole time sweating profusely and leaving wet palm prints all over the Formica kitchen table. He sweated out of nervousness not out of any genetic defect, Suzi knew that, but she always felt a little sorry for him.

Even though Drex was really helping her with her geometry homework, she had to cut the tutoring sessions short. She liked Drex, but not in that way, and she hated to watch him squirm.

"Drex, really, don't sweat it," Suzi said as she stood up with her books in hand. "It's not your fault."

"No, it is my fault," Drex said, adjusting his black-rimmed glasses on his nose and patting dark hair off his forehead. "I should have looked where I was going."

"Well, so should I," Suzi said, shooting a quick glance back at Xavier only to find him still yapping away with Parker. "So should I . . ." she repeated.

"They don't call me Drex the Hex for nothing," Drex said, and Suzi smiled. She thought it was cool that he could make fun of himself.

"So where are you going?" he asked nervously, putting his

pens back into his shirt pocket. He was obviously affected by Suzi's presence, and Suzi thought it was sweet.

"I'm meeting Jett for band practice like five minutes ago," Suzi said, nodding and looking down at her boots. Was she a little nervous, too? No, she told herself. No way. This was only Drex. "I play drums. Jett is guitar," she added, to break the silence.

"Wow, that is so cool," Drex said, a little too enthusiastically. "I compose music on my laptop. It's more like musical scores mixed with sci-fi and electronica, and it's pretty dark but—"

Oh. My. Gosh, Suzi thought. Here we go. Drex was rambling. Time to cut him off.

"Hey, Drex, I really gotta go. Jett's waiting for me," she said, slicing through Drex's story.

"Oh, okay," Drex said, and now he was the one looking down at his untied oxfords. Suzi felt that familiar twinge of feeling sorry for Drex creep back in. He was so sweet, but like she said, she just wasn't interested.

"Well, see you around then," Suzi said, as she tossed her messenger bag over her shoulder and started to walk away. She had just started to hear Jett's guitar riff coming out of the band room, when Drex called out after her.

"Are you going to the prom?" he practically squeaked.

Suzi turned to face Drex. "Nah, not this year," she said, smiling and walking backward toward the sounds of Jett's guitar.

She swore she detected a hint of disappointment in Drex's face.

"The baby BGs erased the evidence," Suzi whined as she walked into the band room, threw down her messenger bag, and plopped down behind a desk. Jett was standing next to the school's drum set, glittery guitar strap around her shoulders, playing her electric guitar, a red Gibson Flying V, a birthday gift from her folks. Jett had the volume on the amplifier cranked up way loud.

"What?" Jett asked, reluctantly turning down her rendition of "Crimson and Clover." "I'm playing Joan here," she said, looking at her friend impatiently.

It was no secret that Joan Jett was Jett's rock-and-roll inspiration. But it was a secret (a secret that Suzi was privy to but not many others) that Jett's real name was Barbara—or Barbie—Black. Of course Jett hated that name with a passion. When she was ten years old, she had discovered the all-girl rock band the Runaways while rummaging through her mom's old records, and she had fallen in love with the guitarist, Joan Jett, the first moment she heard her. She had begged her mom to buy her a guitar, hence the supercool Flying V, and she started telling everybody to call her Jett. The name, along with Jett's genuine devotion to music, had just stuck.

"I said, the BGs wiped Gigi's locker clean. If there ever was a curse note, I'll never see it," Suzi repeated once Jett could hear her.

"Why do you need to see it? You heard Gigi say it happened," Jett countered.

"But I need proof," Suzi said, slumping down in her chair.

Jett nodded to acknowledge her friend's dilemma, then looked Suzi straight in the eye. "You need to relax, Suz," she said, starting in on a song that she and Suzi had been working on for the last couple of weeks. The song was called "Lil' Heartbreaker," and it was fast and furious.

"Forget about it for now. Let's rock," Jett continued, giving Suzi her best rock-and-roll face and cranking the amplifier back up. She closed her eyes and kicked in a perfect rhythm.

Suzi dug her drumsticks out of her bag and sat down behind the snare. The wooden sticks felt good in her hands, solid and powerful. As she unlocked the snare drum and started focusing on the song, all her frustrations about the curse, Gigi's locker, and even Xavier just melted away with the rhythm. Suzi felt her shoulders relax and breath deepen. She waited for just the right moment, and then it was like her sticks knew exactly what to do. Her instincts kicked in, her brain turned off, and she didn't have to think about a thing.

Until Jett cut out of a heated midchorus screech, and she heard the screams.

backhands and blue shampoo

Wow, what a super day, Parker thought to herself as she walked to her gym locker after a killer tennis game. She had practically become high school royalty for being nominated for prom queen, she had squashed her snooty tennis-team rival on the court 21-Love, and the best part of the last twenty-four hours? She had caught Gigi's boyfriend, Chet (whom she secretly had a crush on although she had a college boyfriend in the bag), eyeing her butt and nudging his friends when she walked by in her new bootylicious low-rider jeans that let her black thong peek out against her perfectly flat tummy. Even Xavier Fontaine, the cute French exchange student Kitty had a supercrush on, couldn't stay away from her. Bravo! she thought. She practically ruled this school.

Parker was now strutting her stuff around the locker room, taking out her sweaty, straw-colored ponytail and getting ready to hit the showers after tennis-team practice. A couple of girls came up and congratulated her on her nomination, and Parker just smiled sweetly and took all compliments. Yes, she was awesome. Just when she didn't think she could puff her feathers out any more, "Material Girl" rang out from her floral LeSportsac gym bag. Parker pulled out her cell and looked at the caller ID. She smiled and threw her blond locks back in a rush of excitement. The number was from Puget University. It was Mark! Could this day possibly get any better?

"Hey, babe," Parker said on cue as she flipped open the phone and rummaged through her locker for a clean towel and her shower stuff. "How's college life treating you?" She said this just a little louder than she needed to. She didn't want her tennis team to forget that yes, she was a prom queen nominee, but she also had a hottie college boyfriend.

"Yeah, babe, I'd love to go out to dinner on Friday," Parker continued, slipping out of her Tretorn tennis shoes and into her Roxy shower slippers. "Dolce Vita is awesome . . . hey, I have to go, call me later, okay? Miss you, too, yeah, see you Friday!" Parker finished as she snapped her cell shut and threw it back into her locker. She looked around at some of the girls who couldn't help but hear her conversation and smiled.

"College boys, they're so much smarter than these high school babies," Parker said. She snorted to make her point, then inched out of her white pleated tennis skirt, wrapped her towel around her, and headed for the shower.

Parker let the warm water run over her. After a hard match, she loved unwinding in the shower. The warm water, the steam, the smell of fruity bath products—it was all kind of dreamy and hypnotic.

Parker was listening to a girl with a mean serve talk about how she was trying to talk her mom into letting her have a coed slumber party, when she reached into her shower basket for her True Blue shampoo. Parker always thought the whole blue shampoo thing was a bit weird, but her colorist had told her that it kept blond hair from going brassy, and Parker hated brassy. She squeezed out some shampoo that looked like blue gel toothpaste and put it on her light blond locks.

Parker was reviewing the day's events in her head and playing them back in slow motion for a subtly dramatic effect. She could hear the applause when her name was announced at the prom assembly, and see the hungry look in Chet's eyes when she walked by him in her new jeans. She could see Xavier Fontaine's eyes linger over her bare legs when she talked to him by her locker after school, and she could see the tennis team's eyes turn an envious shade of green when her cell had rung just a few minutes ago and it was her Sigma Chi college boyfriend. She could smell the clean, minty lather of her shampoo and feel it softly slide down her back and over her arms and stomach . . . the overload of sensations put her into a daze. But then one of the girls in the shower stopped talking midsentence, and Parker opened her eyes to see everyone in the shower was staring at her. What was it? She looked down, and even with all the steam making it hard to see much of anything, Parker could see enough to know that there was something dark on her arm. A huge bruise? Jeez, did she smack her arm at practice today?

But on closer examination, Parker saw that it was a stain, not a bruise. It was a blue stain, the color of pen ink, and it was foamy around the edges. Parker frantically tried to rinse and rub it off, but it was too late. Her arms were stained blue, as was her chest, her stomach, and the water pooling around her Roxy shower slippers. Anything that had come in contact with her blue shampoo lather was now also a shade of blue.

Oh my God. Her hair! Her hair! Parker was jumping up and down, squealing and covering her once-blond head with her now-blue hands, and then she saw it. The letters scrawled on a steamy mirror right outside the girl's shower.

The note read, **PROM QUEENS MUST DYE.**

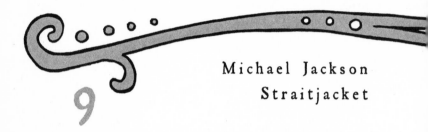

Michael Jackson
Straitjacket

9

"Did you guys hear? The feminist club is made up of witches and they cursed the prom because it demeans all women!" Suzi heard a sophomore girl scream down the halls between second and third period.

It was Tuesday morning, and Mountain High's halls were abuzz with rumors about how Parker Peets had ended up with blue hair. So much gossip was bouncing off the walls, Suzi and Jett couldn't even talk to each other as they walked to class. The scene was way crazy.

The morning's chaos had started when Gigi found out what had happened to Parker in the gym showers the night before. It was an understatement to say she had an absolute cow. Her fears about the curse now validated, Gigi started telling everyone and anybody within earshot about how *she* was attacked by a big bag of spiders and how *she* had received a threat note on her locker telling her to drop out of the race for prom queen or else. The Queen Bee's frantic claims were more than enough to send the entire school into a rumor-infested spin.

What had happened to Gigi and Parker? Was it witchcraft? A jealous lover? A ghost? Everyone was asking the same questions, but nobody had any answers.

Not even Suzi.

"This is so crazy," Suzi said to Jett as they made their way down the hall. It always amazed her just how much people loved to dwell on other people's misery. Even she did it, Suzi admitted, but at least she didn't go around making up stories. She just liked to figure out why things happened the way they did.

"Well, bad dye job, ghosts, *Carrie* incarnate, whatever. I can't believe the girl made it to school today," Jett said, looking around calmly.

Suzi knew what Jett was referring to. When the two of them had found Parker in the gym showers last night, naked, huddled, and screaming in a puddle of blue water, they thought she was going to have to be hauled away in a straitjacket. It took the entire tennis team two hours to even coax her into a robe and send her home. The whole incident had completely freaked Parker out, to say the least. It had freaked everybody out a bit, actually. Even Suzi and Jett. The note that was written on the steamy mirror was way creepy.

"So what does that mean, 'prom queens must die'?" Suzi asked Jett. "Is that a serious death threat or just a prank?"

"Dunno, Suz. But nobody's dead, so that's a good sign," Jett was saying, when suddenly Suzi elbowed her lightly.

"Hey, look." Suzi motioned to a group of girls huddled around Parker's locker. "There she is."

Suzi couldn't help but stare at Parker as she and Jett walked by. Gigi was there, as were Kitty and even Trixie. They were standing around Parker in a circle, as if they were trying to protect her. Trixie had loaned Parker one of her many pink Coach head scarves to cover up her hair in the most fashionable way possible, and she was adjusting it to cover up all of Parker's now-blue locks. But Parker's hair wasn't the only thing that was blue. Parker had wrapped herself up in a long-sleeved, black turtleneck and white gloves to cover up her stained arms and hands, and she was wearing way too much foundation and huge, black Jackie O sunglasses to try to cover up the blue on her face.

Parker was a mess compared to her friends, who were showing as much healthy, glowing skin as they legally could. Except for Trixie, of course.

"Since when did Michael Jackson join the cheerleading squad," Jett said under her breath, and Suzi elbowed her again and gave her a shut up look. But Jett was right. Just looking at Parker bordered on the painful, Suzi couldn't help but think about how not even twenty-four hours ago, she had been walking by this exact same spot and seen Parker, proud as a peacock and in all her glossy blond glory, sporting her sexy tennis skirt and flirting with Xavier right there in front of her locker.

Hey, wait a minute, Suzi thought. She had seen Parker flirting with Xavier last night, but Xavier and Kitty were an item. If Kitty knew that Parker was macking on her boyfriend . . .

Was the vicious Kitty Sui vindictive enough to do something like this?

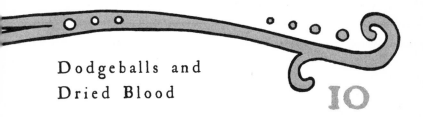

Dodgeballs and
Dried Blood

"Ouch! Take it easy on me, will 'ya?" Suzi said, giving Jett the evil eye and biting her lower lip in pain. She could still taste the remnants of the morning's strawberry lip gloss.

"Suz, you are such a puss," Jett responded, laughing. "C'mon, give me everything you've got!"

Suzi and Jett were partner-stretching in fifth-period gym class, taught by the pervy Mr. Rider. Mr. Rider was considered a "cool" teacher because he liked to hang out with the high school kids, but Suzi noticed that he basically only hung around high school girls, and two senior girls in particular, Evie and Andy. Jett had even spotted the three of them cruising the local mall's parking lot in Rider's red Fiat convertible one weekend. Ick. Rider was also known to wear jeans with holes in the butt, and sometimes he didn't even wear underwear. Double—no, triple ick.

"So is Rider wearing underwear today?" Jett asked as she finished stretching out Suzi's hamstrings. The girls were sitting on an old, smelly gym mat, facing each other, with legs straight out in front of them, soles of their feet touching. They both had their arms extended and were holding on to each other's forearms, pulling and pushing each other back and forth, stretching out their legs. The motion reminded Suzi of a seesaw.

"He is so gross," Suzi said, looking over Jett's stubby red ponytails and at Mr. Rider, who was helping a girl in short shorts climb up a thick rope suspended from the ceiling. Mr. Rider was smiling up at the girl, and while he wasn't touching her, he had his hands placed strategically under her butt.

"Dig up any dirt on the curse yet?" Jett asked, as she lazily flopped one black Converse in front of her and attempted a runner's stretch.

"Nada," Suzi responded, stretching toward Jett. "All day it's been nothing but rumors. It's like an epidemic of ignorance." She tried to touch her forehead to her knees and almost succeeded.

"It's so weird how people get fixated on other people's misery. Like the *National Enquirer* or something," Jett said, rolling her eyes and flopping down onto the mat like a dead fish.

Suzi looked around the gym and soaked up the scene. Boys were snapping girls' bra straps, girls in short shorts were flirting with the boys but trying not to look as if they were flirting, and the jocks were trying to outmacho one another. It was more like a zoo than a gym class, Suzi thought.

Then she spotted Gigi and some other BGs standing in the corner of the gym. They were all huddled together in their matching yoga wear, but while everybody was wearing shorts, Gigi had on a pair of black stretch pants to cover up her legs. The girls all had water bottles in their hands and were gabbing away a hundred miles a minute, most definitely about Parker and the curse, and they were totally unaware of the rope climbing, dodgeball, and gymnastics going on around them.

The BGs always treated Rider's PE class like a forty-minute exercise in gabbing, and Rider pretty much left them alone.

"I'm going to go over and talk to Gigi," Suzi said as she stood up.

"You're going to do what?" Jett asked, still lying on the mat and looking up at Suzi like she was crazy.

"I want to ask her about the curse," Suzi said, brushing off her tee and shorts as if she were trying to make herself more presentable. She had to admit, she was just a tad bit nervous.

"Girl, you really are crazy," Jett said, raising herself up on one elbow and arching one red eyebrow. "Are you sure you want to do this?"

Just then, Gigi screamed out a very unladylike stream of obscenities, and Suzi looked over to find her frowning and rubbing her butt, a dodgeball with the words PROPERTY OF MOUNTAIN HIGH bouncing around her white Tretorn sneakers. Of course not a single dodgeballer came over to reclaim the ball. Nobody was that stupid.

Well, nobody except one very brave or very stupid freshman with pink streaks in her hair.

"Suzi Clue, is that your ball?" Gigi spat out as Suzi picked up the ball at Gigi's feet and bounced it like a basketball.

"Heck no," Suzi said, playing it cool. She took the dodgeball and threw it as hard as she could back to the kids playing the game.

Suzi looked back at Gigi, who was staring at her with her head cocked and eyebrows raised. All the other BGs had stopped talking and were looking at Suzi as well. Suzi swallowed.

"I just hoped I could talk to you for a minute," Suzi said, breaking the silence but not the stares. "I'm a bit confused."

"Obviously," Kitty stated, leering at Suzi.

"No, I mean, I was just wondering if you could tell me what happened to you," Suzi said to Gigi as genuinely as possible.

"Why do you care?" Gigi asked. "You want some gossip to take back to your little freshman friends?"

"No, it's not that at all," Suzi said, and she noticed that she said it a little bitchier than she intended.

"Listen," Suzi continued, shaking her head and taking herself down a notch. "I'm just curious, that's all. I've heard rumors about a curse, and I want to figure out what's going on."

"You've heard rumors, have you?" Kitty snapped rudely, flipping her black hair over one shoulder. "We so don't have time for this. C'mon, girls, let's go change."

Gigi and Suzi were left standing all alone. The tension was thick.

"Who are you? Nancy frickin' Drew?" Gigi shot out, looking at Suzi through small, suspicious eyes. Suzi just shrugged her shoulders and stood there, not sure what else to say or do. She could feel Gigi sizing her up from toe to head: her bright pink Converses, knee-length black shorts, red wristband and shaggy black hair, but Suzi stood her ground. She had never been this close to Gigi before, and she noticed that Gigi wore liquid blue eyeliner, perfectly smudged on the outside corners of her eyes, and blue eye shadow that was so pale you'd only notice it if you were standing as close as Suzi was now. Gigi's skin was almost perfect, like a pimple wouldn't even dare to touch her complexion. Actually, Suzi thought Gigi was pretty. And the girl did speak her mind, which Suzi admired.

"Go back to your girlfriend, Suzi Clue," Gigi finally said, motioning with her eyes at Jett, who was watching them from the other side of the gym. Then she rolled her eyes impatiently.

"Listen," she continued. "I don't know what you have or haven't heard, but it's not *your* problem." Gigi put emphasis on the word *your* and again let her eyes linger over Suzi's clothes. "This is a burden for the prom queens to bear. Not some curious little freshman," she added dramatically. "We're from totally different sides of the cafeteria."

And with that, Gigi turned and walked toward the door to the girls' locker room, leaving Suzi standing in a thick cloud of her designer perfume.

"Uma, wait up!" Suzi yelled as she bolted down the hall after her friend. Thank goodness she was wearing sneakers. Uma had long legs that supermodels would kill for, and she walked at about the same pace that Suzi could run.

"What's up . . . Nancy?" Uma teased, smiling at Suzi and never once breaking her long, confident stride. "The whole school is talking about how you got shot down in gym class," she giggled. "What were you thinking trying to cozy up to Gigi? You'd have better luck petting a piranha," she said as she stopped in front of her locker and dialed her combination.

"I had to try," Suzi said as she leaned against a locker. "I mean, how am I going to figure out what's going on if I don't talk to people?"

"Well, I applaud your efforts. That took guts." Uma grabbed her cell phone, fuzzy lavender jacket, and a bag of dark brown powder out of her locker. "But don't believe a word that Gigi tells you. For all you know, she's behind this curse, picking off her competition one by one," she said coolly.

Suzi heard Uma and let it sink in. She had never really thought that Gigi could be behind the curse. But anything was possible, she guessed.

"Well, she didn't tell me squat, so I have nothing to believe or disbelieve at this point," Suzi huffed, looking down at Uma's hands. "What's that brown stuff?"

"This?" Uma asked, holding up the bag of brown powder.

"This is henna," Uma explained. "While you may choose to dye your hair all the colors of the rainbow, Indians use this. It adds a gorgeous red tint to my hair."

"It's powder," Suzi asked, her mind churning.

"Well, you add water, Einstein," Uma said sarcastically as she dropped the bag into her purple-and-red beaded purse. Suzi wasn't laughing. She was still eyeing the henna.

"Can I borrow some of that? And one of your powder brushes?" she asked, her blue eyes sparkling.

Back in Suzi's neck of the hallway, she and Uma were huddled around Suzi's locker. It was now fifteen minutes after the last-period bell had rang, and the halls were emptying out as students went home.

"What are you going to do?" Uma asked, eyeing the bag of henna and powder brush. Suzi could tell Uma loved the intrigue, although she tried not to show it.

"Well," Suzi said, looking around and trying to be as inconspicuous as possible. "The note on Gigi's locker was written in lipstick. Lipstick is made of oils and wax, which almost always leave a trace."

"Oh, yeah, like how that lipstick stain on my white cashmere sweater never came out." Uma nodded as she watched Suzi untie the bag.

"Exactly." Suzi gave Uma a wink, held up the bag of henna and the powder brush, and then walked two lockers down to Gigi's locker. "Keep an eye out for Gigi," she whispered.

"Gigi? Why?" Uma asked excitedly, but Suzi was already deep in thought.

Suzi bit her lower lip in concentration as she slowly dipped Uma's big, fluffy brush into the henna. Suzi then took a brushful of the brown powder, held it carefully up to the surface of Gigi's locker, and started brushing from top to bottom in light, even strokes.

At first, the henna powder just slipped off the slick metal surface and fell all over Suzi's hands and onto the floor. But eventually, about one foot down from the top of the locker, the henna started to stick in places.

"My God," Suzi could hear Uma say as she clicked her tongue. Suzi kept brushing, then once she had finished, she blew her bangs out of her face and stepped back. Uma stepped back with her. Both girls couldn't believe what they saw.

BEWARE THE CURSE OF THE PROM QUEEN was spelled out in big, smeared, henna-brown letters. Suzi thought it looked a little like dried blood.

"Suz, you're a genius," Uma said, clearly in awe as she looked at Suzi with her big brown eyes. Suzi was just opening her mouth to agree when someone grabbed her by the arm and spun her around.

It was Gigi Greene. And boy, was she pissed.

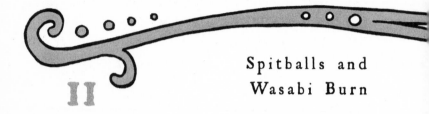

Spitballs and
Wasabi Burn

II

"Just what the hell do you think you're doing?" Gigi spit out. She struck her trademark pose, hands on her hips with her right hip cocked out to the side. Suzi could have sworn she saw smoke coming out of the Queen Bee's nose.

"Beware the curse of the prom queen?" Suzi coyly asked Gigi, pointing at the locker. She knew she had to play her cards right or Gigi would walk all over her. But she also knew the note she had just uncovered on Gigi's locker was her trump card.

Gigi stuttered, and to Suzi's surprise, didn't throw out a bitchy comment or quick comeback. She just stood there, breathing as if she'd just run a three-minute mile and staring at Suzi with a gaze that could have melted metal.

"I just want to know what's going on," Suzi finally said, breaking the silence. "I tried to ask you in the gym," she explained, looking over at Uma for backup. Uma was just standing there with an ear-to-ear grin. She was clearly enjoying the show. A bit too much, Suzi noticed.

"I don't know who you think you are," Gigi finally spit out, leaning in toward Suzi so the students who had gathered around to stare at the locker couldn't hear. "You can't just walk up to me in front of my friends like that, and you sure as hell can't embarrass me in front of the whole school." She motioned to the students standing around them. "I'm Gigi Greene. Got it?" She turned toward the onlookers. "Scram! Show's over!" she yelled, but apparently they didn't move fast enough. "Are you deaf people? Get out of my sight!" she yelled again.

Gigi looked over Suzi's shoulder at the words revealed on her locker. Then, without warning, she grabbed Suzi's arm again, albeit this time less aggressively, and leaned in close to Suzi's ear, so close that Suzi could feel her warm breath on the side of her face.

Suzi half closed her eyes and braced herself for the final insult, the knee-buckling blow from the queen of mean. Here goes . . .

"Meet me in the locker room at four o'clock sharp," Gigi whispered. "And be alone."

And with that, she let go of Suzi's arm and pushed away without a glance. As if the whole thing between them had never even happened.

"Before I tell you anything, what I say in this locker room stays in this locker room. Got it?" Gigi hissed in a threatening voice to Suzi, who was sitting on the yellow plastic bench where she had been waiting patiently for the head cheerleader since the specified time.

It was now 4:23, and Gigi had stormed into the locker room twenty minutes late and in full cheerleader attire: pleated brown skirt (with long black tights to cover her legs), yellow knee-highs (which looked ridiculous over the tights), pony-tails and all.

Suzi knew Gigi was dressed for the big soccer game that was happening later that night. She had seen posters all over school about it. The Mountain High Orcas were playing their biggest rivals, the Evergreen Lumberjacks. Tonight's game was one of the biggest of the year. People painted their faces and everything.

Since Suzi was sitting down, Gigi was towering over her, but Suzi wasn't intimidated. She found it a little hard to be intimi-dated by anybody with pom-poms on her ponytails.

"Yeah, sure," Suzi finally said in response to Gigi's request, looking up at the Queen Bee and shrugging.

Suzi slid her messenger bag off the bench and looked up at Gigi as an offer to sit down next to her, but Gigi ignored her and started pacing back and forth from one row of lockers to the other.

"What do you want from me?" Suzi finally asked. Gigi turned around and stared Suzi down. She had just opened her mouth to say something when a girl dressed in a JV running uniform burst through the locker-room doors, all sweaty and tired. The girl stopped and glanced at Gigi and then at Suzi. Her heavy panting was the only sound in the room.

"What the hell are you looking at?" Gigi spat at her, and the girl jumped and ran toward the toilets. Suzi was starting to feel a bit like a fly caught in a spiderweb.

The locker room was thick with silence once again. When Gigi was satisfied that the JV girl was out of earshot, she finally sat down and slid over next to Suzi, so that her blue eyes and long lashes were only about an inch from Suzi's face. Suzi couldn't help but inch back just a bit. Gigi's presence was almost overpowering.

"I want your help," Gigi finally said as she looked at Suzi with tortured eyes.

"How can I help you if you won't talk to me?" Suzi asked calmly, and she thought she sounded a bit like a school counselor talking to a troubled student.

"Listen, I'm scared shitless," Gigi said, lowering her voice and looking around to make sure nobody could hear. "But I can't just cozy up to you," she continued. "You have no idea how hard it is to be me. I am so popular." Suzi could have sworn she saw Gigi roll her eyes a bit, as if she were being sarcastic about her social status.

"Everybody looks at what I wear to school, how my hair is highlighted, what boys I go out with. People want to be just like me, it's so frickin' pathetic." Gigi shook her head as if she were carrying the heaviest burden in the world. "I started tanning this week," she complained, holding out one arm to show Suzi her freshly bronzed skin, "and now I can't even get an appointment the place is so booked."

Suzi thought of all the people starving in the world, dying from AIDS, and living in war zones, and she had a hard time taking Gigi's problems seriously. But she had to admit, she was seeing a whole new side of the girl. A side that revealed her popularity status for what it really was—silly.

"Look," Gigi continued, nailing Suzi with her hypnotic eyes. "I want you to find out who did this to me," she said, scratching at her legs. "But I can't be seen with you. I'm Gigi Greene; I have a reputation to uphold."

Suzi should have been insulted, but instead she had to look down at the floor to keep from laughing. She wouldn't exactly be laughing at Gigi—she knew that the head cheerleader really believed everything she was saying—but Suzi still couldn't believe that anybody could be so ridiculously full of herself.

"Okay," Suzi said, standing up and walking away from Gigi to get some space. *Focus*, she thought to herself. *Make this crazy meeting productive.*

"Let me ask you some questions," Suzi continued in her most professional, detective-like manner. "Tell me exactly what happened to you in the basement."

"Let me ask *you* a question," Gigi threw at Suzi. Suzi was taken back a bit, but she nodded in agreement. "Did you hear everything I said in the bathroom yesterday?" she asked with small, suspicious eyes. "Were you eavesdropping on us?"

Suzi hesitated a moment before answering. She was all ready to deny Gigi's accusation in order to save face, but then she figured honesty was the best policy. After all, Gigi was opening up to her, the least she could do was to be honest, too.

Suzi shyly answered Gigi's question by slowly nodding her head up and down. She was so busted.

But then, suddenly and unexpectedly, Gigi burst out laughing so hard that a ball of spit shot out of her mouth and landed with a smack on the floor, right in front of Suzi's left sneaker. Suzi looked down at the bubbly wet spot on the concrete, and she couldn't help but bust up herself, which in turn, caused Gigi to laugh so hard she snorted like a pig, which caused both of them to roar even harder.

Before they knew it, both Suzi and Gigi were holding their sore stomachs and wiping their wet eyes. It was as if, in the

thick of the tense moment, both of them had suddenly realized they were taking themselves way too seriously, and that
they both deserved to be laughed at.

Even snorted at.

After a long, lingering laugh at themselves, Gigi dropped some
of her ice-princess pretentiousness and started to treat Suzi like
a real person instead of one of her followers, and Suzi began to
believe that Gigi was actually okay, albeit a little into herself.

Realizing they needed each other in order to get what they
wanted, the two girls agreed to help each other out. They
were now sitting on the locker-room bench, snacking on a bag
of wasabi peas Suzi had found in her messenger bag. The two
almost—almost—seemed like friends.

"So did you notice anything suspicious while you were in the
basement?" Suzi asked as she cracked a hot pea between her
two front teeth. Her teeth were slightly gapped and made the
perfect pea-cracking tools. "Anything out of the ordinary?"

Gigi looked up at the ceiling for a moment. "Nothing but
dust and smelly jockstraps. That basement has always given
me the creeps." She shuddered under her thick cheerleading
sweater as she made a grab for the peas.

"How about the note on your locker," Suzi continued. "It
was written in pink lipstick, right?"

"Yeah, like some supertacky hot-pink color."

"Hot pink?" Suzi repeated, furrowing her brows. Gigi just
nodded.

"How about after you found the note," Suzi continued,
watching Gigi's reactions very closely. "Did you see anybody
strange hanging around?"

"No, I saw the note during third period, when I was on my way to the nurse after . . . you know," Gigi said, looking down at her legs regretfully. "Anyway, the hall was dead. Everyone was in class," she finished, scrutinizing a spicy pea before popping it into her mouth. "Except . . ."

"Except what?" Suzi asked, perking up.

"Well, that creepy janitor was there. You know, the one who whistles all the time . . ." Gigi trailed off, fanning her mouth and nose. "My mouth is on fire. Do you have any water?"

Suzi made a mental note that the janitor was by Gigi's locker and then reached into her bag for her water bottle. "Where is the basement where you found the pom-pom bag?" Suzi asked.

"The gym-equipment basement, over there." Gigi pointed to a brown metal door.

"Who has the keys?" Suzi asked, motioning to the locked basement door.

"Are you crazy?" Gigi asked, choking on a mouthful of the water Suzi had just handed her.

Suzi thought about it for a moment then slowly nodded. She meant to nod her head to show that yes, she was going to go into the basement, but she realized that she had just nodded to imply that yes, she was indeed crazy.

"I need the keys," she repeated. "Who has them?"

"Okay, let me see," Gigi said, shrugging as she wiped red lipstick marks off the bottle's rim with her fingers. "Mr. Rider, Coach Katie, Chet 'cause he's the quarterback, you know, and . . ." Her words trailed off as she smiled mischievously and plunged her hand deep into the cleavage of her cheerleader sweater.

Suzi raised her black brows, completely unsure of what it was Gigi was doing, but then Gigi pulled her hand out of her sweater to reveal a long, shiny, gold chain. On the end of the said chain, dangling from Gigi's perfectly manicured fingertips, was a single silver key.

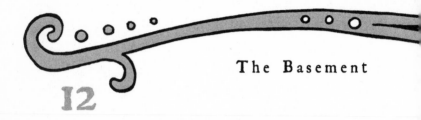

The Basement

12

"Don't leave me alone now, okay?" Suzi told Gigi as she checked her flashlight to make sure it was working. She didn't like the idea of going down into the dark, damp basement alone, but Gigi had told her flat out that there was no way she was ever going down there again. Suzi was on her own.

Gigi's key had worked on the lock, but the door itself was heavy, and the kind that automatically shuts. Gigi had said that she didn't want to stand there holding the door open the whole time, so Suzi had taken one of her drumsticks out of her bag and wedged it in the door. Suzi's wooden drumstick was all that was keeping her from getting locked down in the basement forever.

The thought made her gulp.

"You're going to stay up here the whole time, right?" Suzi asked Gigi again.

"I've got the new *Cosmo* right here. I'm not going anywhere," Gigi said as she plopped down on the bench and starting flipping through glossy, perfumed pages. Suddenly Suzi felt the differences between the two of them start to seep back in.

Okay, Suzi thought. *Here goes nothing.*

The first thing that Suzi noticed was the smell. It smelled like old sneakers.

The wooden stairs creaked as Suzi walked down them one at a time. She shined her flashlight all around her. There were wooden beams on the ceiling with big spiderwebs, rusty nails poking out from the walls, and dust everywhere. Suzi looked back up the stairs for just a moment to reassure herself that the real world, and safety, weren't far away. She could see the light peeking through where her drumstick was holding the door ajar, and she could hear Gigi singing a Beyoncé song. Gigi was off-key to the point of painful, but somehow the voice was still a comfort.

Suzi got to the bottom of the stairs and stepped onto the earth floor. She saw sweat-stained gym mats leaning up against the wall, a set of broken parallel bars, track hurdles lying on their side, and over in the far corner, she could see what must be the cheerleading teams' pom-pom bag. Gigi had described it to a T, brown with yellow stripes and a yellow mini-pom-pom on the top.

Suzi ducked a few cobwebs that were hanging from the ceiling (totally gross) and stopped smack in her tracks when she thought she heard a rustling noise behind her. She whirled around, almost dropping her flashlight, but the room was still and quiet. Nothing but floating dust moved in front of her flashlight beam.

It's all in my head, Suzi thought to herself as she took two deep, calming breaths and forced her feet to move forward.

But then she heard the same rustling noise behind her again, and this time her flashlight found a huge bug, a beetle maybe, caught in a thick spiderweb on the ceiling.

She anxiously shot her flashlight around the basement. She saw more webs, but thankfully, no spiders. Swallowing her fear as best she could, Suzi continued over to the yellow-and-brown bag in the corner. The sooner she got through this, the sooner she could get back to the safety of the locker room. Suzi turned the bag upside down, and one lone pom-pom spilled out onto the dirt floor. A little cloud of dust arose when it landed, and she saw that the threads had dead, black spiders woven into them. Totally gross. Suzi looked inside the bag for something, anything to give her a clue as to what happened to Gigi, but all she saw were webs stuck to the inside fabric. Except, wait a minute. Her flashlight caught something strange. A small tear at the bottom of the bag. No, it wasn't a tear. The edges were clean and straight, almost as if someone had cut a hole in the bag with a knife or pair of scissors.

Suddenly Suzi was startled by a loud crash.

Oh. My. Gosh. The basement door had just slammed shut—and it sounded as if someone was running down the stairs to get her!

Frantically, Suzi shot her flashlight over to the stairs, and almost laughed out loud when she saw her drumstick, the same drumstick that had been holding the basement door open, falling down the stairs, making a tapping sound on every wooden step.

Whew. Suzi's heart started beating again. Until . . . wait a minute . . . she was locked in the basement!

Suzi dropped the flashlight and bolted up the stairs two at

a time. She pushed and pulled and pounded at the basement door. It was securely locked. Crap!

"Gigi!" Suzi yelled as loudly as she could. "Gigi, are you out there? Get me out of here! Get me out of here right now!"

But all Suzi heard on the other side of the door was silence.

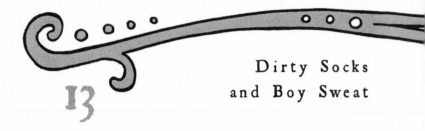

Dirty Socks
and Boy Sweat

Tonight was the big night. All of Mountain High—the preps, the punks, the jocks, the Goths, and the geeks—had shown up, united in their desire to kick some Evergreen Lumberjack butt. Girls painted *M*s and *H*s on their cheeks in brown lipstick, boys painted their entire faces yellow, some of the diehards even dyed their hair yellow. Parents and students alike had packed the spirit bags full of pom-poms, the boda bags full of Starbucks, and their fuzzy warm blankets for the damp Seattle night.

Even Jett Black was there, camera in hand and seated in the top row of the bleachers, where she could go relatively unnoticed and survey the crowd. On principle, Jett refused to wear a tacky yellow sweatshirt or paint her cheeks, but she did manage to don a pair of yellow-and-brown striped socks. She didn't want to be a total party pooper, after all.

Jett had decided to come for two reasons. One, the open buffet of crazy, adolescent antics was prime subject matter for the photo documentary she was working on, and two, she had nothing more pressing to do at the present moment. She and Suzi had a knitting club meeting later that evening, but until then, she was a free agent. The teachers hadn't even assigned any homework. They were all at the game, too.

Uma was also there, seated next to Jett, and she was in top form. She had packed in a love-smitten Li Jung, a wool blanket, and a flask full of caramel mocha.

"Where's Suz?" Uma asked, taking a gulp from her flask and leaning into Li Jung so that he almost toppled over. Uma obviously had Li Jung wrapped around her little pinkie, and her constant flirtation made Jett want to puke.

"She said she'd be here," Jett said, grabbing the flask from Uma and taking a swig. "God, Uma, how do you drink this crap?" she said, wincing.

"It's sweet." Uma giggled. "Just like Li Jung."

Jett sighed her disgust and looked through her telephoto lens for any sign of Suzi. Kids were yelling with their fists in the air, eating red vines and hot dogs, and painting one another's faces, but there was no sign of Suzi. It was weird that Suzi hadn't called Jett after school, but Jett also knew that Suzi had that secret meeting with Gigi, and she just figured the two had gone to Stumptown to talk. She was pretty sure Suzi would meet her at the game.

But the thing was, the game was about to begin.

"Be sure to document this so when we're old and gray we can look back on our glory years." Uma giggled again, pushing Li Jung's long black hair behind his ears and then kissing his lobes.

"Sure thing," Jett said, ignoring Uma and capturing on film a freshman boy spraying beer out his nose. Jett giggled to herself. This was so awesome, she thought. She just wished Suzi were here to share the moment.

The boys' soccer team came out onto the field, and Jett was almost knocked over when everybody stood up and started cheering like mad. She couldn't see the team over the frenzied fans, but she really didn't need to. She saw those guys every day at school.

Besides, Jett was more interested in scanning the crowd with her telephoto lens.

She had a best friend to find.

Suzi was starting to get cold. Really cold. The basement didn't have a heating system, after all. Why would it? There was nothing around except old, abandoned gym equipment, bugs trapped in spiderwebs, suspiciously sliced-open pom-pom bags . . . and her.

When Suzi had first realized she was locked in the basement, she had pounded on the door until her fists hurt, tried to pick the door lock with a rusty nail, and then not knowing what else to do, she had finally slumped down, defeated and tired, on the top step.

That had been maybe half an hour ago, and her butt was really starting to hurt from sitting on the hard, wooden stair. The basement was still cold—and dark as hell.

Suzi had dropped the flashlight and it had flickered off, but there was no way she was going to walk through the dark unknown to get it. Just the thought of feeling her way through all the spiderwebs and creepy gym apparatus made her shiver. She had to stay focused on her breathing to keep herself from hyperventilating.

Out of fright—and anger at Gigi.

How could she have trusted Gigi? Gigi had probably planned this whole thing as a joke, just to get a laugh out of picking on a freshman. Or, as Uma had suggested, maybe Gigi was behind the whole prom queen curse. Maybe she had faked her spider bites to scare away the other prom queen nominees, her main competition. After what Gigi had done to her tonight, Suzi wouldn't put it past her. To think she had actually felt sympathy for Gigi when she had dished out her "people want to be just like me" and all that "I'm so popular" crap. Man, when Suzi got out of this basement, she was really going to give Gigi Greene a piece of her mind.

If she ever got out of this basement, that is.

Suzi could hear the big soccer game, the infamous Kick Wars, starting up on the field. She could hear the crowd chanting, stomping their feet and clapping along with the cheerleaders' cheers. She could hear the announcer—it sounded like Coach Katie, the girl's soccer coach—calling out the names of the players over the PA system, one by one.

Every once in a while, people would run through the gym on their way to the game, and Suzi would hear their footsteps echo above on the gym floor. But no matter how hard she pounded on the door or how loud she yelled, nobody heard her.

Or her cell phone ringing in the locker room, in her messenger bag, which was still sitting on the yellow plastic bench.

Halftime, and still no sign of Suzi. Jett was really starting to get worried.

Uma tried to assure her that Suzi had just gone home after

her meeting, that she was probably exhausted after spending time with the egomaniac Gigi Greene, and that she had just decided to bag the game and call it a night. But then why wasn't Suzi answering her cell phone?

Something wasn't making sense.

On the flip side, Jett had just about had enough of the Kick War circus. Evergreen was kicking Mountain High's brown-and-yellow butt 5–0, Uma was high on sugar and making out with Li Jung under the blanket, and the night was getting drizzly and cold.

It was almost time for Jett to call it game over, but first she wanted to see the halftime show. It was always good for a laugh.

It's halftime, Suzi thought to herself as she lazily made shadow puppets on the basement's dark, webbed ceiling. After sitting on the hard stair for over an hour, she had finally calmed herself down and concluded that her fears were all in her head. Had she seen a single spider? Nope. Any gory ghosts? Nada. Killer cheerleaders wearing hot-pink lipstick? A big negativo.

Squinting her eyes to suck up every drop of light, Suzi had finally walked down the stairs, keeping her arms in front of her in case she smacked into a wall or an old balance beam, and she had managed to retrieve the flashlight and turn it back on. Bingo. She had then tipped over an old gym mat and collapsed down onto it. The mat smelled like dirty socks and boy sweat, but at this point, she could care less.

She might as well get comfortable. It didn't look as if she was going anywhere anytime soon.

Suzi could now hear M. C. Hammer's "Can't Touch This" blaring over the stadium's PA system, which meant the dance team was performing its halftime show. She usually squirmed through such degrading displays of high school spirit, but right now she would have given her right arm to be sitting on the bleachers with Jett, snickering as the dance team high-kicked in their bright yellow leotards.

Suddenly Suzi heard a ruckus up the stairs and in the girls' locker room. She could hear music playing, Madonna's "Dress You Up in My Love," and lockers slamming shut, one after the other. Was the dance team changing after the halftime show? Suzi jolted up off the smelly mat, and taking the stairs two at a time, she flew up toward the door.

But she was stopped in her tracks when one of the stairs collapsed beneath her weight. Her entire sneaker was swallowed up by the deep hole, and she fell, palms first, against the hard edge of the stairs. Ouch.

Suzi pulled her foot out and shined her flashlight into the splintered, dark hollow. The hole appeared to be about the size of a shoe box, and it was filled with dust, thick spiderwebs, and . . . fresh fingerprints? She could see three smudged fingerprints on a dark ledge that curved to the left, but no matter how hard she tried to finagle the light beam around the corner, she couldn't tell if anything more was there.

"Here goes nothing," Suzi said out loud as she put down her flashlight and reached into the dark, damp crevice with her bare hands. She closed her eyes and grimaced as her fingers slid through thick, sticky cobwebs and over rough, rusty nails and damp wood splinters. Then her hand reached to the left, into the dark pocket, and she immediately felt something cold, small, and smooth. She grabbed the object with her fingers and carefully pulled it out.

It was a single, gold hoop earring.

That's strange, Suzi thought, looking at the earring for a long moment before slipping it safely into her bra. *What's a gold earring doing in a secret hollow under the stairs?*

Feeling her adrenaline start to pump, she wondered what else might be hidden under the stair. She dug her hand back in, this time less hesitantly, and her fingers brushed over the nails and through the cobwebs, and then suddenly she felt something else. Something that was . . . sharp. Suzi carefully grabbed an edge with two fingers and gave it one tug . . . two tugs . . . three.

In an explosion of splinters and dust, the second object broke free. Suzi looked down to see that she was holding a pair of shiny, silver scissors. Hanging from the tip was a small, yellow-and-brown slice of Gigi's pom-pom bag.

Oh. My. Gosh. Somebody did cut a hole in the pom-pom bag! Somebody wanted the basement's spiders to crawl in there so that when Gigi opened it up, they'd swarm out and . . . ouch!

Suzi felt a sharp sting on her hand, and when she looked down, she saw a huge black spider crawling onto her hand. She dropped the scissors and shook off the creepy crawler, but shining her flashlight around, she suddenly realized that huge black spiders were everywhere! On the walls, the broken parallel bars—even the smelly gym mat she had just been lying on!

Suzi bolted up the rest of the stairs and practically body-slammed the door.

"Hey!" she yelled as she pounded with every ounce of energy she had left. She could hear someone singing in the locker room, but whoever it was had a terrible voice.

"Is somebody there? Help me!" Suzi screamed. "Get me out of here! I'm being eaten alive."

Suzi pounded and pounded, and she was just starting to think that whoever was in the locker room couldn't hear her screams over their own singing when, finally, she heard a click.

The door opened, and the light seared into Suzi's eyes. She stumbled into the warm locker room, her hands shielding her eyes. She was bent over like she had just run a marathon, and when she stood up, there was a cheerleader standing in front of her. She couldn't tell who it was. All she could make out was the girl's brown-and-yellow uniform and unusually bright pink lipstick.

"Gigi, is that you?" Suzi asked, still squinting as her eyes adjusted to the light. "Man, you are so dead."

But then, as her eyesight cleared, she had to fight the urge to turn and run back down into the basement. The scene in front of her was that frightening.

It wasn't Gigi Greene standing in front of her, or any varsity cheerleader for that matter.

It was Mr. Rider, dressed to the nines in a cheerleading outfit. Ponytails and all.

KITTY'S FIASCO

Kitty had butterflies. It was halftime, the dance team had just performed a killer kick-line routine, and now Coach Katie was announcing the prom queen court over the mike. Every year at the Kick Wars game, the prom queen nominees each received a single red rose, officially marking their nomination. It was a Mountain High tradition.

But this year things were a bit different. Two of the four prom queen wannabes had freaked out and dropped out of the running. First, Gigi threw in the towel, and just before the game tonight, Parker had told Kitty that she was dropping out, too.

Poor Parker, Kitty thought, looking at her blue-haired friend slouched over on the bleachers. Parker hadn't stopped crying all day, and Kitty couldn't blame her. The girl seriously looked like crap. Her hair and skin were really and truly em-bar-rass-ing. She was all wrapped up like a burrito and wearing a head scarf like some hippy dippy.

Kitty couldn't even be mad at Parker for flirting with Xavier. When she had first heard the news, she had made a mental note to key Parker's car or spread a rumor that she had crabs or something. But now that Parker was blue from head to toe, Kitty saw it as Karmic justice and was just going to let it go. Besides, Kitty knew that Xavier was totally in love with her. After all, she was going to be America's Next Top Model.

Kitty had been working at the Orange Julius after school for a whole year in order to save up enough money to hire a professional photographer and finish her modeling portfolio. One more month of serving up greasy hot dogs and salted pretzels and she would be on her way. And being elected prom queen next week wouldn't hurt either. She'd get lots of press, interviews, tour opportunities . . . Oh, she was so excited! Tyra Banks, watch out!

But first Kitty had to get through the red rose ceremony. Read: She had to walk down onto the field in front of the whole school. The thing was, while Kitty love-love-loved being in front of a camera, she hate-hate-hated being in front of a crowd. Hence the butterflies. Or more like hornets, she thought.

Coach Katie, the she-man sports coach, had just called out Trixie Topp's name, and Trixie had walked down the bleachers in her yellow Ralph Lauren rain jacket and matching rain boots and accepted her rose with an ear-to-ear grin. Eech. Trixie was such a Goody Two-shoes, BG-wannabe poser.

Then the moment Kitty had been simultaneously dreading and looking forward to finally came. Coach Katie called her name over the PA system. People started clapping and woo-woo-wooing, and Kitty stood up to acknowledge her applause. She had bought a new, supershort black miniskirt for this special occasion, and she could feel all the guys drooling over her meticulously toned and oiled legs. If only they knew she wasn't wearing any underwear! Truth was, Kitty scarcely wore underwear. Tacky whale tails? So uncool.

Kitty put on her best supermodel's smile, checked her lip gloss, and patted down her slick black hair. Then she walked her bootylicious self down the bleachers and toward the podium, where Trixie and Coach Katie were waiting for her. Kitty took teeny-weenie steps as she walked; there was quite a breeze tonight and she had to be careful so that her skirt didn't fly up. Even one inch could prove disastrous.

Kitty carefully walked up the podium, took the rose, and when Coach Katie tried to hug her, she ducked it like a pro. Trixie smiled at Kitty nervously, and Kitty smiled back while slowly mouthing the word loser. With both Gigi and Parker out of the running, this crown was as good as hers and Kitty knew it.

Coach Katie said a few more words about the prom, and then the crowd went wild. The cheerleaders came out and started kicking, the band fired up, and Kitty felt as if she were a star. She was up onstage, and it was all about her-her-her . . .

Just then, some guy dressed up as a giant orca ran onto the field. That's weird, Kitty thought. She didn't remember seeing the Mountain High mascot at any of the games before. It must be a special Kick Wars thing, she thought. She watched the orca as it danced around the field, cheered with the cheerleaders, and caught a pass from the school quarterback. Then the orca came up on the podium, where

Coach Katie, Trixie, and Kitty were standing. Kitty kept her brilliant smile, but she secretly willed that ridiculous whale away from her. The last thing she needed was to have a giant orca embarrass her in front of the whole school. Way to ruin the moment.

The orca high-fived Coach Katie (the crowd cheered), it waddled over next to Trixie and kissed her hand (the crowd ahhh-ed), and then it ran up to Kitty, picked her up, and twirled her around in its arms. Kitty kicked and screamed, but the orca was just too strong and the crowd was cheering it on. Kitty was mortified, not to mention dizzy, when the orca finally put her down. Thank God, she thought, one more minute of that and she would have puked all over her new patent-leather boots.

She was still a little woozy as she slicked down her hair and tried to compose herself. Wait a minute. Trixie's eyes were bugging out of her head, the band had stopped mid "Louie Louie," and she could have sworn Coach Katie was leering at her. Then she heard the crowd suck in its breath in unison, and it hit her like a brick. Her skirt. She wasn't wearing any underwear.

That was the day America's Next Top Model, Kitty Sui, flashed the soccer team, faculty, parents, and entire student body of Evergreen and Mountain High, and then fainted dead away onstage.

Of course the press was there to cover the event.

Bitchin' and Stitchin'

14

"My God, girl. Where have you been?" Jett asked as she put down her knitting needles, bolted out of her chair, and ran to greet her long-lost friend. "I've been trying to call you all night," she ranted.

Suzi had just walked through Stumptown's doors. It was eight o'clock at night, and while most of Mountain High was still shivering in the drizzly sports stadium, watching the last quarter of the Kick Wars game, Jett had cut out early to attend her and Suzi's weekly Stitch 'n Bitch.

"I've been calling and texting and worried sick," Jett continued while eyeballing Suzi up and down. Suzi was a mess. She had dirt all over her face, stringy cobwebs in her hair, and her arms were wrapped around her like she was freezing her butt off.

"You so need a soy latte," Jett decided as she sat her friend down on one of Stumptown's tattered old sofas and darted over to the barista.

"Where have you been? Under the bleachers macking on Mr. Fry?" Sam Witherspoon teased. Sam was a regular at the

Stitch 'n Bitch meetings. Actually, out of the seven regular members, Sam was the most talented of all the knitters. In the past month alone, he had whipped up a pair of rainbow fingerless gloves, a felted laptop bag, a pair of sparkly leg warmers (which he claimed were for his so-called girlfriend, but Suzi and Jett suspected they were all for himself), and now he was working on his masterpiece—a black cashmere hat with little pink kitty ears on top.

"Where's Uma?" Suzi asked Sam, looking around at the crowd.

"Probably rounding second base right about now." Sam smiled mischievously.

"Here," Jett said, appearing out of nowhere and plopping a steaming cinnamon soy latte in front of Suzi's nose. Suzi grabbed the cup and wrapped her hands around its warmth. She inhaled the sweet, earthy smell and took a sip. She instantly felt better.

"You rock," Suzi croaked softly as she pulled her jacket even tighter around her.

"What's up with your hand?" Jett asked, grabbing Suzi's palm and studying the fresh, bulging spider bite. Suzi winced.

"I was locked in the gym-equipment basement," she finally offered, rubbing the itchy bite against her jeans.

"What?" Jett spit out.

"I said, I was locked underneath the school, in the basement. For what seemed like hours." Suzi pushed Jett's knitting bag over and put her cup down on the table.

"How did you get in there?" Sam asked.

"Well, I had that meeting with Gigi, you know," Suzi began, crossing her arms for warmth. "Gigi had a key to the basement where she was bitten by spiders, so I went down to check it out."

"Did the door slam behind you or what?" Jett asked, clearly concerned.

"Well, Gigi," Suzi said, spitting out the head cheerleader's name. "Gigi was supposed to be watching the door, but she ditched me," she said angrily. She was unconsciously tapping her fingers against her right thigh (a drummer's habit), and Sam reached out, over Jett, and put his hand over Suzi's.

"Or she locked you down there," he offered softly.

"Suz, you know better than to trust a BG," Jett said. "Are you sure you're okay?"

"Yeah," Suzi said, trying not to notice that her hand was starting to itch like mad. "But I was one lucky duck."

Jett raised her eyebrows, silently demanding an explanation.

"Let's just say that the basement is most definitely infested with creepy crawlers," Suzi explained, "but I think they had a little help getting into Gigi's pom-pom bag."

Jett's eyes narrowed suspiciously, and she had just opened her mouth to say something when Sam cut in.

"Well, little Ms., once bitten twice shy," he sang out, holding up his hat to admire his stitches. "Too bad about the detour, because you missed quite the show tonight."

"Why, did something happen?" Suzi asked, scooting forward on the sofa.

"Oh, man." Jett grinned mischievously and shot a look at Sam. "Did it ever."

And then, as if on cue, Jett and Sam erupted into fits of laughter.

• • •

"She was totally commando? You saw everything?" Suzi blurted out.

Suzi almost lost it when Sam and Jett told her the story about how Kitty was attacked by the orca during halftime and ended up flashing her bare butt to the whole school. In turn, Suzi had told Jett and Sam about how she had made it out of the basement only to find Mr. Rider dressed up in a cheerleading skirt and ponytails. Jett had laughed so hard, she sprayed cappuccino foam out her nose. Needless to say, the three friends were sharing a wicked, rolling laugh at their favorite coffee shop, and just like that, the biting spiders and subzero temperatures that Suzi had borne witness to less than an hour before were fading fast.

"Honey, I saw more than I ever hoped to see in my whole life!" Sam suddenly yelled out, referring to Kitty's lack of underwear. Suzi shot him a puzzled look, and Sam resumed knitting ferociously.

"Let's just say that the carpet matches the drapes," Jett snickered.

"Oh. My. Gosh. I can't believe it." Suzi shook her head and looked up at Stumptown's high tin ceilings.

"Believe it," Jett said, giggling and wiping her eyes. "Not even a thong." She snorted again.

"No, what I mean is, I can't believe the prom queen curse has struck again. I'm sure Kitty's fiasco wasn't an accident," Suzi continued, her voice getting serious.

Jett nodded and straightened up a bit, trying to acknowledge the more serious turn of the conversation, but she still couldn't wipe the huge smile off her face.

"So who was in the orca uniform?" Suzi asked, her eyes squinting in thought.

"Don't ask me," Jett replied sarcastically, grabbing for her knitting project, a black mohair scarf with red trim, and pretending to purl profusely. Suzi stared Jett down. She wasn't about to let her friend off that easy.

"Okay, lay it on me," Jett relented, rolling her eyes and sinking back into the sofa. "What are you thinking?"

"Well . . ." Suzi sat upright and leaned forward. "Gigi said that the curse note on her locker, the note that the baby BGs wiped off, was written in bright pink lipstick. When I stumbled out of the basement and my eyes were still fuzzy, all I could see on Rider's face was his bright pink lipstick," she explained.

"Half the school wears pink lipstick," Sam countered.

"Yes, but Rider also has keys to the basement door," Suzi went on, picking her cup off the table and taking another sip. Jett and Sam just looked at her, confused.

"I found a bag of spiders hidden under the stairs in the basement." She shivered. "I think somebody planted those spiders that attacked Gigi. And me." She gulped.

"But how did they get into Gigi's bag?" Jett asked, not missing a beat.

"A hole. Cut right into it," Suzi said, making a scissors with her fingers.

"You think it's Rider who's cursing the prom queens?" Sam asked.

Suzi thought for a moment. "Not necessarily," she said enigmatically as she dug her hand down into her shirt and pulled out the single, gold hoop earring.

She held it up to the light, and it sparkled like a diamond.

"I think whoever is cursing the prom queens has the match to this," she said, looking at her friends and smiling mischievously.

Belgian Waffles and Tighty Whities

15

"Feeling better this morning, kiddo?" Suzi's mom asked as she walked into the kitchen. It was seven-thirty on Wednesday morning, and just like yesterday, and the day before, and the day before that, the Seattle streets were wet and the sky was sulky.

Suzi looked up from behind her steaming stack of Belgian waffles and nodded to her mom. "I'm thawed out now." She smiled, motioning to the plate of extra waffles on the kitchen counter.

Suzi had woken up early that Wednesday morning—and starving out of her skull. She hadn't got home until nine the night before, and against all her mom's pleas to eat something, even just a bowl of cereal, all Suzi had wanted to do was take a hot shower and crawl into bed. She knew she would feel better after a good night's sleep. And feel better she did. But she had also woken up with a growling stomach and she had decidedly whipped up a fresh batch of waffles before her mom had even gotten out of bed.

"Thanks for breakfast," her mom said hungrily as she sprinkled loose green tea into a strainer and poured hot water into her WKPR mug. WKPR was the independent television station where Suzi's mom had worked for the last seven years. Her mom was a documentary writer, and she was always researching and writing about cool subjects like the melting of the ice caps, the theories behind why whales beach themselves, and the ancient city of Angkor in Cambodia. Suzi knew her mom was smart as a whip. After all, she had managed to get her master's in journalism from the University of Washington and keep Suzi shoulder-high in CDs and books all on her own. Suzi knew her dad couldn't help with the bills much. Although her mom and dad got along pretty well, he was a starving artist who lived off grants and the occasional sale of a painting. He currently resided in Amsterdam, and Suzi's mom promised that she could go for a visit when she turned sixteen next year.

"Sounds like you had quite the day yesterday," Suzi's mom said. Suzi had told her mom all about the basement—and the curse—before she had hit the sack last night. She didn't want to worry her mom, but she also didn't like to keep things from her. Her mom usually had spot-on insight and advice.

"But you never told me," her mom continued, stabbing at a fluffy waffle with her fork. "After all that time in the basement, did you find anything?"

"Yeah, I wanted to show you . . ." Suzi began, pulling her prized gold clue out of her bra. She had wrapped it in tissue so that it wouldn't fall out, but it had made one of her boobs look bigger than the other. She ended up filling the other side of her bra with tissue as well, just to even it out.

"I found this . . ." Suzi trailed off, holding the shiny hoop out for her mom to see. "It was stashed in a secret compartment under the stairs," Suzi said, her blue eyes sparkling.

"Hmm . . . thin gold hoops are in style right now, and this one is really small and thick," Suzi's mom said as she studied the earring. Just then, Suzi glanced up at the clock on the wall and jumped out of her chair.

"I have to go. Big day," she said, quickly shoving the hoop back into her bra.

"I'm proud of what you're doing," her mom said. "But please be careful. Your fingertips were almost blue when you came home last night." Suzi could tell her mom was serious.

"'Kay, Mom," Suzi said, giving her mom a quick kiss as she darted out the door. The prom was only three days away, and Suzi had a lot of work to do.

"The waffles are divine!" Suzi heard her mom yell after her as she ran down the front steps. Suzi smiled to herself and pointed her bike toward Mountain High.

Smack!

"Ouch," Uma complained. "Watch it, Suz. I have a wicked headache." Uma made a nauseous face at Suzi as she threw the softball back toward Suzi's mitt.

"It's the sugar in those caramel mochas. You should know better," Suzi teased, jumping as high as she could to snag Uma's terrible throw.

It was once again Mr. Rider's gym class, and although the sky was threatening rain and the field was slick and muddy, Rider had insisted that they go outside and play a game of softball.

Mr. Rider.

As far as the rest of the school was concerned, all was normal with Mr. Rider this morning. He had shown up at work dressed in his usual grotesque getup of jeans with holes in the butt, sans underwear, and with a polyester shirt unbuttoned one button too far so that everyone could witness his abundance of manly black chest hair. Hurl-worthy, but not at all out of the ordinary for Mountain High's pervy gym teacher.

Unbeknownst to the rest of the school, Suzi had been involuntarily enlightened to Rider's miniskirt fetish in the locker room the night before, and it suddenly occurred to her that maybe the reason why it always looked like Rider wasn't wearing underwear was that he wore women's string bikinis instead of the full-cheek coverage of the more manly tighty whities.

But Suzi's all-too-intimate insight into Mr. Rider's dressing habits wasn't the only thing that had changed since last night. The whole school had gone into high red alert since Kitty Sui's halftime incident. The fact that Mountain High had come from behind and ended up winning the Kick Wars game by one point had completely faded into the shadows. Everybody was much more interested in the fact that Kitty Sui had passed out, naked from the waist down, in front of the whole school, and had later found a note written in bright pink lipstick on her Jetta windshield that read, *Kill the prom queens.*

Suzi had heard about Kitty's threat note first thing that morning. She had been walking into the cafeteria before first period to get a dose of caffeine and had noticed the BGs once again causing a ruckus in the back of the cafeteria. After getting her coffee, she had gone to sit with Jett and Uma, and even from where they were sitting almost half a cafeteria away, they could hear Gigi's high, shrill gossiping over every other noise in the room. Suzi had heard everything about Kitty's fiasco: the threat note, the bump on the back of her head from fainting onstage, the rumors about her Brazilian, everything.

Suzi had also noticed that Kitty was a no-show this morning, and she wasn't at all surprised.

Watching Gigi flap her lips, dramatically wave her arms in the air, and madly scratch at her legs, Suzi felt herself steaming inside. She couldn't help but wonder why Gigi didn't come over and apologize for ditching her last night, or at least inquire as to whether she was okay. Every once in a while, Suzi would catch Gigi looking over at her, but as soon as their eyes locked, Gigi would tear her gaze away. Just like Gigi had said, she and Suzi were from totally different sides of the cafeteria.

Smack!

The sound of the ball hitting her leather mitt snapped Suzi back into reality. It was still a cold, drizzly Wednesday morning, and Rider's PE class was still warming up for a softball game.

"So Li Jung and I decided to wear a matching tux and dress to the prom," Uma yelled out as she threw the ball back to Suzi.

"That's great," Suzi answered from right field. She threw the ball back to Uma. It went straight into the glove.

"Why don't you come, Suz?" Uma asked. "You could be our date, it would be a blast," she said as she threw the ball back to Suzi.

This time, Uma's throw was way off. The tip of Suzi's mitt tapped the ball, but it bounced over her head and landed with a wet thud behind her. When she turned around to retrieve it, she noticed that Coach Katie was running onto the field with the girls' soccer team in tow.

The coach was dressed in tight brown long johns and baggy, bright yellow shorts, and her long blond hair was flowing behind her as she blew her whistle and sprinted along with her girls. Suzi had always thought Coach Katie looked more like a pampered suburban housewife than a hard-core sports coach, but she also knew that Coach Katie was highly respected among the sports community. Although the boys' soccer team could hardly find it within themselves to win a game (with the exception of last night), Coach Katie's girls' soccer and volleyball teams were state renowned.

"Balls in, everybody!" Suzi heard her softball team captain yell somewhere behind her. The voice seemed a million miles away.

Suzi looked back at her class, and seeing that most of the students were gabbing away rather than getting serious, and that Rider himself was busy teaching a perky sophomore how to properly move her hips when she swung the bat, she took the ample opportunity to sneak off her position in right field. She could hear Uma yelling at her, asking her where she was going, but Suzi's mind was focused on something else.

Or someone else.

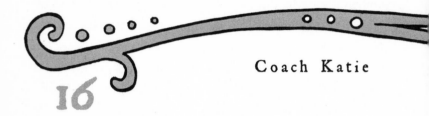

Coach Katie

16

"Coach Katie, can I talk to you for a minute?" Suzi asked politely. She had successfully sneaked out of her softball game and onto the muddy soccer field. Coach Katie was busy watching her team and barking orders, but Suzi had walked up behind her and stood waiting for the right moment to speak.

Coach Katie swung around when she heard her name, her plastic orange sport whistle protruding from her tightly clenched lips. Suzi notice that the whistle had traces of smudged red around the rim.

A gym teacher who shook pom-poms by night and a sports coach who wore bright red lipstick. Mountain High sure had its share of characters. Suzi giggled to herself.

Coach Katie shot her a quick, pissy glance and waved her away, but Suzi was ever so patient. She enjoyed studying her school's only female coach, and she had never stood this close to her before.

Coach Katie watched her girls like a hawk. Whenever one scrimmage team was close to making a goal, she would hunch her big broad shoulders, bunch her manly hands into tight fists, and yell out in a deep, threatening voice, "Sadie, get the lead out!" or "Move it, Piper!" But when she wasn't shouting, when the coach was standing still, Suzi noticed that she had extremely delicate features. She had long, wispy blond hair, a cute button nose, pouty lips, and the perfectly arched eyebrows of a Hollywood starlet.

Just then, Coach Katie reached up and pulled her hair back into an extremely tight ponytail, so tight that it pulled her eyes toward the outside of her face. With her hair out of the way, Suzi also noticed that Coach Katie had her ears pierced.

All the way up the lobe.

"What can I do for you?" Coach Katie finally said. Her eyes gave Suzi a slow, leering, once-over. Suzi cleared her throat and looked up at the towering woman.

"Hi, Coach. I'm Suzi Clue, I'm a freshman, and—" Suzi started to say.

"I. Know. Who. You. Are," Coach Katie answered impatiently.

"Well," Suzi continued, fighting the urge to look down at her muddy sneakers. "I'm sure you've heard about the prom queen curse that everyone's talking about."

"How could I not?" Coach Katie practically snorted, rolling her eyes up at the gray sky. Then suddenly the coach smiled warmly and looked down at Suzi. "What do you care and why are you asking me?"

"I want to know who was in the mascot uniform last night. The orca that assaulted Kitty Sui," Suzi answered directly, feeling her detective intellect giving her a sudden rush of confidence.

Coach Katie let out a huff, a half laugh really, and her breath cloud hung in the cold air for a moment. Then she turned her face back toward the soccer field.

"Give me three laps!" she screamed, and Suzi jumped. "That was quite the scene last night, wasn't it?" Coach Katie said, leaning down so that her and Suzi's faces were just about level. Coach Katie was smiling, but it was a fake smile, and Suzi noticed the coach had a chunk of red lipstick stuck on her front right tooth.

"The truth is," the coach continued, standing up again, "I thought the whole thing was kind of funny."

"Funny?" Suzi asked, surprised.

"I don't mean to seem frigid," the coach said. "It's just that cheerleaders . . . well, they rub me the wrong way," she whispered, shrugging her broad shoulders in a guiltless "what do you do?" gesture.

"Do you know who was in the mascot uniform last night?" Suzi asked, shooting a quick glance back at her softball game now in progress. She needed to get back before Rider found her out.

"Wasn't that whale bit funny?" Coach Katie giggled, but then she saw Suzi's suspicious gaze and her demeanor turned serious. "I have no idea who that orca mascot was. Mountain High officially has no field mascot." Suzi looked up at the coach's face, trying to read her expression, but it was absolutely vacant. Emotionless. Unreadable.

"I like your ears," Suzi said, suddenly changing the subject. The comment was an honest one, but Suzi was also shifting her investigation into new territory. She was looking for the owner of the other gold hoop, after all. "How many times are they pierced?"

"Six times on my right ear and seven on my left." Coach Katie beamed. "I did all the piercings myself, with a stickpin." The thought made Suzi grimace, and Coach Katie laughed, a long, loud, rolling laugh.

"I went to Mountain High, too, you know," the coach said, leaning in. "I know what it's like to want to fit in. Pain is a big part of that." Suzi watched as a dark cloud suddenly came over Coach Katie's face.

"Anyway," Coach Katie said, suddenly doing a little jump and clapping her hands. "I don't know what you're up to, but I like your style and I'm going to help you out," she finished, flashing Suzi another fake smile.

"Follow me," Coach Katie commanded as she started to walk off the field. The heels of her silver-swished Nikes made sucking sounds in the wet mud.

Suzi looked back at Mr. Rider's softball game. There was a big hole in right field. Her hole. But what would Rider do if she ditched his class? Call her in for a teacher–student meeting? Hardly. Not after last night.

"You coming or what?" Coach Katie suddenly snapped, turning around and shooting Suzi an impatient look.

Suzi jumped in her sneaks and followed as ordered.

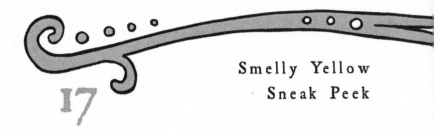

Smelly Yellow
Sneak Peek

"If someone catches you, remember. You didn't get in with my key," Coach Katie said, putting emphasis on the word *my* and sliding her key into the door. Suzi could hear the lock click open.

"Sure," Suzi said as she held back a gulp. She looked up at the sign that clearly read BOYS' LOCKER ROOM. Suzi was way out of her league here, but she knew she couldn't pass up this opportunity. Coach Katie had offered to let her into the boys' locker room so that she could snoop around for the mascot uniform.

"But you're small, so if someone's in there, just duck into a locker and by all means stay quiet," Coach Katie continued, pushing the steel door open just wide enough to shove Suzi's body through. Suzi could feel the coach's massive hand on her left shoulder. It was like a death grip.

"Sure," Suzi squeaked, but it was already too late. The coach had closed the door behind her and locked it quickly.

This time, Suzi did gulp.

Suzi looked around, truly in awe of her surroundings. The boys' locker room was like an explosion of testosterone. The walls were covered with life-size posters of pro sports players in brightly colored uniforms. There was a poster of the Seattle Supersonics, Pamela Anderson in a red bikini, and even one of an oiled, bulging Arnold Schwarzenegger posing in a Speedo.

Unlike the girls' locker room, which smelled of fruity shower products, body lotions, and perfume, the boys' locker room smelled like sweat and feet, and there were dirty clothes, wet towels, muddy football cleats, and jockstraps strewn all over the benches. Suzi wrinkled her nose and flashed back to how her mom used to complain to her dad about how messy he was around the house. She wondered if this was what her mom was talking about.

Suzi took a few brave steps toward the massive row of brown lockers. Some of them were open, as the fifth period conditioning class was in the weight room pumping and ogling their muscles in the mirror. Suzi peeked inside the spaces, feeling powerful and scared at the same time. Wrinkled varsity jackets, huge, dirty sneakers, crumpled-up school papers, lighters, uncapped cologne bottles. A few of the lockers had photos of scantily clad girls whom Suzi recognized from school taped up on the inside of their doors. Suzi shook her head. She bet the girls had no idea their pictures were on public display.

Suzi riffled through each open locker with her eyes, searching for any sign of the orca uniform. Every once in a while, she'd spot a black jacket sleeve that looked like a fin or a white sweatshirt that looked like an orca belly, but mostly she found dirty, stinky clothes and other disgusting boys' things that seemingly hadn't seen soap or the light of day for ages. The orca outfit wasn't anywhere in sight. Bummer, but it was worth a try.

Suzi was just walking around a corner and toward the door that would lead her into the gym when suddenly she stopped dead in her tracks.

"She deserved what she got, the tease." The deep, rough voice was coming from around the corner, and Suzi instinctively jumped back a step and plastered herself up against the wall. The steam seeping out from around the corner told her that the showers had been turned on. Conditioning class must have let out early.

Suzi felt her hands go cold and clammy. Coach Katie had locked the door she had come in through, and if the layout of the boys' locker room was the same as that of the girls', the only other exit was around the corner, and there was a shower-ful of wet, naked boys between her and that door. Not an easy feat to sneak around, no matter how thick the steam. Plus, the guys were sure to come toward her once they finished showering, so she was trapped. What was she going to do? Jump into a locker and stay quiet like Coach Katie had suggested?

Suzi heard the showers start to turn off one by one, and on the verge of panic, she took a dive into the nearest open locker. She had to crouch down to fit, but she managed to wedge herself in behind a big puffy jacket and cover her body with a huge yellow football jersey. Correction: a huge, smelly yellow football jersey.

"I mean, it was going to happen sooner or later. Too many

people hate them," said the same deep voice as before. Suzi heard the slaps of wet feet on the concrete floor, and the sounds seemed to be getting closer. *Here they come*, she thought as she sucked in her breath and held it.

"Dude, Chet. Who do you think did it?" Suzi didn't recognize the voice, but she did recognize the name. Chet Charleston was Gigi's boyfriend, and the buys were obviously talking about the curse.

"Could have been anybody," Suzi heard Chet say.

Suzi stayed still and quiet. She could see through a small crack between the puffy jacket and the football jersey, but everything was all blurry. She mostly saw washboard stomachs and tiny white towels around waists, and she couldn't tell one boy from another.

"I'm sick of the cheerleaders," Chet started to say again. "Gigi's been pulling all this rank shit on me, telling me what I can wear and who I can hang with. That chick is wack." Suzi watched as a figure started to walk toward the locker she was hiding in. As the figure came closer, Chet's voice also got louder.

Oh. My. Gosh. Suzi was hiding in Chet Charleston's locker. She shut her eyes tight. She couldn't watch.

"I'd dump Gigi in a second if she wasn't such a wildcat between the . . . what the hell?" Chet asked slowly and suspiciously. Suzi sucked in her breath and braced herself to be found out.

"Which one of you stole my picture of that naked freshman girl?" Chet asked.

Suzi breathed out a sigh of relief, albeit quietly. She was safe. Just a few more minutes and the guys would dress and leave, and then she could sneak out the door, through the gymnasium, and to class as if nothing had ever happened.

But suddenly Chet started grabbing at the clothes hanging up in his locker, sifting through them to see if the picture had fallen off the door and landed inside somewhere. But instead of finding his picture of a half-naked freshman girl (which Suzi had torn down and put safely in her back pocket), Chet instead found a living, breathing freshman.

Suzi looked up at his shocked face and forced an innocent smile, but then her eyes instinctively dropped from his eyes to his waistline.

Chet was standing in front of her, buck naked.

"What the hell?" Chet repeated, picking up his towel and scrambling to tie it around his waist. He was moving too fast, and no matter how many times he tried to tie it on, it kept slipping off. Suzi knew better than to watch him fumble. She just closed her eyes.

Suddenly Chet grabbed Suzi by the shoulder and yanked her out of his locker in one strong sweep. She stumbled over his supersize football cleats and landed on her knees on the locker room floor, surrounded by half-naked football players.

Suzi stood up, brushed herself off, and cleared her throat to attempt to capture a small air of dignity, but she knew it wasn't working. She was so busted. And so embarrassed.

"Who the %$*#! are you?" "What the %$*#! are you doing?" "Get the %$*#! out of here!"

The boys' reactions all came at once and Suzi felt as if she were being verbally tackled. Some of the boys turned around, shy of being seen in their skimpy towels, while others just stood there, staring her down. It was a circle of testosterone-fueled chaos, and Suzi was standing right in the middle of it.

"Guys," Suzi managed while holding up her hand in a gesture of peacemaking. "I didn't know anybody was in here." She let her eyes fall down to her feet. Maybe if she acted submissive the guys wouldn't tear her to bits. It seemed to work in the animal kingdom, and as far as she was concerned, welcome to the jungle.

"You're not supposed to be in here at all!" Chet yelled. "Is this how you get your kicks?"

"Can't get any action so you gotta sneak it?" another big, muscled guy Suzi knew as Jed spit out at her.

"Guys, guys!" she yelled out as loud as she could, half out of fear and half out of impatience. "I'm not trying to sneak a peek, I'm investigating the curse!" she screamed, holding her hand out to keep the wolves at bay. "I'm trying to find the mascot uniform that someone wore last night to attack Kitty Sui," she finished as quickly and as calmly as possible.

"Curse?" Chet suddenly asked as he took a step back from Suzi and scratched at his head.

"Yes," Suzi answered, relieved that he was at least listening to her. "Have any of you guys seen an orca uniform lying around?" she asked, careful to keep her gaze above the boys' shoulders. She was still very nervous about the naked circle surrounding her.

"I saw the orca dude after the game," offered a voice from the back of the pack, and Suzi stood on her tiptoes to get a better look. It was a senior football player everybody called Cookie because he had the reputation for being such a mama's boy, even though he was as large as a refrigerator.

"Yeah?" Suzi egged him on.

"I saw him, or, uh, it, driving through the parking lot. The dude had this crazy whale mask over his head and almost took me out," Cookie said.

"Do you remember what kind of car it was?" Suzi asked.

"It was some kind of SUV. Black. Big. Sweet ride," Cookie said, grinning at his ability to recall the details.

"Thanks, Cookie. That helps," Suzi said, keeping her voice loud and firm in an effort to maintain control of the situation. "So does anyone have any idea who would want to hurt Kitty, Gigi, or Parker?"

"Coach Katie's probably tired of them turning her down for dyke dates," said one of the smaller guys in the front, and the room erupted in manly laughter.

"Listen, ah, what's your name?" Chet suddenly asked.

"Suzi Clue," Suzi answered.

"Suzi Clue," Chet repeated, nodding and scoffing. "The question you should be asking here isn't who *would* want to hurt the prom queens." He paused for effect. "The question is, who *wouldn't* want to hurt them."

Suzi let the point sink in, and then suddenly finding herself in the middle of another all-too-macho moment, she decided it was her prime time to make an exit.

She quietly bowed her head and had just managed to slip past Chet and about two other big guys when suddenly someone grabbed her left shoulder, hard.

Suzi stopped in her tracks.

"Where ya goin', freshman?" she heard a voice whisper in her ear.

Suzi felt the blood drain from her face. She was scared.

Suzi tried to pull away, but suddenly she felt herself being picked up off her feet and bench-pressed high in the air. The sensation made her sick to her stomach. Then a few other guys came over and suddenly she was being passed around the crowd, over the boys' heads, as if she were a rag doll.

"To the pool!" the boys started to chant in unison. "Pool. Pool. Pool."

Suzi could feel hands trying to pinch her and grab her ass as she was being pushed along, just like when she moshed at a rock concert. And then suddenly she had a brilliant idea. This wasn't the first time she had crowd-surfed, after all. She knew exactly what to do.

In one swift move, Suzi pushed herself up so that she was standing on top of the shoulders of the boy who was carrying her. And then, just as she had managed to get up onstage during a Pearl Jam benefit concert last spring, she ran over the sea of square-shouldered football players and jumped down right as she got to the gymnasium door. With all her body weight, she flung the heavy steel door open and bolted straight into the girls'-gymnastics-team practice, currently in progress.

Ignoring the triple back tucks, handstands, and bar routines going on all around her, Suzi ran like a bat out of hell, leaping over spot mats and springboards and girls doing splits. When she finally did stop for a moment, her sneakers squeaking against the gym floor and her breath coming in sharp pants, she couldn't believe what she was seeing.

Oh. My. Gosh.

The entire gymnastics team had stopped midpractice to witness the explosive and unexpected emergence of the football team into the gym. The girls were giggling, squirming, and pointing as the boys stood there panting, dripping wet, and half naked.

Well, not all of them were half naked.

In all the shuffle, it seemed Chet Charleston had once again lost his little white waist towel.

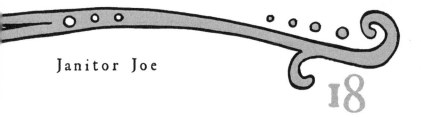

Janitor Joe

18

After her near-death experience in the boys' locker room, Suzi had run down the empty halls as fast as she could and finally stopped outside her geometry class. She then keeled over and stared at her toes, still muddy from the soccer field, and attempted to get her breathing under control. Jeez, she didn't realize how freaked out she had been. Or how close she had come to being thrown into the freezing-cold pool by a bunch of bloodthirsty jocks, thank you very much.

Once she had stopped wheezing, Suzi stood up on her tiptoes and peeked in at her class. Crap. Everybody had their heads down and pencils up. Even Jett's red mop was turned down in sincere concentration. It looked as if Suzi was missing a pop quiz. Just what she needed. She was already barely pulling a B-minus.

Still a little shaky, Suzi decided to catch up with Mr. Crater, the geometry teacher, later. If she explained how she had been practically molested by the pumped-up conditioning class, maybe he would allow her to take a makeup quiz.

Right now all she wanted to do was sit down and collect her wits.

A hallway away, Suzi leaned her weight against a door and pushed it open. The girls' locker room was the obvious choice for peace and safety. Just in case the unruly jock pack had dressed and was combing the halls looking for her, Suzi knew they would never go in there.

Or at least that's what she hoped.

Suzi threw down her messenger bag, collapsed on one of the yellow plastic benches, and stared blankly up at the ceiling. How ironic, she thought, how just one night before, she had been sitting on this same bench sharing wasabi peas and listening to Gigi Greene spill her guts. Then she had been locked in the cold basement for hours. Then she had been cornered as Mr. Rider confessed how he had been dressing up in women's clothes ever since he was tall enough to reach the doorknob on his mother's closet. And today she had been intimidated by a very odd Coach Katie, felt up and almost pooled by the football team, and she had missed a geometry quiz.

Man, she was really on a roll.

Suzi slowly pushed herself up and walked over to one of the many full-length mirrors. She thought she looked pretty good, save for a stray piece of white paper stuck in her hair. Suzi picked it out, opened it up, and realized it was a note, apparently from Gigi to Chet. It must have fallen into her hair when she was hiding in Chet's locker. The note said, *Chet, you are my leather and I am your lace. I'll always love you. Love, Lil' G.*

Now I've heard everything, Suzi thought as she threw the note down onto the floor and flipped her fingers through her knotted hair.

"What are you doing?" a gravelly voice yelled out, as a firm hand gripped Suzi's shoulder and spun her around. Suzi just about had a heart attack. Her second one of the day.

"Who do you think cleans this up!" the man standing in front of her yelled again. Suzi let out a sigh of relief. It wasn't Chet, or any of the football jocks for that matter. It was just the school's mysterious whistling janitor, Janitor Joe.

Janitor Joe was long and wiry, with wrinkled, hollow cheekbones and a pasty, almost yellowish complexion. Suzi watched as the man slowly bent down and picked Gigi's love note up off the floor. He then shoved the dirty piece of paper right into her face.

"Hey," Suzi started to say, taking a step back. "I'm sorry but I've had a really bad day," she apologized, snatching the paper from the janitor's rough hands and then throwing it into the trash can.

"Every day is a hard day, kid," Janitor Joe snapped, grabbing his mop and turning his back on Suzi. He then started lazily mopping the floor and whistling to himself, and Suzi thought it was strange that such a crabby man would whistle. Stranger yet, she thought she recognized the song.

Suzi just sat back on the bench, kept quiet, and watched the janitor work. She was well aware that the janitor had been in the hallway when Gigi had discovered the curse note on her locker, and although he wasn't at the top of her list of suspects, she wanted to study him for a bit.

Suzi had just lifted up her sneaks so that the janitor could reach under the bench she was sitting on, and that's when Suzi heard the noise.

The jingling of what seemed like hundreds of keys.

"That sure is a lot of keys," she said, perking up and looking at the gigantic key ring attached to the janitor's utility belt. Janitor Joe let out a grunt of acknowledgment, but didn't stop his mopping or whistling.

"You must be able to open up just about every door in school," Suzi said again, fighting to get Janitor Joe's attention.

"I got a lot of places to clean, little lady," Janitor Joe finally responded as he stopped whistling, leaned against his mop, and looked at Suzi with tired, stone-gray eyes.

"Well, sir, this will only take a moment," Suzi said politely, extending her right hand. "I'm Suzi Clue. I'm a freshman and I'm investigating what's been happening to the prom queens here at Mountain High."

Janitor Joe looked at her hand as a fish would a bicycle.

"Prom queens?" he finally muttered, squinting as he reached into the torn breast pocket of his dirty blue overalls and pulled out a green pack of gum. He took out a single stick, studied it for a moment, then bent it in half and slid it into his mouth.

Suzi looked at Janitor Joe's fingers. Besides the fact that his knuckles were scabby and his nails had gobs of grease under them, his fingertips were dyed dark blue. Suzi jolted in her sneaks.

Oh. My. Gosh. Blue fingers.

"Janitor Joe, what do you know about a bottle of shampoo that turned a girl's hair blue?" Suzi asked, trying to keep the suspicion out of her voice.

"Blue hair? I thought you kids were into that kind of stuff these days," Janitor Joe scoffed, motioning with his eyes to Suzi's pink streak. Suzi was silent and just stared the janitor down.

"I don't know nothin' 'bout no blue hair or prom queens," Janitor Joe said earnestly. "But I do know about a big mess in the shower. Look what it did to my hands," he finished, holding up a sandpapery, ink-blue paw.

"That sucks," Suzi said, feeling her suspicions wane.

"Damn straight," Janitor Joe replied, reaching up to scratch at a hairy ear. As he did, his sleeve crept up to reveal a thin, sinewy bicep, completely covered with tattoos.

"Wow," Suzi said, squinting at the inked artwork. She could make out a bikini-clad pinup girl that was sagging with age, a bleeding heart with the initials *HP*, and a Gibson guitar with wings.

"You like music?" Suzi asked, raising her black eyebrows.

"Good music," the janitor replied, nodding his head slightly.

"Me, too," she said. "I'm into the Runaways, Death Cab for Cutie, Van Halen before Sammy Hagar. I even play the drums."

The janitor snorted in response, but kindly. "Good for you, little lady," he said, and Suzi swore she saw him crack a small smile as the two sat in silence for a long moment.

"So, someone's hair got turned blue?" the janitor finally asked.

"Yeah." Suzi nodded. "Someone put ink in a shampoo bottle, and the same someone is cursing all the prom queens, doing horrible things."

"Why do you care?" the janitor asked skeptically.

"How could anybody not care when people are getting hurt?" Suzi answered, shrugging her shoulders.

The janitor nodded thoughtfully, let out a dry, tired sigh, and then stood up. After taking a quick look around the locker room, he started walking and motioned for Suzi to follow him.

The janitor stopped in front of an unmarked door, and reaching for his massive key ring, he slid a single key into the lock. The door yawned open, revealing stacks of paper towels, bottles of orange disinfectant soap, mountains of toilet paper, and boxes of maxi pads. The utility closet? Suzi thought to herself. What could be so exciting about the utility closet?

But then she noticed that the janitor wasn't reaching for the toilet paper or the disinfectant soap. His blue fingers were fumbling around with a stash of used personal items, expensive shampoo bottles missing their lids, half-full bottles of designer perfume, fruit-scented hair smoothers, and a disheveled pile of high-end eyeliner pencils and lipsticks.

Suzi heard the janitor give a grunt of approval before he emerged from the closet holding a single shampoo bottle. The bottle had dark blue goo dripping down the sides, and the label read *True Blue Shampoo*.

Oh. My. Gosh. That was Parker's shampoo bottle.

"Is this what you're looking for?" the janitor asked, squinting his eyes and holding up the bottle. Suzi nodded excitedly.

"Well, then," the janitor added, turning back to the closet as he spoke. "That same night I found this bottle in the bottom of the trash, I also found this, right next to it." He picked up a shiny silver tube with his blue fingers.

Suzi grabbed it. It was a tube of lipstick, with a label that read *Prom Queen Pink*.

Pinch me, Suzi thought.

• • •

"You missed a quiz in Crater's class," Jett said as she sank her teeth into a rocket roll. "It was a real bitch," she finished, rolling her eyes at the heavenly combination of spicy uni and sweet ami. The girls had ridden their bikes over to Fishi Sushi after school. After her long, harrowing day, Suzi was absolutely starving.

"I know," Suzi said, swirling her chopsticks to create the perfect wasabi-and-soy-sauce mixture in the tiny dipping bowl. She liked it pasty and fiery hot. "I looked in the window and saw everyone taking it."

"Suz, you're starting to freak me out," Jett said, waving her chopsticks. "One minute you're locked in a spider-infested basement and the next you're crowd-surfing the jocks. And what was the freaky janitor guy doing with Parker's shampoo bottle anyway? Were you going to be his next victim?" she asked, genuine concern lining her voice.

"The janitor's harmless," Suzi answered. "He says he found the shampoo bottle in the trash."

"Oh, sure, he found it in the trash. That's a gem of a story," Jett said sarcastically.

"He says he picks stuff out of the trash to take home to his daughter," Suzi said, shrugging her shoulders and biting into her sushi. "You wouldn't believe the stash of beauty booty he has hidden in that closet." Jett just rolled her eyes.

"He also found this," Suzi continued, putting down her chopsticks to rummage through her bag. She pulled out the silver tube of lipstick and placed it on the table. "Prom Queen Pink." She smiled proudly.

"Is this . . . ? The janitor just so happened to have this, too?" she asked, unscrewing the lipstick and writing *Jett was here* on the Fishi Sushi table.

"Don't," Suzi said, looking around her favorite restaurant nervously and grabbing at the lipstick.

"That's the same shade, isn't it?" Jett said, looking at the bright pink letters on the table. "That's the same lipstick that was used to write the curse note on Gigi's locker and Kitty's car."

"I'm sure it is." Suzi nodded, quickly grabbing a napkin and trying to wipe off Jett's graffiti. The lipstick was too bright and thick, and her efforts merely smeared the pink across the table. Jett waved Suzi's hand away and simply placed her bento box over the mess.

"So," Jett continued, leaning into her friend and raising her brows. "The janitor has the keys, the blue fingers, the shampoo bottle, and this tube of skanky pink lipstick, and you still don't think it's him?" she asked skeptically.

"He has no motive," Suzi said, shrugging as she got back to work on her spicy tuna roll.

"None that you know of, anyway," Jett said.

Suzi let the point sink in.

"So if he didn't do it, then who did?" Jett asked impatiently, but Suzi's only reply was to shake her head and fan at her nose. That last bite was a wasabi overload.

"Suz," Jett said. "I'm just looking out for you."

"I know," Suzi said, after taking a sip of green tea. "And I appreciate it. But the thing is, I don't know who did it. My clues add up to zip," she explained. "Tacky pink lipstick and a gold hoop earring? That describes just about every single person at

Mountain High, even Coach Katie," Suzi said, clearly frustrated.

"And Mr. Rider," Jett snorted. Suzi smiled at Jett's keen insight and the girls ate in silence for a long moment.

"I thought you said the coach wears red lipstick," Jett finally said.

"She does," Suzi agreed. "But just because someone used Prom Queen Pink to write the curse notes doesn't necessarily mean that they wear it."

"What about the car thing? The orca was seen driving a black SUV, right?" Jett asked.

"Have you looked at the parking lot lately?" Suzi said. "It's full of huge, black SUVs. Can anybody say 'global warming'?"

"I mean, there has to be something I'm missing," Suzi finally said, studying a roll between her chopsticks.

"Well, I do have to admit that I've taken some small personal pleasure in seeing Gigi, Parker, and Kitty humiliated," Jett said, sucking on a piece of raw ginger. "Even that girl Trixie Topp can be a real pain in the ass," she slurped.

"Of course!" Suzi suddenly yelled out, popping out of her chair. "Jett, you're brilliant!" She reached over the table, gave her friend a big hug, and started pulling on her jacket.

Jett stared at her friend in utter confusion.

"Are we still on for band practice tonight?" Suzi asked, quickly throwing her stuff together.

"Yeah," Jett said, watching her friend suspiciously.

"Excellent. Then I'll already be at school late tonight," Suzi said, wrapping her scarf around her neck. It was pink mohair with little black hearts that Jett had knitted for her.

"Eat already!" Suzi yelled, hovering over her friend. She was clearly back in detective mode and ready to go.

"Sushi Nazi," Jett said, stuffing her mouth with Suzi's last piece of sushi and then pushing back her chair.

"I hope you know what you're doing," Jett mumbled through her mouthful.

Suzi didn't hear her. She was already halfway out the door.

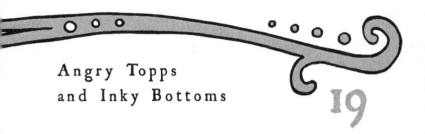

Angry Topps
and Inky Bottoms

19

"Yeah, yeah, yeah, you know it, yeah, yeah, oh!" Jett screamed into the microphone as she gave her red Flying V a final, powerful over-the-head stroke and jumped high into the air. The entire band room—the desks, the windows, even the walls—resonated with her voice and Suzi's drumming.

Suzi grabbed her cymbals to stop them from vibrating. Sweat beads had formed on her forehead and upper lip, her fingers had brand-new blisters from her drumsticks, and her ears were ringing. She and Jett had really rocked out for the last hour. In that time, Suzi had completely forgotten about the curse and lost herself in their songs. Music was such an escape. Suzi couldn't imagine her life without it.

"It's almost there," Jett said, breathing heavily and brushing tight red curls out of her face. She played with her distortion pedals until the feedback cut out and the band room fell silent.

"I agree," Suzi said, twirling her drumsticks between her fingers and flashing a smile.

"We should try to get a gig," Jett said as she swung her guitar off her shoulders and carefully placed it in her black case. Suzi nodded her approval, but Jett didn't see. "Sorry I can't stay after and do the detective thing with you, Suz. I promised my mom I'd make a curry," Jett said, clicking her guitar case shut. "Are you going to be okay?"

"I'll be fine, don't worry," Suzi replied, putting her drumsticks down on the snare and looking her friend in the eye. "Look, as you so brilliantly pointed out, Trixie is the last prom queen standing, so logically, she's the next target. She has drama-club practice after school, and if I'm lucky, whoever's behind this curse will strike again tonight and I can catch him—"

"Or her," Jett interjected.

"Catch him or her"—Suzi nodded—"in the act. And protect Trixie."

"Protect yourself," Jett said seriously. "And what's Trixie doing in the drama club anyway? It so goes against the stoic BG image." She then stood up and flung her guitar case over her shoulder. "Call me if you need anything," she finished, giving Suzi her patented "be careful" look.

Suzi smiled from behind the drums and watched as her friend walked out the door and left her all alone. Suddenly the room was uncomfortably silent.

Suzi took a deep breath and broke into a window-shattering drum solo.

"You taker, you faker, you li'l heartbreaker," Suzi sang under her breath. She had lain down on the band-room floor, propped her head up with her messenger bag, and pulled her hoodie over her head to block out the world. Her pen was on paper and she was deep in thought writing lyrics, but she still kept one eye on the clock above the band-room door. Trixie would be out of drama-club practice in ten more minutes, and Suzi was determined to shadow her that night, wherever she went.

Suzi had to admit she was a bit surprised that Trixie Topp was the last prom queen standing. Trixie seems so fragile and meek, like one "boo" would send her running for cover. But then Jett had enlightened Suzi about the bigger picture. Although the threat of biting spiders, blue shampoo, wild orca mascots, or God knows what else loomed over Trixie's mousy-brown ponytails, the promise of the prom queen tiara over-whelmingly overpowered it. After all, when Gigi, Parker, and Kitty were in the running, Trixie didn't have an ice cube's chance in hell of winning on prom night. But without any competition, the crown was as good as hers.

Maybe, just maybe, Suzi would be able to nab this creep tonight and let Trixie, the underdog of all BG underdogs, win this one.

It was now 4:25. Drama club was out in five. Suzi stood up, threw her bag over her shoulder, and checked her phone. She had two new text messages. Her mom had texted to tell her dinner was going to be at six (perfect), and Jett had texted to tell her to watch her back. Suzi was walking down the hall and toward drama-club practice in the auditorium, texting Jett back and telling her not to worry (again), when suddenly, *bam!* She ran smack into someone.

Suzi managed to hold on to her cell, but someone's plastic calculator went sliding across the floor. A super-high-tech calculator with more buttons than Suzi could count.

Oh. My. Gosh. It was Drex. Drex the Hex.

"Oh, man, I am so sorry. I was computing this logarithm that's been driving me nuts and I finally figured that γ was inverted and . . ." Drex rambled, scurrying after his calculator and inspecting it as if it were made of eggshells.

"Is it okay?" Suzi asked genuinely. Drex nodded his relief.

"We have to stop meeting like this," Drex said, placing the supersize calculator into his brown backpack and then turning his gaze on Suzi.

He looked at her as if she were another problem he wanted to solve.

"Sorry, Drex, gotta go," Suzi said as nicely as possible. She knew Drex would want to chat, but as usual, she was on a mission and didn't have the time. She kept smiling, but also kept her feet moving.

"I heard you missed a geometry quiz," Drex yelled out after her, his voice shaking a little. "If you need help with the makeup, well, let me know."

"How did you know I missed a quiz?" Suzi asked, spinning around.

"Mr. Crater told me. I just got out of the Mathletes meeting," Drex said, shrugging his shoulders.

"Thanks, but I'm okay," Suzi said slowly and curiously. She turned back around and kept walking.

Was nothing anyone did in this school sacred?

"Listen to me you overgroomed, balding, Muscle Beach reject. There is no way in hell that I'm going to let you do this. No %$*#! way in hell!"

The voice was coming from somewhere down the hall. Although it was 4:28 and Suzi was almost at the auditorium, she stopped to listen. The woman's voice was high and shrill. Someone was most royally pissed off.

"I am concerned for the safety of my students, one of them being your own daughter," Suzi heard a voice that was unmistakably Mr. Peasey's reply in a calm, yet stressed tone.

Suzi glanced at the auditorium door and then at her watch. Right on time, the auditorium opened and the drama club swarmed out. Suzi spotted Trixie.

"%$*#! safety, man!" The woman's voice erupted from the opposite end of the hall.

Suzi was torn. She wanted to keep her eye on Trixie in hopes of catching the suspect, but every bone in her body was drawn to the insults and accusations that were coming from the opposite end of the hall.

"I have one girl with spider bites, one with blue hair, and one who's refusing ever to set foot in Mountain High again," Suzi heard Mr. Peasey explain.

They were talking about the curse! No way could Suzi pass on this opportunity to eavesdrop. She decided to catch Trixie at her locker in a few minutes, and she headed over to Mr. Peasey's office. The door was shut tight, but the insults easily penetrated right through it.

"It's not like the %$*#! injuries are life-threatening!" the woman screamed, and Suzi heard a loud thud, as if the woman had stamped her foot.

"I have a responsibility to the students of this school," Peasey explained in a low voice.

"As the parent of the future prom queen, you have a responsibility to me!"

"Mrs. Topp, please . . ." Peasey sputtered. "Canceling the prom is the only way to ensure no more girls are hurt."

"Listen %$*#! face," the woman hissed quietly. "Nothing, I

mean nothing, will keep my baby from being prom queen this year."

Suzi heard an awkward silence, some shuffling, and then footsteps clicking toward the door. It sounded as if the pissed-off woman, apparently Trixie Topp's mom, was making her exit. Time for Suzi to make like a prom dress and take off.

Suzi pulled her hoodie over her head and pretended to ferociously dial the combination on a locker across the hall. She then heard the door to Peasey's office open and high heels click into the hallway.

"If you cancel this %$*#! prom, I will personally make your life a %$*#! hell," the woman said smugly. Her threat echoed off the lockers and down the empty hallway.

Against all better reason, Suzi couldn't help but turn around and sneak a quick peek. Trixie's mom was a short, thin woman with a deep orange tan, clumpy black eyelashes, a slathering of bright pink lipstick, and a platinum blond bob. She was wearing a low-cut white dress, an insane amount of what looked like real gold jewelry, and a shaking Chihuahua was poking its tiny head out of her big white bag.

As soon as the high heels had clicked far enough away, Suzi allowed herself to finally let it go. She threw her back against the lockers, rolled her eyes, and laughed. The whole scene, not to mention Trixie's fashion-handicapped pageant mom, had been quite the show. Man, she wished Jett were here to share the moment.

Just then, the lock clicked tightly on Peasey's door.

"Mr. Peasey? Are you okay?" Suzi asked, darting over and knocking on the principal's door. "Mr. Peasey? What was all that about?"

"Go away," Mr. Peasey said from the other side of the door. He sounded exhausted.

"But, Mr. Peasey, it's Suzi Clue. I'd like to help," Suzi pleaded, jiggling the door handle. It was locked tight.

"Go away, Suzi. I mean it," Mr. Peasey said, sounding pissed now. "I have a %$*#! of a headache."

Suzi stopped knocking. She could always catch up with the principal later.

Right now she had a ponytailed prom queen to drill.

Suzi ran down the hall and toward Trixie's locker. If she hurried, she still might catch the prom queen wannabe, and man, did she have a butt load of questions she wanted to ask. Suzi's sneakers squeaked on the yellow-and-brown tiled floors, but other than that, the only sound in the empty halls was the buzzing of the fluorescent lights and the rain pelting the windows.

Suzi rounded the corner nearest Trixie's locker and sighed her disappointment. The hall was empty. By eavesdropping on the rantings of Mrs. Topp, she had let Trixie slip through her fingers. Damn, she thought, pulling her cell out of her bag. Suzi speed-dialed Jett.

"Speak," Jett answered.

"You won't believe what I just heard," Suzi said excitedly as she started to walk toward the school's exit doors.

"Hit me."

"I overheard Trixie Topp's mom fighting with Mr. Peasey. He wants to cancel the prom, he thinks it's too dangerous after what's been going on, but Mrs. Topp, man, you should have seen her, she's a piece of work. Anyway, she told him that nothing would stop Trixie, her baby, from being prom queen and that if he canceled the prom he'd live to regret it, and oh my gosh, do you think—"

"Breathe, Suz, breathe."

"Do you know what this means?" Suzi asked, still walking down the hallway. She was almost at the door nearest where she had locked up her bike.

"Sounds to me like Mama's got a motive."

"Exactly. Maybe Trixie doesn't need my protection after all," Suzi said. "And she was just here. I missed her, dammit."

"Tomorrow is another day, Suz. Get your skinny butt home and eat something," Jett commanded. Suzi quickly glanced at her watch. Jett was right. She needed to get home for dinner and like right now.

"How's the curry coming?" Suzi asked quickly, switching her phone to her other ear and fishing in her pocket for her bike-lock key.

"I'm up to my elbows in chilies. Call later if you want."

Suzi slipped her phone back into her bag and headed toward the door. She couldn't wait to get outside and into the fresh air, even if it was pouring down rain.

Suzi was just passing by the gym when she heard the voices.

"That tickles!" A girl giggled. "Stop it! You're going to make me pee my pants!"

"C'mon, you know you like it," a guy's voice teased.

The voices were low and coming from the gym, and although the door was closed, Suzi quietly opened it and peeked in. The gym was dark, but she could see one person lying down on the trampoline. Correction, two people lying down on the trampoline. One set of huge sneakers surely belonging to Chet (Suzi would never forget his voice after it hissed in her ear in the boys' locker room earlier), and one set of smaller high-heeled boots, which must have belonged to Gigi.

"Oh, baby, you're so sexy," Chet said. Suzi could hear the springs on the trampoline start to squeak. Totally gross.

"You make me so hot," Gigi's voice cooed so softly, Suzi could barely hear it.

Now Gigi rolled over so that she was on top of Chet. Suzi had seen enough. But just as she was turning to leave, she noticed that Gigi's skirt had hiked up so her butt was waving in the air. Wait a minute, Gigi had a tattoo? Suzi seriously doubted it.

Just then, Chet slapped the girl's butt and she shrieked.

"Watch it or I'll tell your girlfriend," she teased loudly as she wrestled with Chet's huge arms. "I have to go before someone sees me," the girl continued, and Suzi watched as her smaller shadow started to dismount off Chet's massive one.

Suzi took a step closer to try to get a better look, but as she did, her own shadow, caused by the glaring hallway light behind her, passed over the trampoline. She froze like an animal in the headlights.

In what seemed like two seconds flat, Chet was out from under the mystery girl, off the trampoline, and smack in Suzi's face. For the second time that day, Suzi found herself head-to-head, or rather, head-to-pecs, with the quarterback of the football team, Chet Charleston.

"What the hell. You again?" Chet said through clenched teeth. He grabbed at Suzi's hoodie so she couldn't run away.

"Hey, Chet," Suzi said, smiling innocently. "I forgot a book in my locker," she managed to squeak out.

"Book, my ass. You're spying on me," Chet hissed as he pulled Suzi closer to him.

"Why would I spy on you?" Suzi asked. "I was going home

and I heard noises. Let go of me!" she demanded as she pulled herself out of Chet's grasp. Suzi moved her shoulders around to shake off his negative energy.

"What are you doing here after school," Chet demanded, still staring her down.

"What are *you* doing here after school?" she fired back. She was tired of being bullied by this guy. "Who's that girl you're making out with?" she demanded, trying to peek around Chet. He reached out to firmly hold her in place.

"Listen, Suzi Q," he hissed as he held a wiggly Suzi.

"Suzi Clue," she said, struggling against his grip and matching his icy stare as boldly as she could.

"Whatever!" Chet screamed out. Suzi stopped wiggling and stood still. Then Chet leaned into Suzi and whispered in her ear. "You know what curiosity did to the cat?"

Suzi just looked up at him and nodded.

"Good," Chet hissed. "I'm glad we understand each other."

Suzi nodded once again. At this point, agreeing with Chet was the easiest way out, and she gladly took it.

She wanted to live long enough to eat whatever hot dish her mom was putting on the table right about now.

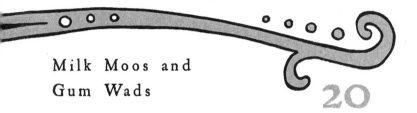

Milk Moos and
Gum Wads

20

Thursday morning started as any other. The sun came up, but nobody really noticed because of Seattle's thick blanketing of sulky clouds. The early-morning recycling trucks clinged and clanged their way down the city streets, noisily emptying bins of glass, paper, and plastic.

Suzi listened to the sounds of the morning from the warmth and safety of her bed. She had pressed the snooze button three times already, and her mom had been by to knock on her door twice. She knew that she had to drag herself out of bed sooner rather than later, but she was just so dang tired.

Suzi had made it home just in time last night to enjoy her mom's famous Indian dish, matter paneer. After stuffing herself with sweet peas in a spicy tomato sauce and fresh hot chapatis, she had recapped the events of her day to her mom (who had looked seriously unsettled when Suzi told her about the boys' locker room and Chet Charleston's most ungentlemanly behavior) and then hauled her butt upstairs to her room to study. She had eight pages to review if she wanted to pass

Mr. Crater's makeup quiz. One minute she was lying in bed with her head propped up on a pillow, trying to find the area of a trapezoid, and the next thing she knew, her alarm was going off in her ear and she had drooled down her arm and all over her geometry book.

Suzi slapped her snooze button for the fourth time. She rolled onto her side and looked tiredly over at her nightstand and all her knitting needles, CDs, and mystery books that were collecting dust.

The gold earring she had found was also sitting on her nightstand. Suzi stared at it and thought about the events of the day before. How she had heard Trixie's crazy mom threatening Principal Peasey, and how, suspiciously enough, Trixie was also the last girl in the running for prom queen and the only one who hadn't been cursed. Suzi felt as if she was finally onto something, and she couldn't wait to track down Trixie and ask her some questions.

That motivating thought was just the jump start she needed to finally get her butt out of bed.

When her mom stopped by her room for a third knock on the door, Suzi was already throwing her clothes on. A black miniskirt, a tight pink tee that said I HEART CUPCAKES (one of her all time favs), a pair of knee-highs, and her black hightops with pink laces.

Suzi knew she didn't have time to take a shower or eat a decent breakfast, but if she hurried, she did have time to stop at Stumptown and get in about half an hour of geometry cramming before school.

The curse and suspicious Trixie Topp aside, Suzi still had a makeup quiz to pass.

• • •

The earthy smell of coffee and the whining sound of the espresso grinders snapped Suzi out of her foggy morning haze. Considering she had been deep asleep less than an hour ago, she had made good time getting ready and riding her bike over to Stumptown. In her rush, she had thrown her hair back into a loose ponytail, and a streak of bright pink bangs hung over her right eye.

Suzi ordered her usual cinnamon soy latte, but with two shots instead of one (she needed the extra jolt this morning). She had just savored her first sip of caffeine for the day and was walking over to grab a napkin when she saw him.

Oh. My. Gosh. It was Xavier Fontaine, sitting at a table in Stumptown, her Stumptown, before school, intently reading a newspaper. He was wearing a weathered brown leather bomber jacket with a white shirt, a soft-looking, light blue scarf, faded jeans, and his signature black loafers. Suzi noticed that his hair was still wet and slick from his morning shower, and it was at this precise moment in time that she realized there was a drug much more powerful than caffeine to kick one into immediate consciousness.

Suzi quickly fluffed out her bangs and licked her lips to get them all glossy. Of all the mornings to run into Xavier, it had to be the one when she didn't take a shower.

Suzi pretended not to notice Xavier as she put her cup down on a table that was not too close yet not too far away, and threw her messenger bag into a chair. She kept her eyes carefully and strategically off of him and on her things as she took off her jacket, opened her bag and pulled out her geometry book. Then, not so carefully, she put the book down on the table. A little too hard.

Suzi felt, yes felt, Xavier's eyes look up when her book hit the table. She sat down and started to flip through the pages with sincere concentration, but she had no idea what page she was looking for, what chapter, or even what section. Heck, Suzi didn't even know what book she was looking at anymore. All she knew was that she could feel Xavier looking at her, and that she had him all to herself this morning, without Kitty, Parker, or any other girl drooling over him. The idea made her nervous and excited as hell.

"*Bonjour,*" Suzi heard Xavier say from his table. She looked up from her book and tried to act surprised. *Oh my gosh oh my gosh oh my gosh.*

"I love the cupcake as well," Xavier teased in his supersexy accent. At first Suzi didn't get what he was saying, but then she realized Xavier was looking at her shirt.

Say something! Anything! Suzi yelled to the inside of her brain, but all she could do was stare at him. She had never seen a boy more beautiful.

"So how are you this morning?" Xavier asked when Suzi didn't respond.

"Fine," she finally squeaked out with a smile that was frozen and incredibly awkward. "How are you?" she asked, and she could have shot herself, she sounded like such a geek.

"I am good, thank you." Xavier smiled genuinely, and Suzi felt her frozen smile relax a little. They stared at each other for a long, awkward moment, and then feeling uncomfortable almost to the point of physical pain, Suzi picked up her latte and took a big, nervous gulp. She spilled some on her chin and quickly wiped it off with her napkin. *Nice move,* she thought, mentally kicking herself.

"You have a little, uh, how you say, moos?" Xavier said to her once she had put her napkin down.

"Moos?" Suzi asked. She had no idea what Xavier was talking about.

"Yes, uh . . ." Xavier muttered as he stood up and started to cross the room toward her. *Oh my gosh oh my gosh oh my gosh . . .*

Suzi grabbed the sides of her chair, fighting the urge to stand up and run out the door. Xavier's presence was almost overwhelming, and he just kept getting closer. She swore she could hear her heart pounding in her chest as he took the napkin from her hand and reached toward her face. Suzi's. Heart. Stopped.

"Mustache!" Xavier said softly. "You have a mustache," he said again as he brushed the napkin softly across Suzi's upper lip.

Suzi looked up at the gorgeous hunk of a man standing over her, and their eyes, his violet and hers watery blue, locked for a long, luscious, lingering moment.

"So we will both be assistants for Señora Picante's class," Xavier finally said, breaking the dreamy moment.

Oh. My. Gosh. Xavier wanted to (gulp) actually talk to her? Suzi pinched her bare thigh to make sure she wasn't dreaming.

"Ouch!" She only intended to think it. But like an idiot, she actually said it.

"Are you okay?" Xavier asked with genuine concern, leaning in even closer.

Suzi just melted. She opened her mouth to speak, but she couldn't manage to get anything out.

"Yoo-hoo, Xavier! Is that you?" Suzi heard the voice, but it sounded light-years away. Neither she nor Xavier moved a single inch.

"Xavier!" the voice said again, this time more demanding, and Suzi looked over to see Trixie Topp bouncing toward them. Trixie seemed uncharacteristically perky and self-confident this morning. She was chomping down on her gum like nobody's business, and her ponytail swung sharply from side to side as she walked.

Gag me, Suzi thought. Way to ruin the moment.

"I'm so glad I bumped into you," Trixie said to Xavier in a bubbly voice. Suzi watched as she pulled her gum out of her mouth, stuck the waxy green mass to the side of her cup, and took a quick swig of her coffee. She then looked over at Suzi and said hi. Suzi said hi back.

"I was wondering how Kitty was doing after, you know, the incident," Trixie said, looking at Xavier and whispering "incident" like it was a big secret. Had she forgotten that Kitty had flashed her bare butt in front of the student body of Seattle's two largest high schools, not to mention that the story was on the second page of the local section of the *Seattle Times*? Kitty's "incident" was anything but a secret.

"I think Kitty is well," Xavier responded, shifting his weight from one foot to the other. "Excuse me, I have to be somewhere."

Xavier abruptly broke away from the girls and went back to his table to get his things. Suzi watched him walk away. Did he just say that he thought Kitty was well? Did he really not know for sure?

"Sure, Xavier, whatever," Trixie yelled after him sweetly, shrugging her shoulders and taking another long swig. "Just tell Kitty I send hugs, okay?"

Xavier nodded to Trixie as he walked past them and toward the door. Before he opened it, he shot Suzi one last, lingering glance. Wowza.

As soon as the door had shut, Suzi took a deep breath, pulled herself together, and focused all her energy on the perky, ponytailed girl standing in front of her table. Trixie was all hers.

"Speaking of Kitty," Suzi said, smiling mischievously and kicking out a chair with the scuffed toe of her high-top. "Trixie, do you have a minute?"

"What exactly are you trying to say?" Trixie asked while batting her gray, saucer-size eyes. She looked like she was about to burst into tears.

"Trixie, I heard your mom threaten Principal Peasey if you're not crowned prom queen tomorrow night," Suzi explained, firmly but gently. She wanted to stand her ground, but the last thing she needed was BG waterworks before first period.

"Just because my mother wants me to be prom queen doesn't mean I've done anything wrong," Trixie snorted defensively, putting her coffee cup to her trembling lips. "I mean, what mother doesn't want her daughter to be prom queen?"

"Well, why are you the only girl who hasn't been cursed?" Suzi asked, still forging forward with her questions.

"I don't know." Trixie looked at Suzi innocently. "Maybe it's because I'm the only girl on the court who's actually nice to people?" she said, her voice squeaking at the end. And then, as if on a cue from a soap-opera director, a single tear silently rolled down Trixie's cheek. Suzi noticed that it cut a wet path over her powdered skin and uncovered the pink bumps of what looked like a mild acne condition.

"Trixie," Suzi started to say, but she was quickly interrupted.

"How can you say this terrible stuff to me?" Trixie asked, wiping her stray tear away angrily with the back of her hand. "I mean, it's not like you have any real proof," she snapped.

"But I do," Suzi said as she reached into her bra and held the gold hoop earring up for Trixie to see.

"What is that?" Trixie asked, and Suzi thought she saw her squirm a bit in her perfectly pressed khakis.

"I have reason to believe that it belongs to the suspect," Suzi said carefully, never taking her eyes off Trixie. This was it. She had the ponytailed prom queen right where she wanted her.

Trixie stared at the earring for a long moment, wiped at her eyes once again, and then clenched her light pink lips tightly. "I don't wear hoop earrings," she snapped righteously as she pushed back her bangs to reveal a pair of perfectly prissy pearls. "I only wear pearls. Ask around if you don't believe me." She smirked.

"Trixie, I . . ." Suzi started to say.

"You what? You %$*#! up, that's what!" Trixie blurted out, suddenly sounding like her mother in Peasey's office the night before. People in the coffee shop turned and stared. "I can't believe you'd accuse me of this. Those girls are my best friends; I'd never do anything to hurt them," she said through clenched teeth. Then she suddenly stood up, almost knocking her coffee cup over, and whipped her arms into a creased khaki trench with bright pink trim.

"I have to look at all the possibilities," Suzi said in her defense. "It's nothing personal, Trixie, come on, sit down."

"I take it very personally. You really should think before you go around making accusations you can't back up." Trixie gave Suzi an angry, yet hurt look and turned on her leather penny loafers to leave.

"Where are you going?" Suzi asked, reaching out to lightly grab Trixie's arm. Even if she was wrong about the other girl's involvement in the curse—and she wasn't entirely convinced that she was—Suzi still wanted to protect her.

"You're just like everybody else in this awful school. You only care about yourself," Trixie said, shaking her head. "Now, if you'll excuse me, I have a tanning appointment before first period, and it was a real bitch to get in."

With that, she shook her arm free and, with a dramatic huff, exited stage left.

All that remained of Suzi's first suspect interrogation was a whiff of her designer perfume and an empty coffee cup sitting on the table. A white paper cup with a wad of green gum stuck to its side and light, ballerina-pink lipstick smudged around the rim.

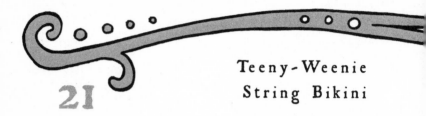

Teeny-Weenie String Bikini

21

"Pencil down," Mr. Crater yelled out, but Suzi kept her pencil charging a mile a minute. She had just managed to squeeze in the answer to problem twelve when Mr. Crater ripped her makeup quiz out from under her. Startled, Suzi looked up at him.

"On the rare occasion that you do grace my class with your presence, Miss Clue, you will abide by the makeup test's stated time restrictions," Mr. Crater said in a condescending tone.

Suzi put her chin down submissively but rolled her eyes. She had apologized to Mr. Crater three times for missing his test yesterday. It wasn't her fault she had missed it. It's not as if she had asked to be mauled in the boys' locker room.

"Yes, Mr. Crater," she replied, still looking down at her desk. She could hear the entire class laughing at her, and she looked up at the clock above the door to see how much longer until the torture was over.

The class's scoffs were the icing on the cake of a total bitch of a morning. Suzi hadn't studied for her makeup quiz because she had run into Trixie at Stumptown, and boy, had that ever turned out to be a total disaster. And now, back in the sad reality of her much-neglected academic pursuits, she had certainly just failed her makeup geometry quiz.

Suzi was still staring up at the clock and wishing herself somewhere else, somewhere warm maybe, when suddenly something strange flashed by the window of Mr. Crater's doorway, something red and all hunched over. Suzi looked around at her class to see if anyone else had seen it, but everybody was chatting it up and totally oblivious. She then jumped up, ran over to the door, and looked down the hallway. It was empty.

"Ms. Clue, you're really testing me today . . ." Suzi heard Mr. Crater say behind her, then suddenly Mr. Peasey's voice poured out of the PA system. The whole class fell silent.

"Attention, students," the principal announced succinctly. "This is just a reminder to please join me in the gym next period for the prom assembly. Thank you," he finished, and the bell signaling the end of class rang out.

"Okay, students, don't forget to finish chapter five," Mr. Crater yelled out over the sounds of books shutting and voices shouting.

Suzi opened the door and shot one more glance down the hall. She was certain that she had seen someone, or something, bolt down the hallway. Then suddenly, as if a dam had just burst, students started flowing all around her. Rivers of bodies started streaming toward the gym. If anybody had been in the hallway, Suzi would never be able to find them now, except . . .

What was that sweet, sickening smell? The entire hallway smelled like . . . singed hair? Burned toast?

Oh. My. Gosh. It smelled like burned flesh.

• • •

"Thank you for joining me for the prom assembly," Mr. Peasey said into the microphone, looking around at the packed gym and shifting his weight from one loafer to another. From her usual seat in the back-corner bleachers, Suzi could tell that he was unusually nervous today, and she couldn't blame him one bit.

"What's going on?" Uma asked excitedly as she scooted down the row to where Suzi, Jett, and Sam Witherspoon were already seated.

"Suzi thinks Peasey's going to cancel the prom," Jett whispered over at Uma.

"Cancel? No, he isn't!" Uma said. "Do you have any idea how many pissed-off people he'll have to deal with? His life would suck."

Suzi knew Uma was right. If Peasey did cancel the prom, it would definitely suck. For most of Mountain High, no prom meant no taffeta dresses, no dyed-to-match stilettos, no limos, and no refunds on hotel reservations.

But for Suzi, no prom meant no answers.

"He won't! He can't!" Sam suddenly screamed out, fanning his flushed cheeks with a notebook. "I just hired the caterer!"

"If he does, he owes me two hundred dollars for my dress," Uma added righteously.

"How much for your date?" Jett teased, and Uma just rolled her eyes.

"Everybody, please, just shut up!" Suzi pleaded, covering her ears with her hands. All the bickering and gossiping was starting to make her head hurt.

Just then, Peasey stopped his throat clearing and tapped at

the microphone. "Order students. Please!" The gym fell silent as the principal slowly pulled a piece of paper out of his sharply creased lavender slacks and opened it up.

"Dear students and faculty of Mountain High. Everybody's aware by now that the prom has run into a few, uh, glitches," Peasey read, pausing and looking up at the audience for effect. "Someone has chosen to terrorize our prom queens, causing unthinkable damage to Mountain High's prized school spirit."

As soon as he finished saying "school spirit," the crowd exploded into angry boos and hisses.

"I came this close to canceling the prom altogether," Peasey continued over the ruckus, and just like that, the entire gym fell silent. Sam looked over at Uma, Uma looked at Jett, Jett looked at Suzi, and Suzi turned to stare down at Principal Peasey.

"And I've decided, that rather than let this spirit spoiler win . . ." Peasey said softly, letting the suspense linger.

"Drumroll, please," Jett whispered, and Suzi lightly elbowed her.

". . . I say we celebrate the prom like never before!" Peasey suddenly roared, jumping into the air and raising his fist over his head like a varsity cheerleader.

"Bring on the prom!" Peasey screamed out again as he attempted a sloppy right stag.

The gymnasium blew its top. Uma, Sam, and the entire school jumped to their feet, screaming, crying, hugging, and stomping their feet on the bleachers. Suzi and Jett remained seated, but they were the only two.

Suzi was more confused now than ever before.

"Told you, told you!" Uma and Sam sang out at Suzi, grab-

bing each other's arms and jumping up and down. The bleachers were literally shaking and causing Suzi's butt to bounce
around as she sat and stewed.

What had happened to Peasey's so-called responsibility to
his students? Had the principal backed down to Mrs. Topp's
rabid threats? The only thing Suzi knew for certain was that
she had been wrong twice in one day, and it was starting to
get embarrassing.

"So, students," Mr. Peasey yelled without losing his big
cheesy smile. "I can't think of a better way to kick off the
prom than by presenting your next prom queen. She may have
been last, but she's by no means least. Let's give a warm, wonderful welcome for the fabulous, gutsy, and a little lucky Ms.
Trixie Topp!" he said, bowing and rolling his arms to sym-
bolize an invisible red carpet upon which Trixie was to walk
down from the bleachers.

The crowd went crazy with whistling, stomping, and cheering, and everyone feverishly searched the bleachers for a first
sighting of their next queen.

But then suddenly the queen herself, perky little Miss Goody
Two-shoes Trixie Topp, popped her ponytails up from the
back of the bleachers—and the screams of excitement turned
to yelps of horror.

Trixie's face was the color of a strawberry. A big, blistery,
overripe strawberry.

TRIXIE'S TAN

That nosy, pushy know-it-all freshman. How dare she!
Trixie stewed in silence as she took off her Ralph Lauren trench and

hung it neatly on the chair in her tanning room. She was so upset, she wanted to just toss it into the corner, but she fought the urge. No need to get crazy.

Boy, was she looking forward to the tanning bed. Trixie loved the hypnotic hum of the bulbs and the fruity smell of her tanning lotion, but she especially loved the bed's safe, cocoonlike warmth, and often fantasized about being on a beach somewhere with a hot, popular guy rubbing cocoa butter on her back. Yes, the tanning bed was her one vice. It took her away to a better place when she needed to escape.

And Trixie needed to escape often.

Trixie was what people at school referred to as a wannabe. Sure, she hung out with the popular crowd, but her supposed best friends walked all over her in their "screw me" stilettos. What, did they think she was stupid? That she couldn't hear them whispering behind her back and making fun of her clothes? Life was so unfair. Trixie scowled. She just wanted to be loved.

And then, as if her life wasn't pathetic enough, first thing this morning, she had been cornered by a freshman (a freshman!) during what was very possibly her worst morning ever.

Long story short: She woke up with the dire need for a nonfat triple sugar-free mocha frappuccino with whip.

The drive-thru line at Starbucks had been insane, so Trixie had driven across the street to Stumptown, the arty-farty place that didn't even have a drive-thru, and next thing she knew, she was standing face-to-face with some short, dark-haired freshman with a ridiculous pink streak in her hair who started accusing her and her mom of being behind the prom queen curse! Just because the girl, Suzi Somethingoranother, had overheard her mom saying that she wanted Trixie to be prom queen. Whose mother didn't want her daughter to be prom queen? Really!

Trixie let out her ponytails and reached into her pink Coach tote for her bottle of tanning lotion. She spread the cool, shiny, strawberry-

scented oil over her skin, and then literally slid into the booth and placed the goggles gently over her eyes. With her right hand, she reached over the edge of the bed, felt for the timer, and set it over one click: twenty minutes. No, two clicks: forty minutes. The prom was only two days away, and she wanted to look MTV spring-break gorgeous.

The bed's bulbs clicked on, and Trixie quickly slipped into her fantasy about prom night. It was going to be so amazing when the crown was placed on her head in front of the entire school. Her mouth curled up into a smug, self-loving smile as her mind drifted away from her sucky day and toward her glamorous, popular, prom queen future. Was it the warmth of the tanning bed or the gym spotlight as the tiara was placed atop her head? Was it the clicking of the bulbs or the crowd as they applauded her magnificence? Was it the sound of the timer going off or the school's band as it struck up a sappy melody for the queen's first dance?

Alas, she would never know. For Mountain High's prom-queen-in-waiting, the well-deserved and long-underdogged Ms. Trixie Topp, had fallen fast, and very peacefully, asleep.

And so Trixie spilled it. Word by word and with brown mascara tears streaming down her red swollen face, she recounted what had happened to her that morning while the entire student body listened, their expressions mortified and butts glued to the bleachers.

Trixie's face was flat-out deep-fried. And worse yet, she was blaming it all on the prom queen curse.

"I was in that tanning bed for forty minutes tops," she cried into the microphone once her story was finished. "There's no way *this* could have happened to me in forty minutes!" Trixie put emphasis on the word *this* as she untied the belt on her khaki trench coat and whipped it open. The crowd shrank back in horror, and it wasn't because Trixie was flashing a surprisingly teeny-weenie string bikini.

"Oh. My. Gosh," Suzi said in sync with the rest of the gym. She looked over at Jett, whose jaw was practically resting in her lap.

"Ouch," Uma muttered, bugging out her eyes. Suzi nodded slowly and looked over at Sam, who looked as if he was in serious need of a barf bag.

Every inch of Trixie's body was screaming red. Her chest, stomach, legs, face . . . the sight of her was so painful, several students had to turn their heads away. A few students even jumped up and ran out of the gym.

"I've been tanning for years, and nothing like this has ever happened to me," Trixie cried as she pulled a tissue out of her bikini top. "This was no accident!" She blew her nose.

After a beat, Principal Peasey rushed over to comfort his school's latest victim, but Trixie jerked away from him as if his hands were hot irons. The principal froze helplessly with his hands in the air.

"Somebody did this to me, don't you see? Gigi, Parker, Kitty—the creep got to me, too! Look at me! I'm a lobster!" Trixie screamed at him, her voice reaching glass-breaking decibel levels. "What did I do wrong? What did I ever do?" she cried, turning back to the crowd and sucking in a long, deep breath.

"*Whhhhyyyyyy!*" she wailed into the mike, throwing her head back and revealing to students in the front row a full mouth of metal fillings.

Once she was out of breath, Trixie went limp. She looked

out at the crowd, her eyes searching for answers, sympathy, maybe just a bottle of aloe-vera gel, but nobody had anything to offer. Everyone was stricken with terror.

Then, on a quick dime, she turned and ran out of the gym.

"Drama geek, all the way," Jett leaned over and whispered in Suzi's ear.

"I thought you were going to protect Trixie!" Uma said under her breath, leaning over Jett and looking at Suzi with confused eyes. Unfortunately for Suzi, the gym was so quiet, Uma's whisper might as well have been a scream. Students for rows around heard the comment and turned to stare at the girl who had failed to protect the school's next prom queen. People started whispering and pointing, and all Suzi could do was shrug her shoulders. She felt like a total loser.

Trixie had been Mountain High's last chance for a prom queen—and last chance for a prom.

The principal started tapping on the microphone in an attempt to regain the crowd's attention. It was difficult because there were so many emotions and rumors raging through the room, and Peasey had to tap for a long time. Once everybody had quieted down, he stood still for a moment with his mouth open, as if he knew he had a bomb to drop but was hesitant about dropping it.

"This is all my fault. I should have done this earlier," he said. "I'm sorry, but the prom is hereby canceled."

With that small mouthful of words, the last glimmer of hope for Mountain High's Go Geisha! prom was lost forever. The gym signed in collective defeat.

Even Suzi herself felt cheated. Now she'd never find out who was behind the curse. She'd never find out who cut the hole in Gigi's pom-pom bag and put the ink in Parker's shampoo. She'd never know who was in the orca uniform and assaulted Kitty, or how Trixie got so dangerously deep-fried. The gold hoop earring and Prom Queen Pink lipstick that she had managed to find? Those clues meant nothing now. The person behind the prom queen curse would get away with it all; Mountain High wouldn't have a prom, and Suzi would forever be known in the halls as the nosy little freshman who couldn't.

Unless . . .

"I'll run for prom queen!" Suzi suddenly screamed, jumping to her feet so quickly that she almost fell forward.

Jett started choking, Uma and Sam looked at each other in disbelief, and every head in the gym turned to see who had just yelled out those five magic words.

Was somebody still willing to run for prom queen even though the other girls had been picked off, one by one? Was anybody really brave enough to put her life on the line to save the prom? Pass that girl the spirit stick and say hallelujah!

Or, Suzi thought as the crowd picked her up, threw her over their heads, and ecstatically carried her down the bleachers to stand at Peasey's side . . .

Pass her a garlic necklace and a lucky rabbit's foot.

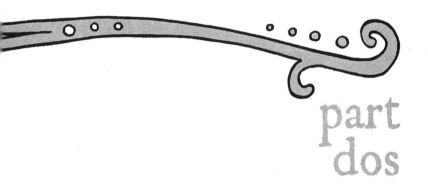

part
dos

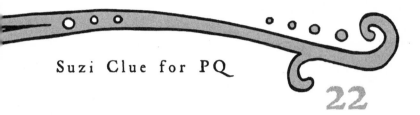

Suzi Clue for PQ

22

The air smelled of wet dirt and pine needles, and the sharp sting of cold rain pelted Suzi's face where it wasn't covered by her thick black hoodie. Suzi loved every second of it. She loved the rain, the fresh, cold air, and the hissing sound of her tires as they glided over the wet, shiny street.

Suzi loved riding her bike. When she was behind the handlebars, she felt unleashed and absolutely free. She loved to take the side streets and ride through parks, passing under low-hanging trees and touching their wet leaves with her bare hands. She loved that she could cut through parking lots, go over curbs, down alleys, and through fields, and basically observe things that people didn't see driving in their fast-moving cars.

On her slow and heavy red Schwinn cruiser, Suzi noticed everything. Riding her bike grounded her and gave her a feeling of security, like the world was tangible, tactile, and predictable.

Unlike the curse.

Suzi had really outdone herself this time. Because she had

failed to figure out who was cursing the prom queens over the last week, she'd been left with no choice but to run for prom queen herself.

But the prom was Saturday night, just two days away, and the thought made her nervous as hell.

Suzi wasn't overly nervous about the fact that she was the only prom queen in the running and thus the prime target for the next attack. She felt ready for that. But the thought that she might unwillingly become Mountain High's next prom queen made her stomach do triple back somersaults.

What if she wasn't able to catch this person and had to get up in front of the whole school and wear a frilly prom dress and that ridiculous tiara in front of everybody?

Suzi wished she could think of a better way to get to the bottom of the mystery, but she couldn't. She had to catch this person, but most importantly, she had to do it before she was (gulp) crowned Mountain High's next prom queen.

"Whoa, Suz. Watch it!" Jett yelled behind her.

"Well, sit still, then," Suzi said, fighting to keep control of her wobbly bike.

Suzi and Jett had just eaten their fill at Fishi Sushi, and Suzi was riding Jett back to school on her bike. Suzi was standing up and pedaling while Jett sat on the seat. Jett's Converses were splayed out to keep her ankles from getting nicked, but her shoelaces were untied and made pinging noises as they flirted dangerously with the turning spokes. As Suzi piloted around puddles and stray branches in the street, Jett was talking a mile a minute and wiggling around, causing the bike to swerve off balance. Suzi had to grip the handlebars with all her strength to keep it from going down.

"Sit still back there," she said again as she took a right and leaned into the turn. They were going downhill now, which made it easier to balance.

"Sorry, I was tying my shoe," Jett replied, wriggling her butt around until she found the perfect fit between the curve of the leather and her Levi's. "So as I was saying," she then continued. "You're nuts. I don't know what part of the word *curse* you don't understand, but it basically means that something bad is going to happen to you. Maybe your hair gel will have bleach in it or someone will throw your drums in the pool or who knows? Maybe the front wheel of your bike will fall off on your way home from school today."

Suzi heard Jett but didn't respond. It had stopped drizzling, and she was enjoying the feel of the fresh air on her face.

"Are you listening to me?"

"I hear you, I just don't think me running for prom queen is that big of a deal," Suzi said over her shoulder. She knew that Jett wouldn't buy her casual dismissal of the situation. She didn't even buy it herself.

"Ask Gigi, Parker, Trixie, or Kitty. See if they think it's no big deal."

"I don't know what else to do," Suzi explained as she took another right and rolled into the Mountain High parking lot.

"Hey, Fiona," Jett said casually, waving to a cute, freckly, dark-haired girl who was hanging out with a bunch of guys under the bleachers. When Fiona heard her name, she looked over at Jett and stopped talking. Everyone around her stopped talking as well, and turned to look as Suzi and Jett rolled on by.

"She was checking me out, did you see that?" Jett giggled as she slapped Suzi's shoulder.

"You wish," Suzi replied, riding up onto the sidewalk and toward the school.

Actually, it looked as if everyone was checking her and Jett out. Kids who were standing by their cars stopped talking to look at them. Even the members of Coach Katie's soccer team had stopped playing and were just standing there staring as the soccer ball rolled out of bounds.

"I just want you to realize that this is a big deal, Suz. For the next couple of days, the entire school is going to revolve around you, and someone is going to do everything in their power to make sure you never make it up on that stage tomorrow night," Jett argued.

"Relax," Suzi said, coming to a stop by the bike rack and waiting for Jett to get off. "I really don't think it's going to be like that. Nobody's going to care that I'm running for prom queen."

"Right. Whatever." Jett gave Suzi an impatient look and walked toward the school doors. She grabbed one, opened it, and waited for Suzi to lock her bike and catch up.

"I mean, nobody even knows who I am, more or less wants to fixate on me," Suzi was still explaining as she walked past Jett and through the open door. "You're totally par . . . a . . . noid." Her last word barely made it out as a choke.

Suzi had to do a double take to make sure she was standing in the right school. The main hall was completely decked out in prom paraphernalia. Red and black streamers were twisted and hanging all the way down the hall, along with little ori-gami swans and rabbits hanging from the ceiling. Each locker had a red paper rose attached to it along with an envelope that said *Go 2 the Geisha Prom!* in thick, black, Japanese-inspired strokes. Suzi noticed that the school's main display case, usually filled with trophies, was now filled with mini bonsai trees and plastic Japanese food. Japanese guitar music was coming through the PA system. The scene was way crazy, but lo and behold, the craziest thing of all was now walking, or should she say waddling, up to her, dressed in a bright red kimono with little gold flowers embroidered on it, with hair slicked back and thick black eyeliner on the eyes.

It was Sam Witherspoon, the prom committee chairman.

"*Konichiwa*," he said respectfully, stopping in front of Suzi and bowing deeply. "Mountain High welcomes our most honorable queen."

Suzi's heart sank deeper and deeper into her chest the farther she walked into the bowels of Mountain High. Sam Witherspoon and his most honorable welcome had been just the beginning. After he had bowed and handed her a single red rose, Suzi had walked around him, making sure Jett followed, and started to make her way toward her locker. But the farther along she wandered into the halls, the more she had to fight the urge to turn around and run straight back out the doors. Sam had obviously put his prom committee to work after the surprise assembly that afternoon.

Posters reading suzi clue for pq in thick black brushstrokes were taped side by side and practically wallpapered the walls.

"Told you so," Jett said as they ducked a junior couple who had rushed into Suzi's face to thank her profusely for keeping the dream of the prom alive. Suzi was too dumbstruck to say anything.

"This is whacked," Jett continued, putting her arm protec-

tively around Suzi's shoulders and steering her out of the way
of yet another grinning couple beelining their way toward
Suzi to show their appreciation. "It's only a dance, what's the
big deal?"

"Did you see the signs?" Suzi asked, bowing her head and
moving as quickly as she could through the crowd. "Oh, man,
what did I get myself into?" she was saying when suddenly she
whipped around a corner and stopped dead in her tracks. She
had almost run head-on into someone.

Of course it was Drex.

"You sure are popular today," he said, bouncing his glance
from Suzi's eyes down to his shoes. He kicked his black
loafers at the floor and the rubber soles made squeaking
noises.

"It's crazy, isn't it?" Suzi replied, looking around at the
whirlwind of activity. She felt as if the entire world were spinning around her, and that she and Drex were the only ones
standing still. Even Jett had moved over to the lockers to chat
up the freckly-faced girl who had been standing under the
bleachers, Fiona Fiercely.

"I think it's brave what you did," Drex said, this time looking Suzi straight in the eye. She noticed that behind his glasses
Drex had the longest, darkest eyelashes she'd ever seen on a
boy. "And I sure feel sorry for what happened to Trixie."

"Yeah," Suzi said. "That's nice, Drex." She tried not to sound
condescending, but as she usually did with Drex, she was just
making small talk and biding time. She wished that Jett would
get her butt back already so that they could go to her locker.
Fifth-period bell was going to ring soon, and Suzi wanted to
ditch her heavy messenger bag.

But suddenly, Drex reached up to scratch at his nose, and Suzi noticed that his fingertips were dyed dark blue. She studied them for a second, a thousand thoughts rushing through her brain. "What's up with the blue fingers?" She furrowed her brow.

"Oh, this," Drex answered, stopping his scratching and studying his fingers. "A pen broke. My favorite, too. It was an extra-fine but it wrote as smooth as—" Suzi opened her mouth to stop Drex from rambling, but just then, Jett ran over and thankfully cut in.

"Fiona wants to know if you'll help pick films for the carnival tonight," Jett said, rocking her hips back and forth and smiling. If Suzi didn't know better, she would have thought that Jett was downright giddy.

"Cool," she said, nodding her head. But then she did a double take. "Wait a minute," she said. "What carnival?"

"Can't you read?" Jett asked, smiling and pointing to a sign above Suzi's head. Both Suzi and Drex stepped back to take a look at what Jett was referring to. The sign was bright yellow and it read:

IT'S CARNIE TIME!
Win Your Honey a Whale!
Dunk the QB in the Tank!
Watch Indie Flicks!
Eat Cupcakes!

"We should go, Suz. There'll be cupcakes," Jett said, shrugging her shoulders, and Suzi shot her friend an amused smile. She knew that Jett had about as much school spirit as the crusty Janitor Joe, and cupcakes wasn't the only sweet thing on her friend's mind. But that was okay. Suzi had her own reasons for wanting to check out the carnival. First of all, Jett was right. Suzi loved a good cupcake. And secondly, as much as the idea made her cringe, she knew she had to get out there and start mingling.

After all, she had to make herself an easy target.

"Sounds good. See you, Drex," Suzi said as she grabbed Jett's shoulder and pushed her toward her locker. The two continued down the hall, sidestepping the gushing couples and staring at the never-ending decorations.

"You're famous, Suz." Jett snickered as they passed what must have been the hundredth SUZI CLUE FOR PQ poster.

"I don't even know how Sam managed to make all these. He must have really cracked the—" Suzi was saying, but then suddenly she stopped dead in her tracks.

She had just turned the corner closest to her locker, and lo and behold, what did she find but an army of BGs blocking her way. Spider-bite Gigi, blue-haired Parker, deep-fried Trixie, and the rest of the mob were gabbing ferociously, and Suzi couldn't see her locker, not to mention get into it.

"Great," she said under her breath.

But then, one by one, as the BGs spotted her, they stopped talking and slowly stepped out of her way. At first, Suzi thought they were giving her the royal treatment, just like everyone else at school, and that maybe this prom queen thing did come with its perks. But then, the final BG blocking her way, Gigi Greene herself, stepped to the side and that's when Suzi saw it.

A slew of SUZI CLUE FOR PQ signs had been enthusiastically

taped up over her locker, completely covering it. That was no big deal.

But at some point, the signs had been violently slashed through with a razor or thin knife, and someone had scrawled the words DIE PQ DIE! across the front of them in tacky, bright pink lipstick.

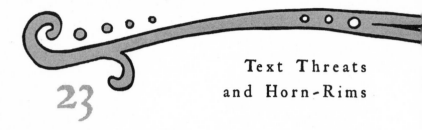

Text Threats
and Horn-Rims

23

"Are you okay? I heard about your locker," Uma said, catching up with Suzi and Jett in the cafeteria after fifth period. She took a seat at the table, brushed her long, dark hair over her shoulder, and gave Suzi a serious look. "Back out, Suz. There's more to life than this prom," she said, looking back toward the BGs, who were all abuzz with prom talk. Suzi had been watching them gossip, preen, and text for a while now. She knew they were planning what dresses to wear, what limos to rent, and which boys they did and didn't want to party with afterward. The thought bordered on dismal.

"Thanks, but I'm okay," Suzi said, smiling at Uma as she dipped her hand into a bag of wasabi peas. Suzi appreciated the fact that Uma was watching her back, even if it meant her sacrificing the one night she had been looking forward to all year. But Suzi had no intention of dropping out. While the scene by her locker had scared her, it had also strengthened her determination to stop this crazy ride. Enough was enough.

"You're too stubborn for your own good," Jett said to Suzi, shaking her head and digging her paw into the bag of peas. "Hey, you going to the carnival tonight?" she then asked, turning to Uma.

Uma nodded slyly. "I heard that Chet Charleston is going to be in the dunk tank, and there's a ball with my name all over it," she said, smiling while all three girls shot a glance over to where Chet was sitting with a giggly Gigi in his lap.

"He's such a rod," Uma added. "He's asked me out like a zillion times. Like I'd ever take her sloppy seconds." She motioned with her head toward Gigi.

"Or thirds," Suzi added, giggling a little.

"Do you know something I don't?" Uma asked, watching Suzi closely.

"I caught Chet making out in the gym last night with some girl with a tattoo on her butt."

"Totally gross," Jett said, making a face and slumping down in her chair.

"What?" Uma asked, perking up. "I heard that Gigi's parents would take away her car if she ever got a tattoo. She can't have any tattoos."

"Exactly," Suzi said, leaning back into her chair.

"Well then, who was it?" Uma asked, but Suzi just shrugged. Uma shot a quick look back over at Gigi and smiled. "Well, I guess we know who it wasn't," she added, erupting in a fit of laughter. Uma's laugh was loud, deep, and contagious. Even Jett cracked a smile.

Just then, Gigi glanced over at Suzi and their eyes locked. Suzi's smile slowly faded as she watched Gigi peel herself out of Chet's grasp, slick her cheerleader skirt down over her black tights, and beeline it across the cafeteria to where she, Jett, and Uma were sitting.

"Is she coming over here?" Uma asked, straightening up.

"She probably heard you ragging on her," Jett said drily, and Uma stuck her tongue out as far as it would go.

"Suzi Clue," Gigi said quickly and firmly, leaning on the table with both hands and cocking her hip to the side. Suzi looked up at her coolly and raised her black eyebrows. She was still pissed at Gigi for bailing on her in the locker room the other night.

"I just wanted to say thanks," Gigi continued. "It takes guts to do what you did."

Suzi was caught off guard by the Queen Bee's nice comment. As far as she was concerned, she was just doing what she had to do.

"But I haven't done anything yet," Suzi stammered, looking up at Gigi.

"You've saved the prom," Gigi said, bugging out her baby blues.

"Yeah, well, I haven't caught who's behind all this."

"You will," Uma said, ignoring Gigi and giving Suzi a little shove. "I hear you have a bunch of clues."

"You've found clues to who did this to me?" Gigi asked, leaning in close to Suzi.

"Well, I figured out that somebody cut a hole in your pom-pom bag, that's how the spiders got in there," Suzi explained. "And I found the pink lipstick that was used to write the curse notes," she shrugged. "Oh, and I found this."

Suzi grabbed the gold hoop out of her bra and placed it down on the table. Gigi stared down at it for a long moment, uncharacteristically silent.

"It's an earring," Jett blurted out, a little rudely.

"I see that," Gigi spit out at Jett before turning her gaze on Suzi. "Is that it? Is that all you know?" she asked, sounding a little pissy. Suzi stared up at Gigi, completely at a loss for words.

"I know that you locked my girl down in the basement for two hours," Jett interrupted again, leaning over the table and giving Gigi the evil eye. Gigi seemed taken aback by Jett's attack for a moment, but only for a moment.

"Hello!" Gigi fired back, almost laughing. "It was the Kick Wars and I'm the head cheerleader. I had to be there," she finished with a self-righteous snort.

"Listen, I'm just trying to be nice here," Gigi said impatiently, looking over at her friends and then back at Suzi, as if to accentuate the fact that she had humbled herself by walking over to a lesser section of the cafeteria.

"Whatever," Gigi finally huffed as she gave Suzi a frustrated look before turning and walking back to her section. The three girls sat in silence for a long moment, recovering from the Gigi Greene drive-by.

"Don't let her get to you," Uma finally offered, smiling at Suzi. "You'll figure it out," she finished, as she picked up the small, gold earring and studied it.

"She's right, Suz. Let little miss perfect see if she can do any better," Jett added. Suzi smiled her appreciation, and just then, her phone beeped, signaling a new text message. "What's this?" she asked, staring at the text in confusion. "Meet me in 105 in five? Who's number is this?" She passed her phone to Jett, who took a quick look.

"Oh, it's Fiona. I gave her your number because you said you'd help with the carnival movie thing. I hope you don't mind," Jett said, shrugging her shoulders and handing the phone back to Suzi.

"Room 105. The media room," Suzi said, nodding. "I should get going," she finished, grabbing her messenger bag off the floor and standing to leave.

"Not so fast," Uma interrupted, still looking at the gold hoop.

"Oh, yeah. I'm such a good detective I almost forgot my main clue. The earring," Suzi said, holding her hand out.

"That's where you're wrong, Suz," Uma said, looking up at Suzi with her big, brown eyes. Suzi just looked at her, totally confused.

"This isn't an earring," Uma finally said, looking from the gold hoop to Jett and then to Suzi.

"What do you mean it isn't . . ." Suzi was saying, when suddenly her phone beeped again.

"I'm coming, Fiona. Get off me." Suzi impatiently pushed a few buttons but then she furrowed her brows as she stared down at her new message.

"Is Fiona hassling you?" Jett asked, straightening up in her chair to grab at Suzi's phone.

"This . . . isn't . . . from . . . Fiona."

Jett's mouth dropped open as she read the message. She then handed the phone over to Uma, and both girls looked at Suzi with their eyes bugging out of their heads.

"What the—" Uma started to say, but the ringing of the seventh-period bell drowned out her last word.

"You're late," Fiona Fiercely said, barely glancing up from behind her silver PowerBook as Suzi walked in the door to the media room.

Suzi stopped in her tracks. She recognized that voice. It was the same low, gravelly one she had heard in the bathroom on Monday, when she had been eavesdropping on the BGs from inside the stall. So Fiona was the mystery girl who had left in a huff.

"Something came up," Suzi said weakly.

"What's the matter, your briefs in a bunch?" Fiona asked sarcastically, looking over her thick horn-rim glasses at Suzi standing in the doorway.

Suzi just shrugged, walked in, and threw her messenger bag on the floor. She had to admit, she felt a little unraveled, but not so much because she recognized Fiona's voice from the bathroom. No, Suzi had other reasons to feel freaky.

Leave it to Uma, her friend who had had her nose pierced since birth, to notice that the earring Suzi had been carrying around these past few days wasn't an earring at all. Back in the cafeteria not ten minutes ago, right after the bell had rang out, Uma had told Suzi that without a doubt, the gold hoop earring was a piece of body jewelry. It was a nose ring, or brow ring, or maybe even a navel ring. The news had sent Suzi into a spin.

And if that wasn't enough, somebody had just sent Suzi a text threat. The message itself, PQ UR NXT, wasn't particularly blood curdling, but the fact that the person behind the curse knew her cell number was enough to make the little hairs stand up on the back of her neck.

"I have some stuff here for you to look at," Fiona said, looking over at Suzi. "Jett says you're a film buff, and Peasey asked me to work with someone on this."

"Sure," Suzi said, walking over next to the monitor. Fiona

was watching a film about a female Roller Derby team, and the players were pushing, screaming, and cursing up a storm.

"I was thinking this might be a good one to lead with." Fiona pointed at the monitor with her pen.

"It's by a local female filmmaker. It's brilliant," Fiona raved. "But I'm also liking a short film about Latino girl gangs in L.A., and a digital piece from a girl in Idaho who wants to play pro football." Fiona handed the film list to Suzi.

Suzi quietly studied the list while Fiona reached into her shirt pocket and pulled out a light blue pack of gum. The pack had a big, black oval in the center, and Suzi thought the design was cool, old school even. Fiona unwrapped a stick and popped it into her mouth. Suzi was surprised that the gum was solid black.

"Licorice gum?" Fiona asked, offering the pack out to Suzi. "I'm totally addicted. Only one place in town carries it, and I buy it by the box."

"This list is impressive, but why are all the films about women?" Suzi asked, waving the gum away.

"Because the sistas need power!" Fiona said, raising her voice and looking at Suzi with unwavering, steel-gray eyes. "I'm peeved that this whole carnival is even benefiting the prom," she continued, scooting her chair back from the monitor and staring point-blank at Suzi. "The school should be raising money for productive endeavors, like self-defense or herstory classes," she explained, tapping her pen against her upper lip and eyeing Suzi from head to toe. "This prom is a slap in the face to women everywhere."

"I don't want to be prom queen," Suzi said, catching Fiona's drift.

"No worries, dear heart. Jett filled me in," Fiona said. "But you're crazy to come to the rescue of those stuck-up bee-yotches. As far as I'm concerned, prom queens are a cancer on the face of the feminist movement. Those girls are getting exactly what they deserve."

"Nobody deserves that," Suzi said, trying to shake off Fiona's negative vibe. "Anyway, I still think the films should have some variety."

"Whatever," Fiona said. It was becoming clear to Suzi that nothing she said really mattered. Fiona obviously had her own agenda, and Suzi's opinions were no part of it. Suzi decided she might as well go to class. She was missing her chemistry lab for this meeting, after all. She turned around and started to walk toward her messenger bag.

"You know," Fiona said loudly, swiveling around in her chair and taking off her glasses to look at Suzi eye-to-eye. "The world would be a better place without cheerleaders and prom queens. Trust me," she said, narrowing her eyes and practically drilling her point into Suzi's forehead. But Suzi barely heard a word Fiona said.

She was too busy staring at the brow ring lodged in Fiona's right eyebrow.

"Who's there, please?" Peasey's voice sang out from behind his closed office door.

"It's me, Principal Peasey. Suzi Clue," Suzi yelled out, standing in the hallway and knocking ferociously.

"Settle down, Ms. Clue, I'm coming." Suzi stopped her knocking and impatiently rolled back and forth on her toes. She realized with a giggle that she was probably the only student in Mountain High history to ever actually look forward to going into the principal's office. Just then, Peasey opened the door and stared down into Suzi's eager eyes.

"Yes, yes. Come in," he said, and Suzi thought she detected a hint of annoyance in his voice.

Suzi walked in and looked around. She had never been inside Peasey's office before, and she wasn't surprised to find it nicely decorated, neat, and orderly.

Books about teaching lined his dust-free shelves, as well as several self-help books, a miniature rock water fountain, and a golden Buddha head. There were home decorating magazines fanned out on a glass table next to a chestnut-colored leather couch, and his office smelled of fresh cedar. All in all, the principal's office was very calming and Zen. Suzi was impressed.

"What can I do for you?" Peasey asked quickly, taking a seat behind a heavy-looking wooden desk. Suzi walked over to the desk and picked up a framed, black-and-white photograph. It was a picture of a gorgeous, dark-haired woman wearing a tiny, zebra-print bikini and playing in the waves of a deserted beach. She was laughing and looking straight at the camera.

"Is this your wife? She looks like a model," Suzi said, looking over the desk and at the principal. Peasey raised his eyebrows but didn't respond. He just continued to look at her expectantly.

"I'm very busy, Ms. Clue. As you know, the prom is in two days. Please just spit it out."

"What do you know about a sophomore named Fiona Fiercely?"

"Ms. Fiercely? Let's see. She's the founder of the feminist

club, the herstory program, Student Queer Pride Day, Vegans
with a Vengeance, female touch football . . ." Peasey answered,
lightly wringing his hands together. "And she's been called to
my office several times for writing her political views in the
stalls of the girls' bathroom."

"So she's a troublemaker," Suzi added, nodding her head.

"Well, I wouldn't exactly say that," Peasey answered slowly,
smoothing down his light blond goatee. "Fiona just feels very
strongly about certain things."

"Did you know she feels prom queens are like a cancer?"
Suzi asked, looking at Peasey excitedly.

"What exactly are you getting at, Ms. Clue?" Mr. Peasey
asked.

"Mr. Peasey, I have good reason to believe that Fiona is the
one behind the prom queen curse," Suzi answered, matter-of-
factly.

"Why do you think that?" Peasey asked, furrowing his
brows.

"Fiona told me that she thinks prom queens are a cancer on
the face of the feminist movement, and that the world would
be a better place without them."

Suzi dug her hand into the front of her shirt and pulled out
the gold hoop.

"I found this hidden in the gym equipment basement. It was
next to a pair of scissors that I think were used to cut a hole
in Gigi's pom-pom bag. So spiders would crawl in there," Suzi
explained. She offered the clue to Mr. Peasey, who held it up
to the light and closely studied it.

"It's a piece of body jewelry," Suzi said, her excitement making her voice breathy. "A nose ring, navel ring, or . . . brow

ring," she finished, pausing to see if Peasey would take the bait. He didn't. The principal just sat there, holding the hoop and staring at Suzi expectantly.

"When Fiona has been in your office, have you noticed that she has her eyebrow pierced?" Suzi asked, taking the ring from the principal and holding it up to make her point.

Suzi smiled proudly and just waited for the principal to pounce out of his chair and shower her with compliments about how clever she was. But to Suzi's dismay, the principal just continued to sit in his chair and squint at Suzi as if he were trying to read very small type that was written on her forehead.

"Mr. Peasey?"

"I appreciate your tenacity, Ms. Clue," Peasey finally said. "But this information that you've acquired, it's all circumstantial."

"Well, it's enough to question her," Suzi countered. "The hate for prom queens?"

"If hate were a crime, half the school would be guilty," Peasey said.

"But the eyebrow piercing!" Suzi said, refusing to back down.

"Ms. Clue, even I have a piercing," Peasey said. The principal's comment jolted Suzi for a second, and she quickly looked at Peasey's nose, ears, and even eyebrows. She didn't see any holes or hoops.

"You can't see it," Peasey added, noticing Suzi's prying eyes.

"The bottom line is that I am not going to accuse one of my students of a crime without adequate proof. That would be unethical," he finished, leaning back in his chair and crossing his arms over his chest.

"Unethical as in how you backed down to Trixie Topp's

mom?" Suzi fired back, and Peasey flinched as if he had just been slapped in the face. "I overheard the fight between the two of you," she continued. "I heard you say how you wanted to cancel the prom to protect your students, but you didn't. Why didn't you pull the plug, Mr. Peasey?" Suzi asked.

Peasey huffed and looked at Suzi impatiently. "I know all about your investigation, Ms. Clue," he said, picking up the ring and looking at it for a quick moment before continuing. "I know you're not cut out for this prom queen business, and that you're only doing it in hopes of finding out who's behind this awful curse."

Suzi sat back down on the edge of the desk and slumped over a bit. Peasey had her pegged, that was for sure.

"Unlike yourself, I am genuinely devoted to this prom. I like school spirit. I even like the perky pep rallies that you and your friends scoff at," he said in a snippy tone. "For your information, I decided to keep the prom alive not because of some hollow threats from Mrs. Topp. I just couldn't bear the thought of depriving my students of the most magical night of their lives, but now look what's happened. What have I done?" he asked, putting his head in his hands. Suddenly, Suzi's hand bumped the photo of his wife, and the frame slammed face-down onto the desk. Peasey's head snapped up.

"Sorry," she said genuinely, picking up the photo and looking at it. The glass had cracked right across the woman's face. Oops.

"We're done here, Ms. Clue," he said, clearly frustrated. "If you find real proof as to who is behind these terrible acts, please let me know. Otherwise, please know that I am extremely busy."

Peasey picked up the photo and surveyed the damage, while

Suzi seized the opportunity to sneak out of his office. When she had reached the doorway, she shot one last, apologetic glance over her shoulder, only to see Peasey still staring down at the photograph.

Suzi felt like such a jerk.

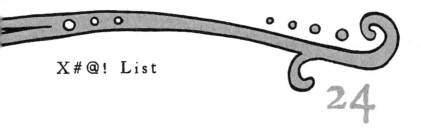

X#@! List

24

"Peasey's pierced?" Jett asked, leaning her back against a locker and cracking a smile. "I wonder where," she said, her voice getting lost in noise of the hallways. Thursday's final period had just let out, and the halls were filled with kids riffling through their lockers and scratching to get out the school doors and into the malls to shop for strappy stilettos, skimpy dresses, and bling galore.

"I don't even want to know," Suzi said, her back to Jett as she riffled through her locker. "But no matter what Peasey says, Fiona is still worth watching. Too much adds up," she finished, throwing her Spanish dictionary into her bag and turning around to face Jett.

"Adds up like a bad idea," Jett countered, kicking at the floor with her sneaker.

"You should have heard her ragging on the prom queens," Suzi said. "The girl has issues."

"Everybody has issues," Jett argued, leaning her head against the metal locker.

"Well, Fiona's also pierced, so I'm going to keep my eye on her," Suzi said, looking at Jett for a moment before turning back to her locker. "Did you know she chews black licorice gum?" Suzi asked, grabbing her iPod.

Jett just scowled.

"I've got to get my butt to Ms. Picante's room," Suzi continued, giving Jett's shoulder a soft nudge. "But knowing me, I could be totally off."

"Damn straight," Jett said with a small smirk. "Go meet your future husband," she added, giving Suzi a little push.

"Right." Suzi threw her messenger bag over her head and started down the hall.

"Call me later. Carnival tonight."

"Of course," Suzi said, whipping around and flashing Jett the rock-on sign. Then she turned back around and couldn't help herself from grinning ear to ear.

Suzi was on her way to her first TA session with Xavier Fontaine. Ever since his elusive "I think she's okay" comment about Kitty at Stumptown the other morning, Suzi had been secretly counting down the hours.

The hunkolicious Xavier and a budding new suspect in her case? Things were finally coming together, and Suzi's sneakers were walking on air.

Suzi rushed into Ms. Picante's classroom only to find she was the first person there. The room was empty and silent. She shot a glance up at the clock over the door. It was 3:20. She was ten minutes early.

Suzi took a seat behind one of the desks at the front of the room, reached into her messenger bag, and pulled out her iPod. She decided on an old Sleater Kinney playlist, pulled out her bright pink, zebra-striped journal (she had glued on the pink paper and drawn the zebra stripes with permanent black ink herself), and then leaned over and tapped her pen against her lips. Peasey and Jett were right. The halls were literally crawling with people who hated prom queens and with people who were pierced. At this point in her investigation, she had so many suspects, motives, hints, and clues, she knew she needed to make a list in order to keep it all straight. She put her pen to paper and wrote it down as she saw it.

X#@! LIST

1. MR. RIDER: HAS KEYS. WEARS BRIGHT PINK LIPSTICK. PIERCED? MAYBE. BUT HE WANTS TO BE A PROM QUEEN, NOT HURT THEM.
2. COACH KATIE: PIERCES OWN EARS. HAS KEYS TO ENTIRE SCHOOL. RED LIPSTICK.
3. TRIXIE: MOM IS A PSYCHO PAGEANT MOTHER. BUT TRIXIE IS DEEP-FRIED AS A WONTON. PIERCINGS? DOUBTFUL.
4. FIONA FIERCELY: HATES HATES HATES PROM QUEENS. PIERCED BROW! ACCESS TO BASEMENT?

Suzi studied her list for several minutes. Fiona was definitely her strongest suspect, but Coach Katie was picking up the tail end. The coach obviously had a thing for piercings, and she did have keys to the basement, after all.

"*Buena tardes.*" Suzi could hear Ms. Picante's voice over Janet Weiss drumming in her headphones. She looked up at her

Spanish teacher, who was smiling down at her with her big brown eyes. Her dark curly hair was free of its usual messy bun and flowing in ringlets over her shoulders today. She looked beautiful, Suzi thought, as she pulled her headphones out of her ears.

"What is that you're writing?" Ms. Picante asked, looking down at Suzi's desk.

"Nothing, Ms. Picante, I mean *nada*." Suzi smiled as she slammed her journal shut. She had nothing to hide from Ms. Picante, but she didn't want to advertise the fact that she was singling out students and teachers and analyzing them.

"*Bueno*," Ms. Picante said sweetly, walking away from Suzi and over to her desk. She took off her fuzzy, bloodred sweater, placed it on the back of her chair, and then opened the top drawer of her desk and pulled out a thick stack of papers. "For your first assignment, I'd like for you to record these grades for me," she said, putting the stack on the edge of her desk. "Please record them in my teacher's log."

"Sure," Suzi said, putting her journal and iPod away and walking over to Ms. Picante's desk. While she was picking up the papers, Ms. Picante reached out and lightly touched her arm.

"You like music," she said softly, smiling up at Suzi. "Why don't we listen to some? It so much helps me to relax."

"Sure." Suzi shrugged and walked back to her desk. She sat down and got to work while Ms. Picante took her own iPod out of a red leather tote and placed it in a speaker deck. Soon the room was filled with music. But not the type of music Suzi would have expected.

"*Soy yo! La jefe! La revolucción es evidente! Y la gente fuerte! Y el gringo muerte!*"

The bass alone was loud enough to make the fillings in Suzi's teeth rattle. Ms. Picante was listening to a totally in-your-face, female rap artist who was going on in Spanish about revolution and death of the "gringo." In English, that meant death of the white man.

"This is different from the music we were listening to last time," Suzi commented, looking up from her papers.

"You remember Dulce Diablo's music!" Ms. Picante said, clapping her hands. "This is her younger sister, Roja Diablo. She is the most famous female rapper in all of Cuba."

"Cool," Suzi said, looking up at the clock. It was almost 3:45 and Xavier was still nowhere in sight. As if Ms. Picante had read her mind, the Spanish teacher suddenly yelled out to her over the heavy bass line.

"Where is your partner? This is not a good start for him." Just then, Xavier whirled in through the door. His dark hair was messy (so hot) and he was breathing heavily (even hotter), as if he had run the entire way. He stood in the doorway panting, and looked from Ms. Picante to the speakers blaring on her desk . . . to Suzi.

Their eyes locked, and Suzi felt herself melt down the back of her chair and ooze out onto the floor like a cone of vanilla soft serve left out in the sun.

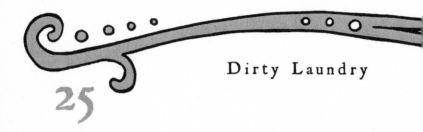

Dirty Laundry

25

This TA thing is going to be a real bitch, Suzi thought as the clock above the door struck 4:13. She and Xavier had been working for almost half an hour now, and Suzi still hadn't finished the simple task of recording the grades into Ms. Picante's log. It wasn't the rap songs blasting out of the speakers on Ms. Picante's desk that were so distracting. It was just that the papers in front of her were so boring, lifeless, and still, while the boy sitting at the desk next to her was so magical, mysterious, and entirely intoxicating. It was just that every time Xavier crossed his legs, rubbed his nose, or flipped a page in his Spanish dictionary (Ms. Picante had asked him to put together words for next week's vocab quiz), Suzi felt little shocks reverberate throughout her entire body. Being so close to Xavier was painful, difficult, and totally distracting.

But Suzi wasn't complaining one bit.

"We are finished for today," Ms. Picante suddenly said as she turned down her music and started to collect her papers and put them in her tote. "My, don't you two look beautiful sitting there together." Suzi felt herself blush, and she didn't dare look over at Xavier. Instead, she stood up and walked over to Ms. Picante.

"I didn't quite finish these," she said apologetically as she handed the papers back to her teacher.

"Roja's music was distracting," Ms. Picante said, nodding her head knowingly. "Next time, we will have quiet."

"The music was cool," Suzi said, leaning in toward Ms. Picante and lowering her voice to make their conversation as private as possible. "I'm just a bit out of it right now," she whispered.

"I understand, *chica*," Ms. Picante said softly, still nodding. "I have seen the signs all over the school. You are running for the prom queen. A very big decision, and one that surprises me very much," she continued, and Suzi thought she detected a slight hint of disappointment in her voice.

"Here are the words for next week," Xavier interrupted, walking up next to Suzi and (purposely?) brushing against her shoulder. He handed his finished assignment over to Ms. Picante.

Obviously, Xavier had no problem concentrating.

"*Gracias*, Xavier," Ms. Picante said. "Next week, you will be on time, no?" she asked in a lightly reprimanding tone, slipping her arms into her red sweater and throwing Xavier's work into her tote. Suzi walked back to her desk to get her stuff together.

"I am very sorry," Xavier said to Ms. Picante. "I was helping with the—how do you say—carnival." He emphasized the last syllable of the word *carnival*.

Suzi couldn't help but giggle a little as she threw her messenger bag over her head and secured it over her right shoulder. She wasn't necessarily laughing at Xavier's accent, she would never do that. It was just that she felt so high on life. She still couldn't believe she was TAing with the hottest guy in school. Suzi was giddy, plain and simple, and the buzz was stronger and cleaner than any triple shot.

"Adios," Suzi said, still smiling as she gave Xavier one last glance and darted out into the hallway. She wanted to go home and get something to eat before coming back to school for the carnival, or "carniv-VAL," as Xavier had called it. The thought made her giggle again, and she stopped for a moment to readjust the strap on her messenger bag.

"I am glad my English entertains you," Xavier said mischievously, sneaking up behind her and whispering directly into her ear. Suzi was totally caught off guard by the feel of his hot breath on her neck. She whipped around lightning fast, but not before noticing that his breath smelled of coffee and chocolate.

"What?" Suzi stammered, fighting to keep her balance after turning to face Xavier so quickly. *There he is, there he is, there he is, there he is . . .*

"I like your pink," Xavier said after a beat, smiling at her as she nervously pushed stray chunks of hair behind her ears. Suzi smiled back, but she was at a total loss for words. Was Xavier making fun of her or hitting on her? She was such a loser when it came to this stuff.

"Thanks," she managed to squeak out. "Um, I have to get home. The carnival's tonight."

Smiling awkwardly and holding up her hand in a casual good-bye, Suzi had turned to go when suddenly Xavier grabbed her left shoulder and gently pulled her back toward him.

Time. Just. Stopped.

"There is something I want to show you," he said, turning her around so that he could look directly into her eyes.

The tone of his voice was dead serious.

Suzi allowed herself to be led through the halls like a puppy on a leash. Her unusual passivity was one part curiosity—and one part hard-core crush. She was practically shell-shocked to be walking down the hall with Xavier Fontaine, their bodies so close that if she only had the guts, she could have reached out and grabbed his hand. The thought made her heart race.

But Suzi suspected more serious matters were at hand here. The tone in Xavier's voice, not to mention the look on his face, had told her that something had happened. He had seen something, something so important that he needed Suzi to see it as well. Whatever "it" was.

Xavier had walked Suzi away from the Spanish room, past the chemistry lab, around the gym and now they were walking toward the locker rooms. They must have passed ten SUZI CLUE FOR PQ signs along the way, but Xavier hadn't muttered a single word about them, and neither had Suzi. They had walked in a complete and not entirely unawkward silence, save for the voices and sounds coming from the cafeteria, where Sam and his prom posse were setting up the craft booths and cakewalk.

Xavier turned a corner and stopped in front of the boys' locker-room door. He reached out to open it, but it was locked tight.

"One hour ago, this door, it was not locked," Xavier said with frustration in his voice, still pulling on the door in hopes of it suddenly breaking free.

"Maybe we can get in through the gym," Suzi suggested, and

Xavier shot her an impressed look. This time, Suzi took the lead and headed toward the main doors to the gymnasium. She opened them without any problem, and she and Xavier walked inside. The heavy doors slammed behind them. It was dark inside, and dead silent.

"Follow me," Suzi whispered, and with Xavier close at her heels, she worked her way around the floor vault, spotting mats, and balance beam. Suzi seamlessly navigated her way through the dark gym, and stopped at the back door to the boys' locker room. At that point, she stepped aside and let Xavier take the lead again. He reached out and took hold of the door, and it opened without a hitch.

"Good job," he said, smiling at her over his shoulder as he walked into the boys' locker room. Suzi gave herself a mental pat on the back as she followed Xavier into the room, making sure the door stayed wide open behind them.

No way was she getting locked in the boys' locker room again. Not even if it was with Xavier.

The smelly room was shadowy and silent. Suzi looked around at the closed lockers, empty showers, and clean, bare benches.

"What do you want to show me?" she asked as Xavier made a beeline past the last row of lockers.

"This way," he responded, motioning with his head to a lone, unmarked door in the far corner of the room. He walked over and stood in front of it, and Suzi stopped next to him. "I was helping with the preparations for the carnival, and a student spilled a plate of cupcakes on the cafeteria floor," Xavier started to explain, looking down into Suzi's eyes. His voice was low and his tone serious.

"Cupcakes?" Suzi asked, her interest sparked.

"I came here to get a mop," Xavier continued, and Suzi noticed that he had grabbed the unmarked door's knob and was slowly turning it. He opened the door, revealing a pitch-black, cavelike room.

"And?" Suzi asked, rising onto her toes and trying to peek into the dark depths.

"And that's when I found it," Xavier said solemnly, stepping aside and motioning for her to enter the room. "How do you say, ladies first?"

Suzi crossed her arms across her chest and rolled her eyes. "The last time I walked into a dark room all by myself, I ended up getting locked in for hours."

"You want to see this," he said genuinely, still motioning with his hand for her to enter the room. Suzi flashed Xavier a kind yet threatening glance, and dove into the darkness, headfirst.

"Some help here?" she yelled back out at Xavier as she stood shrouded in total blackness. She felt around and could feel shelves, large plastic bottles, boxes, and the wooden roundness of either a mop or broom handle. She continued to feel around in the darkness, her fingers brushing over cardboard, rags, and then suddenly something warm, soft, and moving.

Oh. My. Gosh. It was Xavier's hand.

"Sorry," Suzi said, instinctively jerking her hand away.

"It's okay," Xavier said, and Suzi could have sworn by the tone in his voice that he was smiling. Just then, the light flashed on, and Xavier was standing behind her, pulling on a string hanging from the ceiling. And yes, he was smiling.

"Over there," he said to her, pointing to a black plastic bag. Suzi walked over, squatted down, and slowly peeled back the plastic to reveal what looked like a bunch of wet white towels. Or at least they used to be white. Now they had very questionable brown smudges all over them. Totally gross.

"Dirty laundry, Xavier? Is this what you want me to see?"

"Just look," Xavier urged, and Suzi hesitated for a moment.

"Pass me those gloves," she finally said, and Xavier grabbed a pair of yellow rubber gloves off the shelf next to him and gently tossed them over.

Sweaty gym shorts, smelly socks, old jockstraps . . . it didn't take long for Suzi to lose her interest, and almost her lunch. She was just about to stand up and give Xavier a piece of her mind when all of a sudden something inside the bag caught her eye. Something big and black. Suzi grabbed for the dark fabric, pulled at it with all her might, and it broke free in an explosion of socks.

She jumped to her feet, holding the black fabric out with her hands. It took a good couple of shakes to completely unroll the fabric so that she could get a good look at it. Suzi eyed it up and down, up and down. She then slowly looked over at Xavier, who was silently nodding his head.

Suzi was holding the black-and-white orca mascot uniform.

Sweaty Palms and
Strawberry Shortcake

26

"How did you know I would want to see this?"

"I have heard the girls talk about how you are trying to catch the person who has hurt them," Xavier responded, squatting down so that he was eye to eye with Suzi. "Kitty has told me about this uniform. She has nightmares about it."

So Xavier was still going out with Kitty, Suzi thought, feeling her stomach sink—but only for a minute. More pressing matters were at hand. She hungrily rummaged through the inside of the orca uniform, then the outside, but she found no hints as to who was wearing it the night Kitty was attacked.

"There's nothing here," Suzi finally said, looking up at Xavier. A long, not entirely comfortable moment passed between them and then suddenly, without any kind of forewarning, Xavier started leaning in toward Suzi . . .

Oh my gosh oh my gosh oh my gosh . . .

Closer . . .

Oh my gosh oh my gosh . . .

And closer.

Suzi inhaled Xavier's musky scent and held her breath as she watched him close his eyes and bring his lips close to hers . . .

"I gotta go," Suzi suddenly said, standing up and darting her eyes away.

"So soon?" Xavier asked, standing up so that he was once again close to Suzi. He looked deeply into Suzi's eyes, and she felt her legs weaken.

"Carnival," Suzi added, nodding her head nervously and taking a small step back. Although her skin was tingling and her chest was heaving, Suzi knew she had to get herself out of this situation before she did something stupid—like kissing vicious Kitty Sui's boyfriend.

Suzi held the uniform in front of her to purposefully create some space between the two of them, gave it another quick shake, and she was just about to shove it into her messenger bag when she noticed something.

The orca uniform had a small side pocket. It was difficult to see because the fabric was so dark, but it was a pocket nonetheless. Suzi dug her fingers in and felt a small, crumpled piece of paper. She pulled it out and eagerly opened it up.

"What is that?" Xavier asked, leaning in close.

Suzi's brows furrowed in complete concentration—and confusion.

"I have to get home," Suzi said again, ignoring Xavier's question and shoving the piece of paper safely into her back pocket. She was turning around to leave, when suddenly, the lights in the shower flickered a few times, making a horrible buzzing sound. They flickered once, twice, and then went out completely.

Suzi was swallowed in total darkness. She couldn't see

Xavier, the exit door, or even her own hand in front of her face.

"Crap!" Suzi said, feeling around in her bag for a pack of matches. She didn't smoke, but she was known to use a match on her eyeliner pencils from time to time.

"Do you have a lighter?" she was asking Xavier through the darkness, when *whap!* Something hit the wall next to her, and a sound rang out in her ears.

"Crap!" she yelled again, ducking down. Suzi quickly reached out to feel the wall, only to find it was covered with something wet, warm, and sticky. Her stomach sank, and she suddenly felt faint.

Oh. My. Gosh. It felt like blood.

"Xavier?" Suzi asked weakly.

"Look! There!" Xavier suddenly yelled out, and Suzi exhaled in relief. Back in the gym, someone had turned on a single, dingy yellow bulb, and (gulp) Suzi could see the shadow of a person holding a huge gun.

Her senses kicked into automatic overdrive. She reached out into the darkness until she felt the thick skin of Xavier's bomber jacket.

"Get down!" she whispered forcefully, pulling his arm down to the ground.

Still holding on to his hand, Suzi squinted toward a row of lockers near the showers. She then ducked her head and made a dash, with Xavier in tow, toward their cover.

Ping! Ping! Ping! The sounds exploded all around them and Suzi practically jumped out of her skin. She and Xavier made it to the lockers, and then quickly ducked behind them. Suzi's sneaker slipped a little on the floor. She reached down to touch the small puddle and recognized the sharp smell.

"It's a paint gun," she whispered to Xavier, fighting back the urge to laugh with relief.

"I'm sure it still hurts," Xavier said, and Suzi nodded.

"Let's make a run for the gym doors," she said.

"We want to stay in the dark," Xavier countered.

"We want to get the hell out of here," she insisted, creeping forward a couple of steps. "C'mon."

Suzi went first. She stayed low and ran from behind the dark lockers, through the back door, and into the dimly lit, open range of the gym.

Ping! A bullet shot out somewhere from the right and hit the floor about five feet in front of her. Suzi kept running as fast as she could and stopped behind the leather bulk of the floor vault. *Ping!* Suzi heard another bullet hit the balance beam, which was halfway across the gym.

"Stop it!" she yelled out angrily, and her voice echoed throughout the empty gym. Even with the yellowish glare from the one lightbulb, she still couldn't see who was shooting at her.

Suddenly Suzi heard the paint gun go off again and again and again as Xavier came running over and crouched down with her behind the vault.

"*Merde!*" he hissed, panting after his narrow escape. "Who is doing this?"

"I have no idea," Suzi answered, giving Xavier a quick once-over. It looked as if the person with the paint gun had missed him, too. "Stay here," she said to Xavier, doing a quick scan of the gym.

"Where are you going?"

In one quick move, Suzi zipped out from behind the vault, cartwheeled across the mats, and ducked down as she ran the length of the balance beam. Spotting the springboard the gymnastics team used to mount the beam, she jumped on it with all her weight and made a midair grab for the thick climbing rope hanging from the ceiling. She caught it with both hands and swung like Tarzan for a good five seconds before letting go and landing safely on the other side of the gym.

Before Suzi even had a chance to reflect on her most awesome display of agility and strength, yellow paint bullets started exploding all around her. She spotted a big, plastic hamper filled with rubber balls nearby, and she dove, headfirst, behind it.

The gym fell silent.

"Here, kitty, kitty." The low, creepy voice came out of the darkness and from somewhere by the main doors. Suzi carefully peeked around the plastic hamper to try to get a good look, but as soon as she did, a paint bullet exploded about an inch from her skull, and she quickly ducked back.

"C'mon, pussycat." The voice giggled menacingly. "I won't hurt you."

Suzi stayed put as her stalker's words bounced around the gym. She closed her eyes and tried with all her might to identify the voice, but she just couldn't. Whoever it was, they were masking their voice, talking unnaturally low and deep.

"I can see you," the voice sang out. Suzi could hear the sound of soft footsteps on the wooden floor, and they were moving (gulp) in her direction. She shot a quick glance over at Xavier. He was still crouched down behind the vault and didn't seem to be going anywhere anytime soon.

"Why are you doing this!" Suzi yelled out from behind the

hamper. She could feel her heart dancing in her chest, and her breath was coming in short pants.

No answer. Just more footsteps, getting closer . . . and closer . . .

"Who are you!" Suzi yelled out again, and she had to fight the urge to jump out from behind the hamper and confront her attacker face-to-face. She hated being hunted like an animal, but she had no weapons, and thus, no choice.

"You won't get past me, girlie girl," the voice teased, and Suzi knew her stalker was right. There was nothing but open space between her and the gym doors. Well, nothing except a psycho with a loaded paint gun.

She was trapped. Unless . . .

It took every ounce of her patience to stay low and wait for just the right moment. She counted the seconds, one Mississippi, two Mississippi, and then, as soon as she could hear her stalker's footsteps on the other side of the hamper . . .

"What do you want from me?" she screamed, shooting up from her hiding place and staring her attacker straight in the face.

Oh. My. Gosh. Suzi quickly eyed her attacker up and down.

It was definitely a girl—the short skirt and knee-high boots told her that much—but as for the face? Her attacker was wearing a cheap, plastic Strawberry Shortcake mask, and it had the most sickeningly sweet smile Suzi had ever seen.

"I want you to stop snooping around," Strawberry Shortcake hissed at Suzi, planting her boots hip width apart and holding the gun at half mast. "I want you to forget everything you know about the curse."

"Sorry, can't do that," Suzi said. She whipped her right hand up to reveal her own secret weapons, a pair of nicked-up wooden drumsticks. She held one up over her head, and at first, Strawberry Shortcake seemed alarmed and took a quick step back. But when she realized Suzi was threatening her with sticks, she threw her head back, let out a long, evil, rolling laugh, and continued to close in.

Suzi took her drumstick, and instead of throwing it at her attacker, she threw it as hard as she could toward the single lightbulb on the ceiling. Strawberry Shortcake stopped midstep to follow its path, and scoffed when it missed its target by a long shot. She slowly raised her gun and aimed it at Suzi, who was now standing not more than two feet away. Those paint bullets were going to hurt like hell . . .

Suzi took her second drumstick and threw again, this time with more determination and strength. With one eye, she watched as Strawberry Shortcake's finger slowly grabbed for the paint gun's trigger. At the same time, she saw her drumstick fly through the air and arch toward the gym's single light source.

Crash! Suzi hit her target dead-on. The gym went black.

Suzi quickly dropped to the floor, and as she did, paint bullets started spraying out in all directions. Picturing the layout of the gym in her head, she held her breath and made a run in the direction of the exit door.

"Where the %$*#! are you!" Strawberry Shortcake screamed through the darkness. Suzi heard a loud thud, an even louder curse word, and a flurry of bouncing sounds. She realized that Strawberry Shortcake must have kicked over the hamper full of rubber balls.

"Xavier! Run!" Suzi screamed out as she was running through

the open gym, and then all of a sudden *bam!* She slammed headfirst into a wall.

"Damn," she hissed as she felt at the wall, trying to figure out where she was and how to get out of there. Wait a second. She felt a handle. She was at the gym's main doors, where she and Xavier had first come in. Bingo!

Suzi threw all her weight against one of the doors, and as it opened, light poured into the gym, allowing Xavier to find his way out. Suzi looked over toward the hamper for Strawberry Shortcake, but her masked, psycho paintball stalker was nowhere to be found.

The gym was empty and silent, save for a bunch of rolling rubber balls.

"What happened to you?" Suzi's mom said with genuine alarm in her voice.

Suzi didn't answer at first. She just sat at the kitchen table, inhaling the delicious smell of her mom's garlic shrimp and jasmine rice. She was starving.

"I don't know if I'm cut out for this detective thing," Suzi finally said.

"Are you hurt?" her mom asked, examining the yellow splatters on Suzi's hair, jacket, and shoes.

"No, but whoever it was had a paint gun and trapped us in the gym."

"Us?" Suzi's mom asked, putting two fingers under Suzi's chin and gently raising it so that she could get a good look at her daughter's face.

"Me and Xavier Fontaine, the French exchange student," Suzi said, looking into her mom's eyes. "The psycho wouldn't stop shooting at us," she finished.

"Did you see this person?"

"They were wearing a mask."

Suzi's mom gave her daughter one last look-over and then, satisfied she wasn't hurt, turned her attention back to the sizzling shrimp and vegetables. "I know I've said it before, but I don't like this. Aggressive boys, threat notes, a masked person with a paint gun?" She paused for a moment, leaned the wooden spoon against the edge of the wok, and looked her daughter straight in the eye. "I'm worried about you."

"Well, maybe you can help me," Suzi said, sitting up in her chair. She dug into her back pocket and pulled out the crumpled piece of paper that she had found in the pocket of the orca uniform.

"What do you make of this?" she asked.

"What is this, an e-mail address?" Suzi's mom asked, furrowing her brow. She studied the paper for a few moments before handing it back to her daughter.

"Maybe," Suzi said, shrugging her shoulders. "I'm not sure. All I know is that it belongs to the person behind the curse," Suzi said, eagerly studying her newest clue.

It was a small piece of notebook paper with the mysterious code "T@UU" scribbled on it in dark blue ink. Suzi had no idea what T@UU meant, but her mom was right. It could be some sort of an e-mail address.

"Well then," her mom said, walking back toward the stir-fry. "Now you have two clues, that paper and the earring," she added, seeming impressed.

"Actually the earring is a brow ring," Suzi said, still studying the paper. "Or maybe a nose ring or something."

"It sounds like you know what you're doing, sweetie," her mom said, scooping a huge mound of shrimp and snow peas

onto a plate. "But, please be careful. Somebody out there obviously doesn't like you poking around."

"So I've noticed." Suzi huffed. "But I'm okay. I even have a
hunch about who's behind this."

"You do?" her mom asked, carrying the plate over.

"Yeah," Suzi said, nodding. "But Principal Peasey says I need
more proof."

"Proof?" her mom asked, putting Suzi's plate down on the
table. "So what are you going to do?"

"I'm going to follow a lead," Suzi said, smiling as she pierced
a particularly juicy shrimp with her fork. "And decipher what's
on that paper."

bombs away

*Man, this thing is hard to see through, she thought to herself as she
removed the plastic mask and hung it on a rusty nail sticking out
of the wall. She liked the way it looked with its mushroomed strawberry hat and sweet grin contrasting against the black, soulless holes
for eyes. It was as if the mask knew exactly how she felt every day
at Mountain High: smiling on the outside but dark and empty on the
inside.*

*She removed the paint gun from its harness and noticed that she
only had three rounds of paintballs left. That meant she had shot sev-
enteen rounds at those two, and still it wasn't enough. That nosy girl
still seemed all too intent on finding out who was behind the curse, and
well, considering it was hers truly, that couldn't be allowed to happen.*

It was time for Plan B.

After stashing the gun and mask where nobody would ever find them, she crept up the creaky stairs, through the locker room, and down the deserted halls, keeping her eyes peeled for volunteers setting up for the carnival. Whenever she heard voices or footsteps, she would duck into a bathroom or behind a garbage can. She was very careful not to be seen. It would be sloppy of her to be placed at the scene of the crime.

The cafeteria had been completely set up. The volunteers had moved on only to discover the mess in the gym (Oh my God, who would do this!?), and she knew that they would be kept busy scrubbing paint off the gym walls long enough for her to do what she needed to do. The cafeteria was empty, and all hers.

She walked by the crafts table, running her fingers over the hand-knit hats and handmade journals. Nice work, she thought as she picked up a black cashmere hat with pink felt kitty ears. She stuffed it down into the depths of her oversized bag.

She looked around at all the banal carnival decorations. The childish "Fishing for Prizes" game with its stupid red fishing poles and giant plastic hooks, the tacky, bright yellow lemonade stand, and the over-size glass jar filled with big bubble-gum balls, the number of which people were supposed to guess. Minus one, she thought smugly as she dipped her hand in, pulled out a bright blue ball, and popped it into her mouth.

She spotted what she was looking for. Over in the far corner and on a card table covered with a pink paper tablecloth were dishes piled high with delicious-looking, delicate cupcakes. Vanilla, chocolate, and strawberry, each with a creamy dollop of icing and sweet sprinkles on top. The cupcakes were innocent-looking and perfectly irresistible. They better be, she thought. Her whole plan was banking on it.

She walked over to the cupcakes, sampled some of the frostings with her finger (the vanilla on the strawberry cupcakes was by far the best), and then she made her way over to a neat row of nine foldout chairs.

This was the cupcake walk. Tonight the music would start, and the players would walk around the chairs in a circle. Then the music would stop abruptly, and the players would scramble to sit their butts down in a chair. Players who were left standing would be asked to leave, and one chair would be removed from the row. It would all come down to two people and one chair. The middle chair was always the last one.

Taking one last look to make sure she was still alone, she reached into her bag and took out a plastic bucket, a roll of thin rope, and a small garbage bag that was tied very tightly at the top. Kneeling down, she tied one end of the rope to the bucket handle, and then looked up at the ceiling. She eyed the long light fixture, that would work perfectly, but where could she hide the other end of the rope? By the bubble-gum balls? Behind the Fishing for Prizes curtain? No. She spotted the perfect place. A place where she could hide safely and pull the rope at the exact right moment. The student store would be open for business during the carnival, selling tacky school sweatshirts, baseball hats, candy bars, and cold water. It was the perfect place to linger unnoticed. Plus, she noted, it was located right next to an emergency exit door, making her quick escape a snap.

She grabbed a chair, put it solidly on top of a table, and carefully climbed up. From here, she could easily throw the rope over the light fixture and properly set up her little surprise. Her plan was going to work exactly as she had planned, and the thought excited her.

Tonight that nosy, pink-haired freshman would finally stop snooping around, and she would be off the hook. Sweet and innocent, just like these beautiful little cupcakes. She smiled, picked up a vanilla with shiny pink sprinkles on top, and shoved the whole thing into her mouth at once.

Success tasted so sweet.

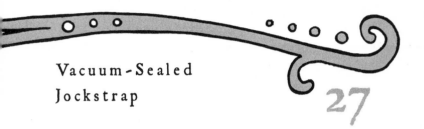

Vacuum-Sealed
Jockstrap

27

"Two points!" Jett screamed while shoveling popcorn into her mouth. Suzi had just thrown her third straight beanbag between the cardboard lips of a giant, smiling clown, and she only needed to sink one more in order to win an oversize, purple octopus. Suzi had no idea what she would do with the stuffed octopus if she were to win it, but she had to admit, it felt good to be winning.

For the first time in four days, Suzi was finally beginning to feel like herself again. She had managed to escape from psycho Strawberry Shortcake, a bit yellowed but relatively unharmed, and she even had an idea about who it might be behind the menacingly sweet mask. Plus, she had found another clue, the piece of paper, and although she didn't know exactly what T@UU meant, she knew it had to be important. Suzi was super antsy to figure it all out and get the proof that Peasey demanded, but she knew her investigation would have to wait until morning. Tonight, the Mountain High carnival was going, full force.

Suzi took a deep breath and squeezed the last bag in her left hand, feeling the individual little bumps slipping around between her fingers. She focused on the grinning hole in the painted cardboard, shifted her weight to her back foot, focused again, and then launched the bag. It landed half in and half out of the clown's mouth, and after dangling on the lip's edge for a moment, it finally slipped and fell to the ground with a hushed thump.

"I can't take you anywhere," Jett said, throwing a piece of popcorn into the air, and catching it on her tongue.

"Is there a prize for three out of four?" Suzi asked, ignoring Jett's comment and looking at the junior student who was running the beanbag toss.

"Sorry, little lady," the junior responded in true-to-form carny lingo. "It's for a good cause," he added in a righteous tone.

"The prom, I know," Suzi said, turning toward Jett and huffing at her bangs. "Man, I can't wait until this thing is over."

"The carnival?" Jett asked coolly as she scoped out the scene.

"The prom," Suzi said, rolling her eyes. Jett nodded knowingly.

Suzi and Jett stepped away from the beanbag toss and slowly strolled around the crowded gym. The entire space had been converted into a full-on festivity bonanza, with everything from a dunk tank and kissing booth to a head-scarfed tarot-card reader and mini–skate park in the far corner. Students buzzed around excitedly, licking puffy nests of cotton candy, bragging about prizes, and swapping game tickets. Except for a few stray splotches of yellow paint that Sam's volunteers weren't able to scrub off the walls, nobody ever would have guessed that a paintball shoot-out had gone down in that same space not even two hours before.

"Did I tell you that Xavier tried to make the moves on me?" Suzi suddenly asked, grabbing a handful of Jett's popcorn.

"No way!" Jett yelled out, popcorn falling from her lips.

"Way," Suzi said, smiling slyly. "It's like I've dreamed about it forever, right? But when it actually happened, it was just too weird. The last thing I need . . ." Suzi was saying, when suddenly, preppy Ewan Sinclair bumped into Suzi from behind, knocking her into Jett. Popcorn spilled everywhere.

"Watch it, jockstrap!" Jett yelled out while throwing the remains of her popcorn in Ewan's direction. Ewan was oblivious and just kept bulldozing through the crowd, holding a sawdust stuffed blue whale over his head.

A bouncy Gigi pulled up behind Ewan, strangling a pink stuffed dog in her left hand and holding a tangle of orange game tickets in the other. Gigi was gabbing a mile a minute at her friend in tow, Parker, who had managed to pull her blond wig into her trademark ponytail. Behind Parker was a tall, blond mystery man wearing a navy sweatshirt with Greek letters printed on the chest. Suzi realized he must be the college boyfriend Parker was always bragging about. He was smiling from ear to ear, and Suzi noticed that he had quite the roaming eye when it came to checking out the other girls in the gym.

And behind Parker's ogling boy toy, and bringing up the tail end of the A-list parade, was none other than Kitty Sui, who was making her first school appearance in two whole days. Usually at the front of the crowd and packing enough attitude to shoot anyone down, Kitty was quietly sulking behind her friends, with her arms crossed tightly across her chest and her glossy black hair looking uncharacteristically stringy and limp. As soon as Suzi saw Kitty, she began scanning the crowd for Xavier, but Mr. Fry was nowhere to be found.

"No wonder French boy was macking on you," Jett said as soon as Kitty had passed. "She looks terrible."

"She lost face," Suzi said, studying Kitty closely.

"Yeah, for starters," Jett said sarcastically. "But someone needs to take that jerk Ewan down a notch," she quickly added, holding her middle finger up in the air and flipping off the crowd in Ewan's direction. Unfortunately for Jett, Ewan's direction was also the current direction of Principal Peasey.

"Principal Peasey," Suzi said politely, suppressing a giggle as he walked over to confront the two girls.

"Ms. Black, that is hardly the type of behavior—" Peasey started to lecture.

"Who's your friend?" Suzi interrupted, referring to a good-looking bald man standing at Peasey's side.

"This is Keith McCain," Peasey said. "He's the security guard I've hired to keep an eye on things. He's the best there is," Peasey beamed. Mr. McCain flashed Suzi and Jett a quick, confident smile, puffed out his chest, and then resumed looking around the gym.

"You two look like family," Jett said with a smile.

"Yes, well, about your behavior, Miss Black," Peasey said, raising his voice and looking at Jett very seriously.

"Mr. Peasey, I'm glad you hired Mr. McCain here because somebody tried to shoot me with a paint gun not two hours ago," Suzi interrupted.

"Were you hurt?" Peasey asked, raising his brows.

"Well, no, but . . ." Suzi started to say.

"Did you get a good look at them?" McCain interrupted, in a tone that was so detective TV show, it was almost comical.

"Well, no, but," Suzi started to say again. "Maybe I can borrow Mr. McCain tonight, pick his brain about the curse?" Suzi finished, looking up at Peasey.

"I'm sorry, but I will personally be needing the services of Mr. McCain this evening," Peasey responded, lifting his chin with an authoritative air. "We need to, uh, go over background information, important stuff like that," he finished.

"Background information?" Suzi asked, totally confused.

"Don't worry, Ms. Clue," Peasey said. "I'm sure nobody will try anything tonight with these muscles patrolling the area," he finished, admiring McCain's strong physique.

Then Mr. Peasey cleared his throat, held out his palm to suggest that McCain take the lead, and the two men walked away in the direction of the cafeteria. Suzi and Jett watched them leave and then looked at each other.

Jett opened her mouth to say something, but her comment, whatever it might have been, was completely swallowed by the loud, shrill sound of a girl screaming.

It was a happy scream, the scream of someone who was on top of the world and loving it. It was the scream of their friend Uma Ashti, and it was coming from the vicinity of the dunk tank.

Suzi and Jett squeezed their way through the masses to find Uma, standing in the center of a circle, armed with a softball and grinning madly from ear to ear. In the dunk tank sat a very wet, very unhappy Chet Charleston, and Suzi had to slap her hand over her mouth to keep from erupting into laughter.

Uma had indeed lived up to her promise and just dunked the two-timing school quarterback.

Chet's white hairy legs were dangling over the edge of the seat, his toes just inches from the water. His curly blond hair was plastered wet across his forehead, and his polo shirt was practically vacuum-sealed to his body, making his bulky size look unusually wimpy.

"Hang in there, baby!" Jett yelled out, elbowing Suzi in the arm and laughing so hard, Suzi thought her friend was going to pee her pants.

Uma shot a glance over at her two friends and gave them a sly wink before she raised her arm, threw a wicked-fast curve-ball, and hit the target lever right in the center.

"No!" Chet screamed as the seat collapsed and he dropped with a heavy splash into the water.

"Two for two!" Uma yelled.

Suzi giggled as she watched Chet dog-paddle over to the tank's ladder. He grabbed onto one of the rungs and looked helplessly through the glass at Uma, who was clapping her hands and jumping up and down.

"Please," Chet pleaded, his feet struggling to grab the bottom rung. "The water's so cold."

"I'd like to buy two more, please!" Uma responded enthusiastically, waving a five dollar bill in the air.

"Maybe this carnival thing is for a good cause, after all," Suzi whispered into Jett's ear, but Jett's attention was obviously elsewhere. Suzi followed her friend's gaze over to Fiona, who was standing by the kissing booth, surveying the crowd.

Suzi eyed the freckly feminista suspiciously. "Want to check out the crafts in the cafeteria?" she asked.

"Huh?" Jett's attention clearly elsewhere.

"The craft booths. I want to see if my stuff is selling," Suzi continued.

"I'm going to hang here for a while," Jett said, motioning unconvincingly with her eyes toward Uma and the dunk tank.

"Right." Suzi nodded knowingly. "I'll catch you later," she continued, giving Fiona another once-over before heading toward the cafeteria.

On her way out of the gym, Suzi exchanged a quick glance with Ms. Picante, who was standing next to a man tossing coins into little glass bowls in hopes of winning a giant red heart balloon. Suzi smiled and her teacher smiled back. Then Ms. Picante's friend turned around, and Suzi noticed two things. One, that he was wicked cute, with curly dark hair and gorgeous olive skin; and two, that he was wearing a red tee with a picture of a beret-wearing Che Guevara on the front, the famous South American revolutionary.

Ms. Picante was just full of surprises, Suzi thought to herself.

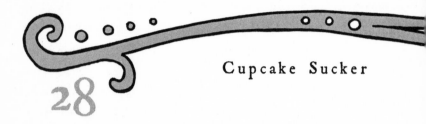

Cupcake Sucker

28

Aside from being the site of the snack bar, school store, and more carnival games, the cafeteria was where all of the student craft booths were happening. Tables filled with hand-knit sweaters, recycled-paper writing journals, and vinyl messenger bags lined the walls, and as far as Suzi could tell, business looked pretty good. And in the far corner, over by the student store, was a table piled high with plates of delicious-looking cupcakes. She started to walk across the gym . . . but almost as if a hook were reeling her in, Suzi found herself lured closer and closer to the cupcake table. She had always been a sucker for a good cupcake.

"Ouch," someone yelled into her ear. In all her cupcake hypnosis, Suzi had smacked right into Trixie Topp.

"That really hurt," Trixie snapped as she rubbed the side of her arm.

"I am so sorry," Suzi said genuinely as she tried to look through Trixie's huge, dark sunglasses and into her eyes. "Are you okay?"

"I'm fried from head to toe, no thanks to you," Trixie said angrily.

Now it was Suzi's turn to say ouch. Trixie's comment, no matter how unfounded, cut into her like a knife. She knew in her heart that she had done her best to protect Trixie, but apparently it hadn't been enough. She only hoped that Trixie would be able to forgive her once she caught the real culprit behind all of this pain and suffering.

But first, the cupcakes.

Suzi walked over to the table and ogled the precious little cakes. Vanilla with pink frosting, chocolate with chocolate frosting, strawberry with white frosting and pink sprinkles on top. Suzi felt as if she had died and gone to heaven.

"How much?" she asked in a whispery breath as she dug around in her pocket for some cash.

"They're not for sale," Suzi's chemistry teacher, Ms. White, said from behind the table.

"How much?" Suzi said again, high on the smell of cake and icing.

"They're for the cakewalk, dear." Ms. White spoke again, this time a little louder. "You buy a ticket and you win the cupcakes." She looked at Suzi over the top of her bifocals.

"Count me in," Suzi said, quickly forking over her money.

"Herb, here's our last player," Ms. White yelled out at the school's bald librarian, who was manning the turntable. Mr. Jones, or Herb as he was apparently called by his coworkers, nodded his approval, and the players rose to stand beside their chairs.

Mr. Jones dropped the needle on the record, and the music started playing. Suzi just stood there, not sure what to do, but then a student nudged her from behind, and she started following the others in a circle around the chairs.

Suzi eyed each of the chairs as she passed, ready to drop her butt to safety as soon as the music stopped. When the sound of a needle scratched against vinyl and the music stopped abruptly, Suzi, quick as a bullet, plopped down into a chair and looked around at the other players. She was safe, but a junior girl with braces wasn't so lucky and was forced out of the game. Ms. White walked over and removed one chair.

Fifteen minutes and seven sit-downs later, the cakewalk had been reduced to only three players: a big senior girl whose secret weapon was to use her booty to push people out of her way, the quick and spry Suzi, and none other than the school's plum-jacketed principal, Mr. Peasey. Suzi had noticed Peasey's presence in the game from the get-go, but she had never anticipated just how competitive the principal would be.

One more sit-down, and the big-bootied girl was left standing. As Ms. White escorted her out of the game, the girl threw a fit, complaining that Peasey had cheated by lingering in front of the chairs. Several students gathered around. Suddenly, Peasey and Suzi had an avid audience.

Herb gave the record its final spin, and Peasey and Suzi started circling the single chair like two coyotes around a deer carcass. Suzi kept low and loose, focusing on the chair and the sounds of music at the same time.

Suzi passed by the seat of the chair, her senses keen and reflexes ready . . .

Peasey stopped in front of the chair and lingered a second longer than he should have, but Suzi gave him a friendly nudge . . .

Suzi and Peasey were standing on opposite sides of the chair when the music stopped. Quick as lightning, they both made a mad dash for the last chair, their bodies slamming together, butts first.

Suzi really wanted those cupcakes. But apparently, so did Principal Peasey.

Peasey's superior physical prowess paid off, and in one unusually bullish gesture, he managed to throw Suzi aside with his weight. He didn't push her all that forcefully, but as Suzi struggled to keep her feet beneath her, she tripped over her shoelace, slammed down onto the floor, and rolled into the crowd like a big bowling ball. As she was rolling, she caught a glimpse of Peasey smiling victoriously as he sank his butt into the last remaining chair.

But suddenly, a gooey slimy mess oozed down from the heavens and landed with a wet splash right on top of Peasey's head, and the principal stopped smiling real fast.

"Aarghhh!"

"Eeeww!"

"Blughugh!"

Suzi was still rolling across the floor when the slimy goo splattered all over Peasey, but she had smelled it before she even saw it. Suddenly, the entire cafeteria was overwhelmed with the thick, putrid smell of rotten fish, and Suzi felt herself gag.

Covering her nose with one hand, Suzi jumped up, pushed a few retching students out of her way and ran over to Principal Peasey, who had quickly scrambled away from the pile of fish guts and was now sitting by the cupcake table, surrounded by a wall of gaping students. He ranted as he frantically brushed the thick, putrid slime off his slacks and perfectly pressed, purple shirt. Suzi noticed that while the principal looked absolutely abhorred by his current condition, he also looked unharmed.

Still covering her nose from the stench, Suzi turned her attention back to the puddle of fish guts. Totally gross, Suzi thought. But even more gross, and something that made her spine shiver from top to bottom, was the fact that right in the middle was Suzi's very own pink sneaker. The one that had fallen off when she had tripped over her shoelace.

Her mind reeling, Suzi threw her head back and looked up at the ceiling. Hanging from the fluorescent light was a plastic red bucket, the type a child would take to the beach. The bucket was dangling from a thin rope that ran over the top of the light casing and into the student store, where the rope hung down behind the doorway.

Suzi shot another quick glance up at the bucket, which she noticed was still rocking from side to side, and she watched as a stray gob of green goo dripped out and landed with a wet splat, right inside her slime-covered sneaker.

Suzi felt something inside of her shift. Time to wrap this party up.

Suzi scanned the cafeteria with her eyes. Students and teachers were buzzing around everywhere. Over to her right, Peasey had his arm around McCain's broad shoulders and the security guard was gently lifting the rambling principal to his feet. People were leaving through the cafeteria's main doors, but nobody was running or suspiciously fleeing the scene. But then Suzi's eyes noticed the red emergency exit sign right next to the student store. She looked down at the door. It was clearly ajar and shutting, as if someone had just gone through it.

Suzi took off through the exit door and onto the school's wet, muddy lawn.

It was raining outside, and dark and quiet. Suzi's feet made sucking noises as she stepped to her left and right, not sure what to do or which way to go. But she looked down and saw a trail of footprints leading across the muddy lawn and into the parking lot, and then she heard a car engine fighting to turn over.

She ran in the direction of the sound, kicking up mud all around her.

She hit the pavement and her speed increased, but suddenly tires started squealing. Suzi watched as a shiny, black SUV lurched out of a parking space and up onto the curb. Suzi heard the transmission grind as the driver struggled to put the car into first gear, and the SUV started peeling out of the parking lot.

Suzi ran for her bike, which was parked close by, and in one swift move, she unlocked her bike and started running with it at her side. She then mounted her seat while her bike was moving, stood up, and pumped her legs as hard as she could. She wasn't about to let that SUV get away so easily.

She felt mud spattering off her back tire and up the back of her jacket as she jumped a curb and took a shortcut through the school's lawn, past the outdoor pool, and then she wheelied off another curb and landed on the same street as the escaping car, just a few feet behind it. She kept pedaling ferociously, but Suzi's legs were no match for the SUV's horses, and the car easily gained ground and sped away. Suzi's back tire skidded as she brought her bike to an abrupt stop and squinted after the car. Maybe she could at least get the license plate. Maybe not. The SUV's back, just like Suzi's, was completely covered in mud.

"Dammit! Come back here!" Suzi yelled at the shrinking taillights of the SUV. She blinked through the cold rain until the lights of the SUV had completely faded away, and the only sounds were those of her own, desperate gasps for breath.

Suzi put one muddy pink sneaker on one pedal and one soaked sock on the other and started slowly riding back toward the cafeteria.

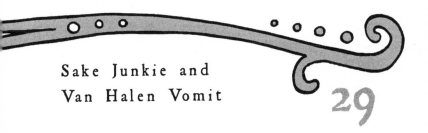

Sake Junkie and
Van Halen Vomit

29

"That was too damn close," Jett said, peeking out from behind her computer and across the table at Suzi. She gave Suzi a scowl before ducking back behind her monitor as Mr. Jones, or Herb as Suzi now knew him, the school librarian, walked by with a sour look on his wrinkled face.

"I'm fine," Suzi said, bugging out her eyes but not looking up from behind her monitor. She was too busy typing.

It was Friday morning, computer lab in the library, and Suzi had been waiting for the chance to get on a computer ever since she found that mysterious note in the orca's pocket the day before. She had a secret code to crack.

UR INSANE, Jett instant-messaged over to Suzi's computer, and Suzi heard her friend clear her throat in an effort to drive her point home. Jett was in quite a foul mood this morning, and Suzi felt bad because she knew she was the reason behind it.

"Look," she finally said, firmly but gently, looking over her monitor at her friend. But before she could get another word out, Jett cut her off.

"You could have been doused by fish guts or flattened by that SUV!" she yelled out, and the entire library turned to look at her.

"Ms. Black, do you have something you wish to share with the class?" Mr. Jones said, turning his attention from a student he was helping and nailing Jett with his discerning gaze. Jett crossed her arms over her chest, stared up at the ceiling, and stewed in silence.

"Ms. Black?"

"Mr. Jones," Suzi interjected as politely as possible. "My friend is just upset over the events of last night," she explained. "Surely you understand."

"I understand that this is the library and your friend has work to do," Mr. Jones answered. Suzi rolled her eyes and looked back at her monitor in defiance.

"And don't call me Shirley," Jett added under her breath, and Suzi erupted in laughter. Mr. Jones shot them both a dirty look, but then turned his attention back to his students. The girls laughed again.

"I know you're not doing homework over there," Jett whispered after a long silence. "You're slapping at that keyboard like a redheaded stepchild," she continued.

Suzi couldn't help but crack another smile as she hit the enter key one more time. Unfortunately, her screen displayed the same frustrating line she had been getting all morning.

No matches found.

"Damn!" Suzi said under her breath as she pushed the keyboard away and looked over at Jett for a long moment. "I'm trying to figure out what this code is on the piece of paper I found in the orca uniform, but I'm not finding anything," she whispered.

"You still think it's Fiona, don't you?" Jett asked, shaking her head. "You think Fiona's one twisted sister."

"I don't know, but I'm trying to find out, no thanks to this crappy computer," Suzi said, giving the ancient, pea-green monitor a little slap. Just then, Drex walked by with an armful of thick, heavy-looking books.

"Hey, Drex!" she said, motioning with her hand for Drex to come over. Drex stopped in his tracks and looked in Suzi's direction. He seemed to be surprised, or maybe nervous, as he made his way over to where she was sitting.

"Hey," Suzi said again, scooting her chair over so that Drex could squeeze into her space. "You're good with computers, right?" Drex put his books down on the floor with a thump, pushed his glasses up on his nose, and nodded. "Come here," she said, pulling him down so that he was squatting next to her monitor.

"What's going on?" Drex asked, clearly confused, but not altogether unflattered. Even Jett peeled out of her chair and walked over to see what Suzi had in mind.

"I've been trying to find out what this is, but the computer isn't telling me anything," Suzi said, showing Drex the piece of crumpled paper. "Can you help me?"

"What is this?" Drex asked, studying the piece of paper.

"It looks like an e-mail address," Suzi said, putting her hand on Drex's shoulder. "But I can't figure out what the UU stands for. I've check country codes, Uruguay, Uzbekistan. I've checked university codes . . ."

"Have you checked private domains?" Drex interrupted, looking nervously at Suzi's hand. "Small Internet providers and stuff?"

"Go for it," Suzi said, smiling at Drex and moving over so

that he had access to her keyboard. Drex started quickly typing away.

"What if it's not an e-mail address at all, but a password?" Jett asked.

"Passwords usually don't have symbols," Suzi answered, picking up the note. "But it could be one of those word puzzles where each character has an assigned letter," she finished.

"A cryptogram," Drex answered, not looking away from the monitor. "They're usually all symbols or numbers, not a combination."

"So what is it?" Suzi asked, huffing the bangs out of her eyes and staring at the paper intently. A moment of heavy silence passed, with the only noises being those of Drex's fingers on the keyboard.

"Well, it's a *T* and an 'at' symbol and a *U* and another *U*," Jett finally said, thinking it through out loud.

"*T* at *UU*," Suzi said. "*T* at *UU*," she said again, slumping in her chair and looking up at the ceiling.

"Maybe it's an abbreviation or something," Jett was saying, when suddenly, Suzi jolted to attention.

"*T*-at-Two-*U*," she said, bugging her eyes out at Jett.

"*T*-at-Two-*U*?" Jett responded, wrinkling her nose.

"*T*-at-Two-*U*!" Suzi said again. "That's it! Tattoo You! That's what it says!"

"That's an old Rolling Stones album," Jett said.

"It's also a tattoo studio that just opened," Drex piped in, and both Suzi and Jett turned to look at him. "I found no matches on domain names, so I searched some local blogs. There's a mentioning of a new tattoo studio on Pike Street with the same name as what's written on that paper." He shrugged. "The 'at' symbol, two *U*'s, everything."

"Drex, you're a genius!" Suzi yelled, giving him a big kiss on the cheek. This time Mr. Jones did hear and cleared his throat to express his disapproval.

"I need the address," Suzi whispered, her voice breathy with excitement.

Jett stood by and watched in silence, but she couldn't help but notice that it took Drex three whole tries to click on the correct link, even though it was clearly right in front of him.

Drex's fingers were shaking that badly.

Suzi bolted down the hall, her pink sneakers nothing but a blur as she darted in between bodies, through lovebird couples, and around the occasional road hazard of an open locker door. The bell had just rung, announcing the end of third period. It was lunchtime. Students were swarming everywhere, and Suzi was beginning to feel like she was navigating her way through an obstacle course.

In her left hand, she held the one clue that, as far as she was concerned, might well be her golden ticket to solving the curse. Drex had managed to pull up the address on the tattoo studio, T@UU, and Suzi had written it down on the same piece of paper and then rushed out the library door.

Although Suzi was starving, she had decided to skip lunch today to go check out the studio. She wanted to talk to the people who worked there, look around, and see if she could find anything that might shed light on the curse. The studio wasn't that far away, and if she pedaled fast enough, she'd be able to make it back just in time for geometry class. The exit doors were just coming into view at the end of the hall . . .

"*Konichiwa!*" Sam Witherspoon screamed, jumping in front

of Suzi so quickly and unexpectedly, she almost smacked right into his red-and-gold kimono.

"Sam!"

"Our honorable prom queen," Sam continued, making a calm, deep bow as Suzi stood there panting.

"Sam, I'm kind of busy right now."

"My committee has been busy as well." Sam smiled and motioned with his hand to the gym, which, Suzi suddenly noticed, she was standing directly in front of. "The presence of our most honorable queen is requested immediately."

"Now?" Suzi asked impatiently, taking a step away from the gym. "Sam, I really can't—"

"We have sushi for you to taste, origami for you to ogle," Sam whined, suddenly breaking his calm, Japanese exterior. "It all hinges on you! You have to approve everything!" He grabbed onto Suzi's arm and gave it a firm tug. "We're running out of time!"

Sam was right. It was Friday morning. The prom was tomorrow night. Suzi was most definitely running out of time.

"Sam, I can't."

"Not acceptable," Sam argued, holding her arm even tighter. "You are the prom queen. Now act like it!" he huffed, lightly pushing Suzi into the gym.

"Lovely, isn't it?" Sam beamed as Suzi got her bearings. He was holding out his arms and twirling around in circles.

Suzi nodded slowly and silently, scoping out the gym from wall to wall, streamer to streamer, basketball hoop to basketball hoop. She then folded and tucked the tiny piece of paper that held the tattoo studio's name and address safely into her back pocket and softly patted her butt a couple of times. This might take some time; she smiled to herself, eyeballing a long thin table in the far corner of the gym.

And would someone please let her get at that most auspicious sushi buffet?

Ten minutes and twenty spicy tuna rolls with extra wasabi later, Suzi was standing in the middle of the gym, sipping on a cup of steaming green tea and discussing the prom decorations with Mountain High's benevolent yet bossy committee captain. While she had been hesitant to offer her opinions at first, she had quickly succumbed to Sam's prodding when she realized that it felt kind of good to put in her two bits. It made her feel like what she was doing for the school really was appreciated and, in some small way, maybe even important.

Sam was in rare form, rambling a mile a minute about where he had found the perfect tatami mats, discounted kimonos for the dance team, children with fingers small enough to make all the origami rabbits hanging from the basketball hoops, and how the Japanese guitarist he had hired turned out to be a sake junkie, so he had to find a world-music DJ at the last minute, which was totally out of his budget, but something he deemed necessary, so he had made an executive decision and he hoped Suzi was okay with it.

Suzi just nodded in agreement as Sam went over every last detail of the prom decorations. She was liking the huge flat screens that would flash a dancing clan of Harajuku Girls, and she also liked the dry, woody smell of the tatami mats (much better than the smell of sweat and feet, which was usually how the gym smelled). She gave her enthusiastic approval of the delicate-looking Japanese paintings of clouds and trees and flowers that hung on the walls, red-and-black strokes on the posters announcing the silent raffle, and the rice-punch bowl that was disguised as a trickling waterfall fountain.

But Suzi's favorite part of Sam's Go Geisha! prom scheme was the amazing sushi buffet. Maki, sashimi, spicy, crunchy, tuna, shrimp, ami, and uni, the committee had thought of every-thing under the sea and made samples for Suzi to approve. The lingering wasabi burn in her sinuses proved it.

"So, my queen, you approve?" Sam asked, once again pre-senting his calm, "I think I'm turning Japanese" air. He looked around at his busy worker bees and smiled proudly.

"I do," Suzi said, nodding. "As you know, I'm not really a prom person, but you've done an amazing job," she finished, taking a long, slow sip from her cup.

Sam jolted in his toe socks and sandals. "Do not hex the auspicious prom with your negative mojo," he said sweetly, although his eyes contained an edge of concern. "Listen, I know this prom isn't your thang, but I am certain that all will change once you're standing in front of us tomorrow night, under the lights, reigning over your subjects," he rambled, turning and motioning to the one part of the gym that Suzi had so far avoided. The area where tomorrow night's crowning would take place. With the tiara. And a dress. And the spot-lights. In front of the whole school.

Suzi gulped.

She looked across the gym and over at the elevated, eerily empty wooden stage. The only decoration on it so far was a poster sagging from one side to the other that read CONGRATU-LATIONS GO GEISHA PROM QUEEN!

She suddenly felt sick to her stomach. The little hairs on the back of her neck jumped to attention and a creepy chill ran down her arms. She tried to hold her stomach and make a run out the gym doors into the safety of the hallway, or even better, the girls' bathroom, but it seemed her stomach, and its contents, were moving faster than her legs.

Right there, in the middle of the painstakingly, impeccably, and most auspiciously decorated gym, Suzi heaved once, then twice. Third time a charm.

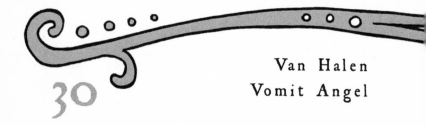

Van Halen
Vomit Angel

30

The next thing Suzi remembered was waking up on a sofa in someone's office somewhere. A fluorescent light flickered overhead.

Moving her eyes only, she looked around the room and saw a dark wooden desk covered with file folders, a white leather chair, a dead palm plant, and a full-length mirror. Posters of Venus Williams, Mia Hamm, and Anna Kornikova covered the walls, as well as framed pictures of the Orca's girls' soccer team.

Suzi was in Coach Katie's office, and she had no recollection of how she got there.

She looked down toward her feet and saw that her sneakers were covered in vomit, and that's when it all came back to her. Instinctively, she reached up to feel her Van Halen *Diver Down* tour tee. It was wet. And sticky. And Oh. My. Gosh. The smell made her want to vomit all over again. Remembering how Jimi Hendrix had died, she quickly rolled over onto her right side to keep from choking.

And that's when the pains kicked in.

The cramps seared like lightning through every inch of her body, from her head to the tips of her toes, and all she could do to keep from screaming out was to grab her stomach and writhe around in pain. She turned from her right side to her left and onto her back. *Make it stop make it stop make it stop.*

Time as she knew it slipped away, and when she finally opened her eyes again, she was seeing big, fuzzy black spots. No, wait a minute. That black spot to her right was a person. It was the school nurse, Nurse Pettibone, and she was standing over her, feeling her forehead. Nurse Pettibone looked like an angel with her blond hair and kind blue eyes. Then suddenly Nurse Pettibone's white nurse hat sandwiched down into a French beret and it was Xavier standing there, staring down at her with his violet eyes. Then Xavier's violets went stone gray, and it was Fiona Fiercely, chewing on her black gum and leaning maliciously over Suzi's limp, helpless body. Then Fiona stood up, turned her head toward the door, and when she looked back at Suzi, she had turned into Coach Katie, sporting a wickedly tight ponytail and a fresh slathering of fiery-red lipstick.

Was Suzi hallucinating? Was she dead? Was this hell?

Coach Katie looked unhappy about something, pissed off even, as she told Suzi to open her mouth, and Suzi gagged as a cold, smooth instrument slid over her tongue and hit the back of her throat.

"Close your lips," Coach Katie demanded. Suzi looked up at her with heavy lids.

"Coach?" Suzi whispered. Oops. The thermometer slipped out of her mouth and onto her barfy chest.

"I said, shut it!" Coach Katie snapped, shoving the thermometer back into Suzi's mouth and turning around.

Suzi lay still as ordered and quietly watched as the coach grabbed a rag and poured some bottled water over it. The coach was talking to herself the entire time.

"Little Miss Know-it-all," Coach Katie hissed, as she walked over, squatted down, and started wiping off Suzi's neck with the wet rag. Suzi kept quiet, although the coach was rubbing real hard.

"Clean up the patient for me, Kathryn," the coach spit out in a high, mocking voice as she kept rubbing that same spot on Suzi's neck. "Do this for me, Kathryn. Do that, Kathryn."

Suzi had to bite her lower lip to keep from screaming. Her neck was being rubbed raw.

"I'm a nurse. I'm little Miss Smarty Pants," the coach continued, making an ugly face and rubbing, and rubbing, and rubbing—

"Coach!" Suzi suddenly screamed out, the thermometer bouncing around in her mouth.

"Oh, we're talking now, are we?" Coach Katie said, looking down at Suzi. "Oh, I'm so glad. We wouldn't want anything to happen to our precious little prom queen, now would we? No, no no!" the coach continued, clicking her tongue. "Prom queens get the royal treatment because they're special," she finished with a malicious whisper.

Suzi felt creepy chills run down her arms again. This time, it wasn't because of any bad sushi. It was because Suzi sensed danger. Imminent danger.

"I tried to help you, prom queen girl. I was so nice to you. And this is how you repay me? I'm wiping vomit off your face?" The coach huffed, standing up and walking back to her desk.

Suzi felt herself let out a quiet sigh of relief. The coach was acting way crazy, psycho even, and the farther away from Suzi she was, the better.

Her head still heavy, Suzi watched as the coach sat down at her desk and picked up a single piece of bright yellow paper. Coach Katie stared at it for a moment, huffed, and then picked up a pair of shiny, silver scissors.

Suzi gulped. Scissors.

"I should be running my girls, but instead I'm told to cut out these ridiculous prom decorations," the coach huffed, chopping away at the yellow paper and practically massacring it. "This whole prom is bullcrap. Absolute bullcrap."

Suzi kept quiet as the coach took her aggressions out on the paper. The woman sliced and ranted and swore and shredded until almost nothing was left. Then she picked up a fresh piece, but instead of tearing into it, she froze, the scissors pointy-side up in her hand, and leered over at Suzi.

"What is it about you prom queens that makes you think you're better than everybody else?" the coach asked. The sharp tip of the scissors caught the light and gleamed into Suzi's wide, frightened eyes.

Suzi sat up with a jerk, the thermometer shooting out of her mouth and landing on the floor with a glass-shattering crash.

"Look what you've done, you naughty prom queen," the coach scolded, still holding the scissors as she got up and walked toward Suzi.

Oh my gosh oh my gosh oh my gosh.

"Kathryn." A light, sweet voice cut through the tension in

the room and descended upon Suzi's ears like an angel from heaven. She looked over at the door. Enter the beautiful Nurse Pettibone, in all her glowing, sunny blond glory.

"Porsche," Coach Katie said nervously. "I'm so glad you're here," she lied, smiling through clenched teeth.

"I've cleaned the patient, as you asked, and taken her temperature. But we had a teeny tiny accident," Coach Katie apologized, looking down at the broken thermometer on the floor.

"Accidents happen," Nurse Pettibone replied, nodding. "I'll get someone to clean it up. Thank you Kathryn. You've been of the utmost help," the nurse said, smiling genuinely.

"Do you need me for anything else?" the coach asked, fidgeting with the end of her ponytail. The nurse smiled, looked down at Suzi, and shook her head. Coach Katie ducked her head and quietly left the office.

As the coach made her exit, Suzi fell back into the sofa and breathed out a long sigh of relief.

"You're an angel," she heard herself say as the nurse gently slipped the glass tube under her tongue.

"No, I'm a nurse." Nurse Pettibone giggled. "And you have quite a case of food poisoning, poor thing," she said as she gently touched Suzi's face. Suzi closed her eyes and soaked up the love.

"How are you feeling?" the nurse asked.

"Better," Suzi answered. "But weak."

"Hasn't anyone ever told you about the dangers of eating raw fish?" the nurse teased, pulling the thermometer out of Suzi's mouth. "Well, I'm going to get you some electrolytes, and I want you to go home and get some rest. Nurse Pettibone's orders."

Suzi just nodded. She was suddenly very, very tired.

"I know you have a big night coming up," Nurse Pettibone continued, leaning down so that her face was close to Suzi's. Suzi inhaled the nurse's sweet, powdery scent. "But no worries. With a little rest, you'll be in top form for the crowning. I promise."

Suzi's eyes darted open. Oh. My. Gosh. The prom.

"No time to rest," she blurted out, trying to sit up.

Nurse Pettibone laughed as she gently pushed Suzi onto her back. "I know you're excited," she said, looking dreamily up at the ceiling. "You want to primp and pretty yourself for the beautiful tiara."

"But I don't want to be prom queen," Suzi croaked, feeling a little woozy. She heard Nurse Pettibone giggle again.

"Don't be silly, sweetheart," the nurse said gently, looking at Suzi with her huge blue eyes. "Everyone wants to be prom queen," she finished, and Suzi noticed that she shot a lingering glance at Coach Katie's door.

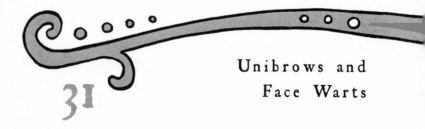

Unibrows and Face Warts

31

Nurse Pettibone left Suzi alone while she went in search of packages of powdered electrolytes that Suzi could take home with her. Suzi lay on Coach Katie's sofa, staring up at the flickering fluorescent light. Its erratic buzzing was the only sound in the room, and the rhythm made her sleepy.

Thank God she was feeling better. The piercing cramps had mellowed, the nurse had said her temperature was down, and she no longer felt the uncontrollable need to barf all over everything—and everyone.

Poor Sam, she thought as she vaguely remembered the horrified look on the prom committee chairman's face as she had hurled sushi chunks all over his precious red-and-gold silk kimono, not to mention his brand-new toe socks and bamboo sandals.

But no cramps and normal temperature aside, Suzi was still feeling pretty tired. Physically, because of her recent bout of food poisoning (she made a mental note to have a long talk with Sam about his choice of sushi caterers), and emotionally, because of her unsettling experience with Coach Katie.

Coach Katie. Suzi had sensed the woman was a little off after speaking with her on the soccer field a couple of days ago, but she had no idea of the extent of the coach's mental problems. Obviously the coach had a serious problem with Nurse Pettibone, a personal vendetta for prom queens, and a serious dislike of Suzi, by prom queen association.

What would have happened to Suzi if Nurse Pettibone hadn't come in at that precise moment to save the day? Suzi flashed back to the image of Coach Katie viciously shredding the paper with her scissors and shivered.

Coach Katie was definitely a resuscitated suspect.

Suzi sat up and dug into her back pocket. She pulled out the little piece of paper and studied it. T@UU. Suzi had been on her way to the tattoo studio when she had suddenly felt sick. She knew the studio might hold answers to her questions, and maybe even to the entire curse, but Suzi felt like she had been hit by a bus.

Suzi shoved the clue safely back into her pocket and swung her legs over the side of the couch. She felt a momentary rush as she moved, but she put her head down and it passed. She looked around the room, searching for her messenger bag. Instead, she spied something else.

Coach Katie had left her purse sitting on top of her desk. Suzi studied it from afar, the expensive Italian leather, the perfect stitches, and big silver buckles.

The temptation was just too strong.

Suzi slowly peeled herself off the sofa and walked over to the coach's desk. She looked down at the purse and paused for a moment, caught in a judgment conundrum. Should she? Shouldn't she?

She decided she most definitely should.

Suzi sat down on the desk and started riffling through the coach's bag. She pulled out several tubes of bright red lipstick, ponytail holders with clumps of blond hair wound around them, a leather date book (which she flipped quickly through, no dates pending on Coach Katie's calendar), a Mountain High key chain (which, she noted, had a shiny silver Jetta key on it), and a cell phone. Nada, she thought to herself as she picked up the cell phone and casually flipped it open. She almost laughed out loud when she saw the coach's screen saver.

A huge black Doberman with a pink spiked collar.

Suzi started punching buttons on the phone, checking out the address book, which was full of women's names, probably soccer players', and then suddenly, but very clearly, she felt a twinge of regret about snooping around in the coach's personal belongings. Sure, she was investigating the curse, but surely she could find a more tactful way of going about it than digging into people's purses.

Suzi threw the phone back into the coach's purse and pushed the bag back where she had found it. She then scooted toward the edge of the desk and started to jump down, but her ankle caught something on the way down, something sharp, and she cried out in pain.

Suzi had nicked her leg on the corner of a desk drawer that was sticking out, and she was bleeding a little. She rubbed her ankle and gave the drawer a little kick of frustration, but the drawer didn't move. She kicked at it again. Still, it didn't budge.

Suzi then leaned down and gave the obtrusive drawer an

angry shove with the palm of her hand, but something seemed to be stuck behind it. Something big and solid.

Suzi squatted down and pulled the wooden drawer all the way out. She then reached her hand into the dark hollow and felt something solid and with hard edges. It felt like a book, and Suzi pulled it out. She looked down at the words that were spelled out on the cover:

MOUNTAIN HIGH ORCAS 1988

Suzi was holding an old yearbook from twenty years ago. The cover looked as if it had once been a bright and cheery yellow, but time had faded it into a dirty cream riddled with rips and tears, scraggly ink marks, and brown coffee-cup rings. But even with all the wear and tear, Suzi could make out the image on the cover. It was an old, black-and-white exterior photo of none other than her school, Mountain High.

Coach Katie had told Suzi that she had gone to Mountain High. Was this the coach's yearbook?

Her curiosity peaking, Suzi opened the book and heard the spine crackle and pop with age. She looked at the faculty page and giggled at the picture of Mr. Crater with a full head of hair; she flipped through the seniors' photos with their big bangs and puffy-sleeved shirts (so cool), and she surveyed the football team and their poses of prowess and machismo. But then suddenly, as she was still flipping through the pages, the yearbook jawed open to reveal a bunch of items that had been stashed inside.

More accurately, it looked like a collection of old prom paraphernalia that had been pressed inside the prom section.

Suzi picked up a crackly, browned corsage, remnants of a

carnation maybe, and she lifted it to her nose to smell it. Its scent, along with its natural color, was long faded. She then pulled out a glossy prom program (the 1988 prom theme, *Totally Bitchin' Prom*, was totally awesome), and then she studied an old paper napkin with a big, dried-up lip print kissed onto it. Even after two decades of time, Suzi recognized the color of the lipstick.

It was Coach Katie red.

Suzi placed the pressed items on the floor and turned her attention to the prom photos. She looked at pictures of people dancing, kissing, moonwalking, and toasting the camera with cups full of punch. Suzi studied the photo of the prom queen court, studying the girls' awesome asymmetrical haircuts, heavy makeup, and big jewelry, and then her eye caught on something. One of the girls on the court. She had bangs teased to the ceiling, a huge corsage that covered the lower half of her face, and she was wearing a puffy-sleeved, polka-dot dress, but all the eighties appendages in the world couldn't disguise the tight ponytail and competitive leer on the girl's face.

The girl in the puffy-sleeved, polka-dot dress, standing in the middle of prom queen court and towering like an Amazon over the other girls, was a younger, thinner, totally new-wave Coach Katie.

Oh. My. Gosh. Coach Katie had never mentioned anything about running for prom queen. The thought seemed totally ludicrous, actually. But there she was, and photo captions didn't lie. The line beneath the picture read, *Mountain High's prom queen court 1988, from left: Bobbie Baker, Carlie Meader, Kathryn McGee, Porsche Pettibone.*

Kathryn must be the coach's first name, Suzi thought. But what about Porsche Pettibone? Could it be?

Suzi looked closer at the petite, blond woman called Porsche, but her picture had been drawn on with a set of horns, a mustache, and a beard, so Suzi couldn't make out the girl's face. She looked around some more, and she saw that the caption under the picture of the crowned prom queen read, *Mountain High Prom Queen, 1988: Porsche Pettibone*. Suzi looked closer at the photograph. This girl's picture had also been defaced, but Suzi could still see the girl's eyes. They were sweet, kind, and all too familiar.

Porsche Pettibone, Mountain High's prom queen way back in 1988, was none other than Mountain High's modern-day Nurse Pettibone.

Bigger picture: Nurse Pettibone had beat out Coach Katie for prom queen twenty years ago.

Suzi quickly turned the page and saw more photos of the young Nurse Pettibone, and each had been defaced in some way. One had arrows drawn through her head, one had a tongue hanging out of her mouth, and big boobs bursting through her dress. A couple of the nurse's photos had also been given bubble captions that said *I'm better than you!* and *Off with their heads!*

Suzi gulped.

So Coach Katie's hatred for Nurse Pettibone, and apparently all prom queens, dated back nearly twenty years. What if this year, the coach had finally collapsed under the weight of all her anger? Would it be enough to drive her to do crazy things, like curse the prom queens?

Just then, someone barged into the room.

Suzi jumped out of her skin, thinking it might be Coach

Katie returning to find her snooping through her personal stuff, but whew, it was just Principal Peasey. The principal looked at her for a long, solid moment, and then he must have read the daze and confusion on her face, because he darted over and grabbed the old yellow yearbook right out of Suzi's white-knuckled hands.

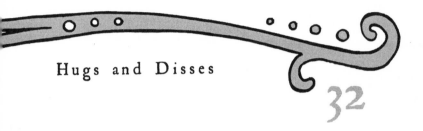

Hugs and Disses

32

"You're a genius! A raving genius!"

"You kick ass, man!"

"Hooray for Suzi!" The roar and energy of the students was overwhelming as Suzi walked down the hall, with Jett's leather sleeve protectively around her. She was so glad Jett was there. She was still weak and a little woozy from the food poisoning—and the whirlwind of events surrounding the indictment of Coach Katie.

Indictment was a gentle word, actually. It had been more like a witch hunt.

Suzi wasn't even given a chance to explain to Principal Peasey what had happened. Seconds after the principal had grabbed and flipped through the defaced pages of Coach Katie's yearbook, he had whipped out his cell, hit a speed-dial number, and next thing Suzi knew, security guard McCain had appeared out of nowhere and started drilling her with questions.

"Name, please?" McCain had asked, looking down at his small pad of paper.

"Uh, Suzi. Suzi Clue," she had stuttered. "But I met you . . . ?" she started to say.

"What happened here? Were you attacked? Assaulted? Do you have proof?"

"Well, not really. I think I had food poisoning, and Coach Katie was here, and then she had scissors, and—"

Suzi had just started to tell her story, when Peasey threw the yearbook, prom section open, down on the table and screamed out, "Now this is what I call hard, irrefutable proof!"

"It is?" Suzi asked weakly.

"You don't need any more proof than this," Peasey snapped at McCain, totally ignoring Suzi's question. "Now get moving."

And that was that. McCain had asked Peasey for a description of Coach Katie, which Peasey had happily divulged, and then the man had turned to Suzi and asked her what the coach was wearing when she last saw her.

"Red lipstick," was all that Suzi could spit out. She honestly couldn't remember what the coach had been wearing. Things were happening way too fast.

Jump forward fifteen minutes. Suzi was still sitting in the infirmary with Principal Peasey when the call had come in. McCain had trapped Coach Katie in the girls' locker room, and he had, in his exact words, secured the suspect.

Next thing she knew, Suzi had heard sirens, and two more security guards busted through the school doors and hauled away a spitting, kicking, screaming Coach Katie.

A mob of students had gathered and were throwing insults as she passed by, and their screams drowned out many of the coach's last words. But Suzi was certain that she had heard the coach protesting her innocence, saying that she hated prom queens, that they were stuck up, self-serving, silver-spooned girls who deserved whatever was dished out to them, but that she had never touched a single hair on any of their precious heads.

And then once Coach Katie had left the building the students had turned their feverish attention to Suzi, little Miss Freshman Nobody turned Mountain High heroine. The mob completely encircled her, exploding with cheers and tears and handshakes and hugs, when all Suzi wanted to do was go home, eat something, and take a nap.

"Let me get that," Jett said as she gently leaned Suzi up against the lockers and started to dial the combination. "What do you need?" she continued, staring into the bowels of Suzi's locker. "Books? Jacket? Whiskey?"

"I need to eat," Suzi responded, still in a daze. "I need to think. I need to sleep."

"Well, that's why I'm here," Jett said, grabbing a few random books and Suzi's thick black hoodie. "I'll get you home and you can sleep to oblivion."

"Something stinks," Suzi continued, staring blankly at all the giddy, prom-happy students buzzing around her, kissing, hugging, and holding hands.

"Well, you are wearing your lunch," Jett added, smiling. "Or maybe it's someone else you smell," she continued, wrinkling her nose. "Gigi Greene at three o'clock."

Suzi looked behind her and at the friend-or-foe cheerleader coming straight at her. Gigi was wearing her staple cheerleading outfit (although there wasn't a game tonight) and black tights, and Suzi noticed that the Queen Bee looked a little haggard around the edges.

Suzi knew just how the head cheerleader felt.

"Suz!" Gigi yelled out, although she was still a good five feet away. Suzi braced herself against the lockers. She was so not in the mood to deal with Gigi right now.

Gigi opened her arms wide and sucked Suzi up into a huge hug, enveloping her in fuzzy cheerleader sweater and the smell of designer perfume. "Congratulations!" she squealed. "You did it!" Suzi looked over Gigi's shoulder at Jett, who was eyeing the head cheerleader very suspiciously.

"Coach Katie, who would have guessed!" Gigi said, looking Suzi straight in the eye for the first time. "Not me!" She laughed, stomping her foot on the floor. Gigi's Tretorns had brown and yellow pom-poms on them with tiny little bells, and when she stomped her foot, Suzi thought she sounded a bit like a horse.

"I had my money on that creepy janitor or one of the hard-up football jocks, not the girls' soccer coach." Gigi laughed, throwing up her arms in disbelief. She was totally amped up, Suzi thought, like she had just slammed a six-pack of Red Bull or something.

"My girl has had a hard day, saving your precious prom from the throes of destruction and all, so if you wouldn't mind." Jett stepped up to interject.

"I'm fine," Suzi said, shooting her friend a calm look before turning back to Gigi. "But I am tired, so please just tell me what you want."

"I just want to say thanks," Gigi continued, shooting Jett a glare before looking back at Suzi and smiling. "You have no idea what everyone thinks of you, what I think of you. You saved the prom!"

Suzi eyed Gigi carefully. The Queen Bee was being sweet as saccharine, and it was leaving a bad taste in Suzi's mouth.

"So," Gigi continued, cocking out her hip and getting all serious. "On behalf of all the prom queens, thank you," she said again. "But we'll no longer be needing your services."

"What?" Suzi was totally confused.

"Yeah, what?" Jett repeated a little louder.

"Well." Gigi shrugged. "With the curse over, the prom will go on as originally intended, with the nominated court in the running," she said, flashing Suzi a fake smile. "Parker, Kitty, Trixie—and me."

Suzi looked at Gigi in disbelief. Was she being fired?

"It's no big mystery that you don't want to be prom queen anyway," Gigi quickly added, sounding a little pissy.

Gigi had a valid point, but still. Suzi hadn't even been given a chance to step down. She was simply being . . . dissed.

"Yeah," Suzi said, trying to get a grip on the situation. "You're right. I don't want to be prom queen. I don't even want to go to the prom."

"Great, then we're on the same page," Gigi said with a smile. "But thanks a bunch for your help. We couldn't have done it without you!" She gave Suzi another dramatic hug in the hallway, for the whole school to witness.

So that's why Gigi was so wired, Suzi thought as the cheerleader's arms practically suffocated her. Gigi was out-of-her-mind excited about finally getting what she had waited for her entire life. She wanted to be prom queen, everybody in school knew that. And tomorrow night, thanks to Suzi's tenacity, bravery, physical agility, and life-threatening efforts, it was finally going to happen.

Gigi let go, and Suzi attempted a smile that came out lopsided. Just then, Principal Peasey's voice came on over the PA system.

"Attention, students." His voice was clipped and energetic. "I'm sure you've all heard the glorious news by now, that our prom queen culprit has been caught and will soon face the punishment she deserves."

Suzi heard the whole school let out a simultaneous cheer.

"On behalf of this most brilliant occasion, and in an effort to make the needed preparations for the big night, I've decided to give everyone, students and faculty, the rest of the day off," Mr. Peasey continued proudly. "After all, it's practically a holiday! So go home, everybody! And see you tomorrow. At the prom!" The PA system clicked off.

More cheers and yells of excitement echoed through the hallways and off the school walls.

"Now I can help my mom prepare for the huge prom party she's throwing," Gigi said.

Parker, Trixie, Kitty, and a mass of BGs suddenly came yelling and bouncing down the hall toward Suzi's and Gigi's lockers, and Gigi let herself be swallowed up by them. Suzi and Jett watched as they bounced, en masse, down the hall and out the school's exit door.

And then, thankfully, they were gone.

"Gag me," Jett said drily, turning to Suzi. "Hey, you're off the hook for prom queen."

Suzi just shot her a look.

"I think somebody needs a nap," Jett digressed, pulling a few more books out of Suzi's locker and rolling her eyes.

"I still say something stinks," Suzi said again, and Jett opened her leather jacket and smelled inside it.

"Not you." Suzi laughed, and the movement made her stomach ache again. "It's Coach Katie," she continued, grabbing her messenger bag and hoodie from Jett. "Something's just not right."

"I'll tell you what's not right," Jett said, grabbing Suzi by the shoulders. "The vomit in your hair. Now get home and take a shower. This case is closed," Jett finished, swerving her friend around the masses of hyperactive students.

Suzi stayed quiet and allowed herself to be led down the hall and out the doors, where her mom was parked and waiting for her. She agreed with Jett, she needed to go home, take a long shower, and sleep it off. But that was about the only thing she agreed with Jett on.

As far as Suzi was concerned, this case was most definitely not closed.

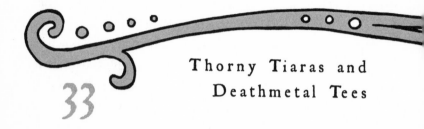

Thorny Tiaras and
Deathmetal Tees

33

"Hey, baby, what's shakin'?"

"Hi cutie pie, what are you in here for?"

Suzi kept her eyes on her sneakers as she followed the massive security guards down the seemingly never-ending hallway. Through her bangs and out the corner of her eyes, she could see hands pawing at her, trying to grab her hair and her shirt. The one time Suzi dared to look up, she had seen nothing but missing teeth, messy hair, and scary crazy eyes. The crowd screamed and moaned and ran their tin coffee cups along the bars, and Suzi just kept putting one sneaker in front of the other. Man, what was she doing here?

But Suzi knew exactly what she was doing there. She had a few unanswered questions that she wanted to talk to Coach Katie about, and considering Coach Katie was in prison, well, their rendezvous options had been a little limited.

Suddenly, the security mob in front of her stopped walking. Suzi watched as one of them reached down, grabbed a huge key chain, and unlocked a single, windowless, metal door. The guard then shot her a look of genuine concern.

"You sure about this?" he asked.

Suzi's throat was dry with fear, so she just nodded her head. The guard opened the door and stepped aside. Suzi paused for a moment, then took a deep breath and walked into the room. The door slammed shut behind her.

Once again, Suzi and the coach were all alone.

"Coach?" Suzi squeaked, squinting through the dim light.

Coach Katie was wearing a red jumpsuit and sitting on the edge of a single bed that was pushed up against a dirty concrete wall. Her head was bowed, as if she were praying. The coach didn't move.

"Coach, are you okay?" Suzi asked again.

The coach slowly raised her head and turned to look Suzi in the eye. Her gaze was blank and lifeless, and strangely enough, she was wearing her orange sports whistle around her neck and her patented fiery red lipstick. The coach's hair was pulled back into a tight ponytail, and on top of her head, she was wearing a prom tiara.

But it wasn't just any old prom tiara. It was a tiara made of thorns.

"Coach?" Suzi asked for a third time.

Coach Katie still didn't respond. Instead, she pulled the thorny tiara off her head, pricking her fingers but not even flinching when they started to bleed, and then she stood up and started to slowly walk toward Suzi.

Suzi took a quick step back and felt the door against her shoulder blades. No. Way. Out.

"This is for you," the coach finally said in a monotone voice. She kept moving closer, looking like a zombie in a bad horror movie, and holding the tiara out to Suzi with her bloody fingers.

"Now you'll know the burden of the crown," the coach continued, as she kept walking closer and closer . . . she was just inches away . . . she grabbed Suzi's head and forced it down to receive the crown . . .

"Yo, baby, what's the haps?"

"Huh?" Suzi asked, rolling onto her back and throwing her arm over her eyes.

"Hello?! I said what's going on? How are you feeling this morning?"

The voice was Jett's. She was calling Suzi on her cell. Suzi must have heard her phone ringing and grabbed it while she was still half asleep, because suddenly, and thankfully, Suzi wasn't in prison with Coach Katie anymore. Instead, she was safe and warm in her own bed. It was Saturday morning, and to answer Jett's question, Suzi was feeling much better. Well, except for the nightmare she just had.

"I am so glad to hear your voice," Suzi said, blinking her eyes.

"I bet you say that to all the girls," Jett teased through the phone.

"I mean it," Suzi continued sleepily. "I was having this really weird dream about Coach Katie. It was totally disturbing."

"Don't worry about that anymore," Jett replied. "It's all over, and I thought we could celebrate by rocking out this afternoon, before the school is infested with prom-goers."

Suzi was silent on the other end. Sure, she had just woken up and was still a little out of it, but also, she just couldn't shake her terrible dream. Everybody grabbing for her and wanting a piece of her . . .

"Suz," Jett continued. "What do you say?"

The dead, vacant look in Coach Katie's eyes . . . the bloody tiara made of thorns . . .

"Hello? Did your mom slip you a Tylenol PM?" Jett asked.

"I have something I have to check out," Suzi finally said, jumping out of bed and looking around for the jeans she was wearing yesterday. She found them and dug her fingers into the back pocket. Bingo.

"Let it go, Suz," Jett whined on the other end. "I know what you're going to do, but why do it? Coach Katie is behind bars."

Suzi pulled out the little piece of paper and studied the address of the tattoo studio she had written down Friday afternoon, before the bout of food poisoning. So many things were rushing through her head: her dream, the coach, the coach's defaced yearbook.

"I said, why do it?" Jett repeated, still trying to dissuade her friend. "Coach Katie is behind bars."

"But that's exactly why I have to do it," Suzi said quietly, still studying the address on the paper. "Don't you see, Jett? That's exactly the reason I have to do it."

Two hours later, and Suzi was locking her bike up outside the tattoo studio, T@UU. It was another cold, rainy afternoon, but this time, Suzi had come fully prepared with gloves, a hat, and rainproof jacket. It has been one hell of a week, and Suzi had had enough of being wet, muddy, sick, tossed around by macho jocks, dissed by Gigi, and almost doused in fish guts. This time, Suzi was playing it safe.

Well, as safe as possible, considering she was still investigating the curse.

Although Jett had tried to persuade her to let it go, that

Coach Katie was guilty and that the curse was over, Suzi just wasn't satisfied with the way things had played out. She agreed with Peasey that the coach was definitely a prime suspect, but she disagreed about the conclusion of the evidence. Since when was a defaced yearbook considered cold, hard proof? What if an innocent woman ended up losing her job or even doing time, all because Suzi wanted to play the drums instead of following through with a lead? Suzi would never be able to forgive herself.

She had to know the connection between the tattoo studio and the prom queen curse.

Suzi blinked the rain out of her eyes and stared up at the sign taped in the window. It was a handmade sign, a piece of white cardboard with T@UU written on it in thick, black ink. This was definitely the place. Suzi opened the door and heard a bell go off as she walked inside.

Except for the sound of a high-pitched buzz coming from somewhere in the back, the place was quiet and completely empty. Suzi looked around at the vintage vinyl couches, the faux-fur throw covering the concrete floor, and the music magazines and art books stacked on the coffee table. She shot a glance behind the counter; nobody was there, but she did notice a huge sign that very clearly stated: NOT 18? NO TATTOO. I.D. REQUIRED.

That was okay. Suzi wasn't here to get a tattoo. She was on official business.

Suzi walked over to the walls and studied all the tattoo art that was displayed behind glass. She looked at tattoos of anchors and pinup girls, dolphins and fairies, Coney Island landmarks and religious motifs. Suzi had never been in a tattoo studio before, and she was fascinated by all the different styles.

"Can I help you, little lady?" a voice with a thick, Irish accent suddenly called out behind her.

Suzi whipped around and found herself looking at a tall, thin guy standing across the room and behind a long, glass counter. He had messy, pond-black hair and was wearing a ripped deathmetal tee. Even from across the room, Suzi could see that his arms were completely covered with tattoos.

"Wow, did you do all those tattoos yourself?" Suzi asked, walking toward the counter.

"These?" he asked, glancing at his arms as he peeled off a thin surgical glove. "Nah, a friend did them. Are you thinking about a tattoo?" he continued, throwing the glove in the trash. "Or maybe a piercing?"

"Piercing?" Suzi asked, stopping at the edge of the counter. She looked down into it, and realized that it was filled with rows upon rows of body jewelry. She ogled over all the different sizes and thicknesses of hoops and bars and other unidentifiable objects. Some were silver, some were gold, some were bright pink, some had diamonds, and some just looked really, really, painful.

Suzi smiled. She had hit the body jewelry jackpot.

"So it's a piercing you want?" the guy behind the counter asked, reading Suzi's face. "I thought you looked a little young for a tattoo."

"Actually, I just have some questions," Suzi answered.

"It's your first time is it?" the guy asked, arching one black brow.

"Actually," Suzi said, digging into her bra for the gold body ring, "I'm looking for the owner of this," she finished, holding the ring out.

"This is a run-of-the-mill piercing ring, not an ID tag," the man said, looking at Suzi as if she were crazy. "It could have come from anywhere."

"I have reason to believe that it came from here," she continued in her most professional manner. She wanted the tattooed man behind the counter to know that she was very serious. "I was hoping you'd let me look at your appointment book to see if the person I think it belongs to is a client here."

Suzi took the ring back and looked up at the man with her big, blue eyes. If only he would let her take a peek at the list, she could check and see if Coach Katie, or Kathryn McGee rather, was on it. Then she would know for sure that Coach Katie was pierced here, and that the gold ring belonged to her, and well, case closed.

"I'd really like to help you, little lady," the man started in. Suzi heard a big "but" coming and held her breath.

"But," he continued, and Suzi felt herself deflate. "The piercing artist isn't in today. I'm Mack. I'm just the tattoo guy. I have no idea where she keeps her books," he finished, shrugging.

"Will she be in later?" Suzi asked hopefully.

"Later tomorrow," Mack replied. "She's in a band and has a gig tonight."

Damn, Suzi thought. Tomorrow the prom would be over, and it might be too late.

"Anything else I can do for you?" Mack asked, but Suzi just shook her head. Mack shrugged again and turned to talk to a girl who had just appeared out of the back. She had a white bandage on her arm, and Suzi realized that Mack must have just given her a tattoo.

Suzi ran her fingers over the glass counter, looking at all the body jewelry to see if she could at least find a match for the gold ring. She looked over the endless rows of rings with beads, rings with semiprecious stones, rings with initials, and then suddenly, Suzi saw something she recognized. But it wasn't a piece of body jewelry.

Suzi noticed a small candy box sitting on top of the counter, on the other side of the cash register. It was a light blue box with a long, black oval printed on it. Suzi recognized the old-school design, but she couldn't quite pinpoint from where.

"What's this?" she asked, walking over for a closer look.

"It's called Black Jack gum," Mack answered, shooting a look back at Suzi. "It's licorice-flavored. We're the only ones in the city . . . who . . . carry . . . it."

Mack had to yell the last half of his sentence to the back of Suzi's head. Not to be rude, but she was already halfway out the door.

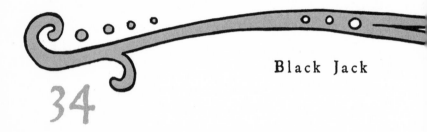

Black Jack

34

"Over here," Suzi yelled out the second she saw Jett walk in the door. Suzi had been waiting for Jett at Stumptown for almost twenty minutes, and although she had ordered herself a fresh cinnamon soy latte, the wait was driving her crazy. Suzi watched as Jett went over to stand in line for a cappuccino, and she just couldn't take it any longer.

"Jett!" Suzi yelled out again, giving her friend an impatient glare from across the room. Jett scowled but then walked over.

"You're depriving me of caffeine?" Jett asked, sliding into a chair next to Suzi and putting her messenger bag on her lap. "Ruthless," she murmured, reaching into her bag and pulling out a manila envelope. "But I'm glad you called me. I was just about to call you."

"I have something to tell you," Suzi said excitedly, leaning over the table.

"Take a look at these," Jett said, ignoring Suzi and pulling a stack of glossy paper out of the envelope. She placed the stack in front of Suzi, and Suzi noticed that they had small, black-and-white photos on them. Apparently, they were contact sheets.

"Since you didn't want to practice," Jett said, still monopolizing the conversation, "I spent the morning in the darkroom printing the film I took at the Kick Wars," she continued, handing Suzi a small magnifying loop.

"But I have something . . ." Suzi started to say again, but Jett cut her off.

"Just take a look," Jett insisted, motioning with her eyes at the contact sheets.

"I don't have time for this right now," Suzi protested. "I have something important . . ."

"You have time," Jett insisted calmly.

"Jett, listen to me. Coach Katie isn't the one behind the curse!" Suzi finally yelled out, placing the magnifying loop down on the table.

"That's exactly what I've been trying to tell you," Jett said, picking up the loop and pushing it back into Suzi's face.

Suzi shot a confused look at her friend, but then she grabbed the loop and felt her bangs fall into her face as she leaned over the contact sheets. One by one, she studied the pictures Jett had taken the night of the Kick War soccer game, the same night that she had been locked in the basement. Suzi looked over the pictures of boys spraying beer out their noses, girls with big Ms painted on their cheeks, and Uma nibbling on Li Jung's earlobe.

"What is it that I'm looking for exactly?" Suzi asked, her patience waning, but then suddenly, wait a minute . . .

Suzi zeroed in on a photo of the prom queen rose ceremony. Suzi could see Kitty, standing up onstage and looking very nervous, not to mention very cold, in her short skirt and high boots. Kitty was standing next to Trixie, who was smiling from ear to ear and wearing a long rain slicker, and Trixie was standing next to none other than Coach Katie.

In the background and to the left, Suzi could see the orca climbing the stage stairs, waving its fins obnoxiously in the air.

"Coach Katie wasn't in the orca uniform that attacked Kitty," Suzi said, suddenly shooting an excited look up at Jett.

"Because she's standing onstage, next to Kitty while Kitty is being attacked," Jett added, nodding her head knowingly.

"This is brilliant," Suzi said, giving Jett a quick smile before looking back down at the photos.

Suzi moved the loop from photo to photo, studying the orca as it climbed up onstage, high-fived the coach, and then lunged for an unsuspecting Kitty. Suzi's eyes scrutinized the uniform, searching for something, anything that might give her proof as to who was wearing it, but nada. Suzi couldn't see the orca's shoes, hair, hands, or face.

All Suzi could see was Kitty Sui's bare butt.

Poor Kitty, Suzi thought, studying the expression of sheer horror on Kitty's face as she was picked up and twirled around, baring her butt to the entire crowd. Wait a minute . . .

"What is it?" Jett suddenly asked, reading her friend's face.

"Did you look at Kitty's butt?" Suzi asked, her face still down.

"Uh, no," Jett said unconvincingly. "Why?"

"Remember when I said I saw Chet making out with some girl in the gym . . ." Suzi started to say.

"A girl with a tattoo on her butt," Jett added.

"Kitty has a tattoo," Suzi finished, looking up from the photo and bugging her eyes out at Jett. "Chet and Gigi, Chet and Kitty? Kitty and Xavier, Xavier hitting on me? Is nothing sacred?" Suzi said, exasperated.

"Welcome to high school, Suz," Jett said drily. "It's an epidemic of meanness, and meaningless meanness at that."

Suzi put down the loop, grabbed for her latte, and took a long, thoughtful sip. She knew that no matter how cynical Jett's comment seemed, it carried a lot of truth, and the idea was slightly depressing.

"So what did you want to tell me?" Jett suddenly asked, grabbing Suzi's latte and taking a gulp herself.

"Oh, yeah," Suzi said, suddenly perking up with excitement. "I went to the tattoo studio this afternoon . . ." she started to say.

"Black Jack," Suzi said, after explaining to Jett how the tattoo studio also did piercings, but that the piercer hadn't been in, so Suzi had looked around for a match to the gold ring and . . .

"Black Jack?" Jett asked, raising a lone, red brow. "As in gambling?"

"As in gum," Suzi added, her eyes sparkling. "Licorice-flavored gum. The studio is the only place in the city who sells it."

"And your point is?" Jett asked, still not getting it.

Suzi looked at her friend and cocked her head. She knew she had to approach this situation with a little tact.

"You know who chews that gum, don't you?" Suzi asked, trying not to show the extent of her excitement. "Licorice?"

"Damn, girl," Jett said after a pause. "You still think it's her?" she finished, looking down at her motorcycle boots.

"I think there's a good chance," Suzi said gently. "I think that Black Jack gum links Fiona to the studio, which links directly back to the piece of paper I found in the orca uniform and the gold ring that I found at the beginning of this whole mess," she finished.

"Speaking of mess," Jett said, shaking her head. "But how would Fiona get into the basement and all that?" Jett asked, looking up to meet Suzi's gaze.

"Good question," Suzi answered, slowly nodding her head. As usual, her redheaded friend was right. Suzi still had a few details to hammer out before she would have the cold, hard proof she needed.

"I wish I could just talk to her," Suzi continued, grabbing her latte and leaning back in her chair. "Do you know her address?" she asked, taking a sip.

"I don't," Jett said, narrowing her eyes as she stared out Stumptown's front windows. "But I know someone who does," she finished slowly.

Suzi looked outside to see what her friend was staring at.

Oh. My. Gosh. It was the devil herself, the bespectacled and freckled Fiona Fiercely. She was across the street, mounting her low rider bike and heading east. Due east.

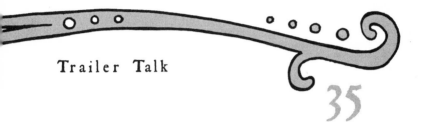

Trailer Talk

35

"I shouldn't be here," Jett whined, leaning her head against the trunk of a thick tree and looking impatiently down at Suzi.

Suzi heard Jett but didn't answer. She was busy placing her rain jacket down on the wet grass to make a place where she could lie down and survey her surroundings. In short, Suzi was creating a stakeout, and the idea had her more than a little excited.

After spotting Fiona back at Stumptown, Suzi and Jett had quickly hopped on their bikes and followed Fiona past the school and about three miles east. They had been careful to keep their distance and not be seen, and Suzi was pretty sure they had been successful.

"You realize this is stalking, don't you?" Jett asked, looking at her friend now lying belly-down on the ground. "I'm officially a stalker now, thanks to you."

"We're not stalking. We're spying," Suzi replied, looking up at her friend.

"No, *you're* spying. *I'm* stalking," Jett said, kicking at a pinecone with her boot. "Fiona told me to get lost yesterday."

"What happened?" Suzi asked.

"I walked into the Vegans with a Vengeance meeting in my leather jacket," Jett explained, shrugging her shoulders. "It was so over."

Suzi looked at her friend sympathetically, but she couldn't help but giggle a little. Thankfully, Jett giggled, too.

"Well, then, since you have no personal attachment to my main suspect any longer, let's see what we can dig up on this licorce-gum-chewing, vegan extremist," Suzi said with a wink, patting the rain jacket and gazing down the grassy embankment at her target. Jett got down next to Suzi and followed her friend's gaze.

The two girls were staring down at a small, gray trailer with a broken fiberglass porch, on which sat a single foldout metal chair.

Suzi and Jett had followed Fiona to an inner city trailer park—and to this lone little trailer.

"You're sure this is it?" Jett asked Suzi for the umpteenth time.

"I saw Fiona go in there," Suzi said, sweeping her eyes over the trailer and its surroundings. She scoped out the entire area, the old shopping cart left to rust in the yard, the weeded-over garden, the dusty Wonder Woman sheets covering the window.

"Who would have guessed that Fiona lived in a trailer park," Jett said, rolling over onto her back and looking up at the sky. "But one thing still bothers me."

"What's that?" Suzi asked, not taking her eyes off the trailer.

"How did you know that it wasn't the coach?" Jett asked. "I mean, after you found the yearbook, what made you keep looking?"

"Well," Suzi explained, doing another quick sweep of the trailer. No movement. "Coach Katie only wears red lipstick, and the lipstick used in the curse notes has consistently been bright pink, that Prom Queen Pink," Suzi explained, looking over at Jett.

"But you said it yourself, just because someone used bright pink lipstick to write the notes doesn't mean they wear it," Jett countered.

"True, but when I was sick in the coach's office, I looked through her purse," Suzi started to say.

"No way," Jett snorted.

"And," Suzi continued, fighting for her friend's attention, "the coach has a Jetta key on her key chain. A Jetta doesn't exactly fit the description of a huge, black SUV," she finished.

"But the coach could have a second car," Jett argued, raising her red brows.

"All good points," Suzi said, smiling at her friend's tenacity. "But I saw the person who attacked me. They were wearing a mask, but they weren't big like Coach Katie. They were smaller, thin," Suzi said.

"I think Peasey was eager to peg the blame on someone," Suzi continued, shooting another look down at the trailer.

"And save his precious prom," Jett said, looking up at the sky.

The girls lay in silence for a spell. Suzi just stared down at the trailer, waiting for something to happen, and Jett grabbed a pinecone and picked off its thick, wooden petals.

"Suz, what are we doing here?" Jett finally said, grabbing a hat out of her bag and pulling it tightly over her red curls.

"I'm still trying to figure that out," Suzi said truthfully and slowly.

"Well, figure fast because it's colder than sh . . ." Jett was saying, when suddenly, a screen door squeaked beneath them and Fiona Fiercely walked out of the trailer and onto the broken fiberglass porch.

Suzi jumped to her feet and took cover behind a tree. She watched Fiona's every move as the bespectacled suspect walked out of the trailer, stretched lazily, and then reached into her front shirt pocket and pulled out a small, light blue package. It was Black Jack gum; Suzi was sure of it. Fiona then peeled the wrapper off a stick, popped it into her mouth, and planted herself on the top step of the porch, her legs splayed out in a wide V.

"There's our girl," Suzi said under her breath, not taking her eyes off her target.

"What's she doing?" Jett asked, standing up next to Suzi and squinting her eyes.

"Just enjoying a stick of gum on her front porch," Suzi answered casually. "Black Jack gum," she finished, shooting a knowing look over at Jett. Just then, the screen door squeaked again.

"But wait, here comes someone else," Suzi said, looking back down at the trailer.

"Who is it?" Jett asked, squinting harder and standing on her toes. "Whoa, that isn't . . ."

"It is," was all Suzi could say. She looked over at Jett, her jaw practically hanging down to the ground.

Oh. My. Gosh.

It was none other than the school janitor, Janitor Joe. The janitor was minus the overalls and plus a pair of black jeans and a tight black tee, but it was definitely him. Just a cooler version of him.

"Wow, Fiona is Janitor Joe's offspring," Jett said slowly, turning to look at Suzi.

Suzi watched as the janitor took a seat in the foldout chair. Fiona held out the pack of gum to the man, and he took a slice.

"That's Fiona's dad?" Suzi repeated disbelievingly.

"I think it's safe to say she gets her good looks from her mother," Jett added with a giggle.

"That's it!" Suzi suddenly said, feeling so excited she wanted to burst. "That's how Fiona got into the basement, the locker room, everywhere! She used her dad's key ring!" she finished. "The janitor has keys to everything!"

"What a waste," Jett agreed, shaking her head.

"It all makes sense," Suzi said, looking back down at Fiona and the janitor. "Now all I need is proof to take back to Peasey."

"Proof?" Jett asked fearfully. "What kind of proof?"

"The kind that comes from drilling your suspect face to face," Suzi said, mustering up determination in her voice. Suzi knew what she had to do. What she had come all the way to this trailer park to do. She couldn't back down now.

"I'm going for a confession," Suzi continued, suddenly taking an aggressive, yet slightly apprehensive, step toward the trailer. Jett reached out and caught Suzi's sleeve.

"Wait a minute," Jett said, shooting Suzi a warning glance. "You're not going to just bust in down there."

"Got a better idea?" Suzi shot out, looking down at Jett's hand on her arm. "The prom is tonight and . . ." she was arguing.

"Okay, I digress," Jett said, stepping away. She knew from

past experience that it was useless to try and hold Suzi back. "But I can't go with you. I don't want Fiona to think I'm some nut job who can't take a hint."

"You don't want Fiona, a girl who very possibly tried to shoot at me and douse me in fish guts, to think that you're crazy?" Suzi asked.

"I have a reputation to uphold," Jett said, flipping up the collar of her jacket.

"Well, I'd hate to ruin your reputation," Suzi rebutted, taking another look down at the trailer. Fiona and the janitor were hanging out and calmly chatting it up. They clearly had no idea what was coming.

Giving her friend a wink for good luck, Suzi turned on her heels and started to make her way down the slippery embankment, toward the trailer.

"Hey, Fiona," Suzi said coolly as she approached the tiny trailer. There was no way around the fact that she was completely busting in, as Jett had so eloquently pointed out, and she wanted to make her presence known to Fiona and the janitor before she was right on top of them. No need to rattle any cages.

"What the hell?" Fiona spit out, chomping on her gum as if her life depended on it. Other than her mouth, Suzi noticed that no other part of Fiona's body moved. Her main suspect seemed unshaken and remained firmly planted on the top step of the porch. Janitor Joe also stayed right where he was, seated in the chair. Although he watched Suzi closely, he didn't say a word.

"Sorry to barge in on you like this," Suzi continued, stopping when she reached the bottom step of the porch and looking up at both Fiona and the janitor.

"May I?" Suzi said politely, looking up the steps at Fiona.

Fiona shot a look over at the janitor, and he nodded silently. Fiona shrugged and moved her butt over a few inches.

Suzi smiled her thanks and demurely walked up the steps, noticing how they sagged under her weight. When she reached the top step, she looked over at the janitor and tipped her head. "Hi again, Janitor Joe," she said, smiling.

At first the janitor just looked at her, seemingly confused. Then all of a sudden Suzi saw a flash of recognition in his eyes and he said, "You're the girl from the locker room. The one who likes The Runaways."

"Anything but young country." Suzi laughed, holding up her hands.

"Glad to see you here," Janitor Joe said, his eyes smiling approval. *Wow*, Suzi thought. The janitor was being surprisingly hospitable.

"How did you find out about this place?" Fiona asked suspiciously.

"Uh, my friend Jett gave me the address. I hope it's okay," Suzi lied. She knew Jett would have her head for dragging her name into this, but the last thing Suzi wanted to do was tell Fiona she had followed her home.

Fiona gave her a confused look, but it faded after a few seconds.

"So, I'm off the hook for being prom queen tonight," Suzi finally said, trying to act casual. "Thank God," she added dramatically.

"Right," Fiona snorted, putting another slice of black gum

into her mouth. "That whole prom charade is just plain sin-ister. Give women something better to believe in, puh-lease!" she yelled up at the sky.

"Weren't you trying to find out who was hurting the prom queens?" Janitor Joe suddenly piped in, leaning forward and resting his elbows on his knees. "Any luck?"

Suzi gulped. Janitor Joe had opened the can of worms. Now it was time for her to get her hands dirty.

"Some," she admitted with a tactful smile. "Actually, janitor, that's the reason I came here today. To talk with your daugh-ter about this mess with the prom queens."

Janitor Joe cocked his head in crystal-clear confusion.

"I know Peasey thinks Coach Katie is the suspect in ques-tion, but I think there's more to this mystery, and I think your daughter may have some very valuable information."

"My daughter?" Janitor Joe asked.

"Fiona," Suzi said, looking at her main suspect. She paused for a moment and took a deep breath to build courage.

"Yes?" Fiona said sarcastically.

"I understand the hatred and anger you feel toward the prom."

"And?" Fiona said, her patience seemingly wearing thin.

"Well, prom queens may not be your type of people, but they're people nonetheless. They feel pain and hurt." Suzi stopped for a moment to search Fiona's eyes for a sliver of recognition or remorse, but the girl gave her nothing. "I think you know what I'm talking about," she added gently but firmly.

"Wrong!" Fiona said, snickering. "I have absolutely no idea what you're talking about."

"Why do you want to talk to my daughter about the prom

queens?" Janitor Joe suddenly said. Suzi was grateful for the interruption. The surrounding air was growing thick.

"I'm sorry, janitor," she said, looking away from Fiona and back at the girl's father. "But I have reason, good reason, to believe that your daughter is the one behind the prom queen curse," she finished solidly, shooting a firm glance back at Fiona.

"My daughter?" Janitor Joe asked, scratching at the dark stubble on his chin. Suzi nodded but kept her eyes firmly on Fiona. She wanted to be ready in case Fiona made a run for it—or for her.

"But my daughter doesn't even go to Mountain High," Janitor Joe said, looking at Suzi as if she were losing her mind.

"What . . ." Suzi started to say. She looked at Fiona, to the janitor, and then back at Fiona again.

Oh. My. Gosh. Was she losing her mind?

"Cut the crap, Suzi Clue," Fiona finally spit out. "Why are you really here," she asked, narrowing her eyes. "It's obviously not for the lessons."

"Lessons?"

"Joe's guitar lessons?" Fiona said in a condescending tone. "This is Joe Smith, lead guitarist of Honeypot, the best grunge band on the planet? Before Nirvana? Maybe you've heard of them?"

Suzi quickly looked over at the janitor. Oh. My. Gosh. Fiona was right. Janitor Joe was Joe Smith. The Joe Smith! How could she not have noticed?

"In the flesh," the janitor said humbly. "I sweep floors for the health insurance."

Suzi was stunned into an uncharacteristic silence. She was trying to put all the pieces together—Joe Smith, Fiona Fiercely, the band Honeypot—when suddenly the screen door squeaked again and a third person emerged from the trailer onto the saggy porch.

"And this here," Joe Smith continued, his posture perking and gray eyes brightening. "This is my pride and joy, my little pumpkin," he said, holding his rough palm in the air to showcase a girl in torn jeans, a Team Dresch tee, and scuffed, heavy boots. The girl had choppy, neon-green hair, rings through her nose and brows, and a snarl on her tight, thin lips.

"Meet my beautiful daughter, Pearl," Janitor Joe said proudly as Pearl sat down next to her father.

"Hey," Pearl said, giving Suzi a cold sneer and snapping her gum. "You here for the lessons?"

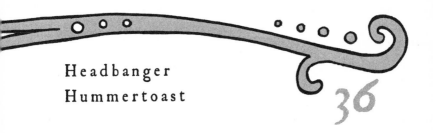

Headbanger
Hummertoast

36

"Stupid. Stupid. Stupid," Suzi said, repeatedly banging her head against the table. She was sitting at Stumptown with Jett. After the trailer park/Fiona/Joe Smith fiasco, Jett had finally talked her into getting caffeinated out of her skull. Jett knew that her friend needed it. Nothing like three shots of espresso to lift the spirits.

"Stupid. Stupid. Stupid," Suzi continued.

"Don't be such a masochist," Jett said, grabbing Suzi's head and holding it still. She tried to peek at her friend's face, but all she could see was shiny black and streaks of pink.

"Stupid," Suzi moaned one last time, through her hair.

"You are not stupid!" Jett said, rolling her eyes and then putting her steaming cappuccino to her lips. "C'mon. Drink your poison before it gets cold."

"I'm not thirsty."

"Get over yourself," Jett said, whisking a cloud of foam off the top of her cappuccino with a finger. "You went out on a limb and it whacked you in the face, but so what? It took guts to do what you did."

Suzi sat upright, yanked her hoodie over her head, and then slumped down into her chair. She clasped her hands around her warm cinnamon soy latte.

"I can't believe what a fool I made of myself," Suzi said, shaking her head. "We followed Fiona to what we thought was her house, which was actually Janitor Joe's house, then we thought Fiona was Janitor Joe's daughter, but the truth is, Fiona just takes guitar lessons from Janitor Joe, who is actually Joe Smith, the lead guitarist of Honeypot, the most famous band on the face of the planet." Suzi rambled, holding her hands up to the ceiling.

"Does it get any more messed up than that?" Suzi huffed, clearly exasperated.

"Hollywood couldn't write it any better." Jett smirked.

"I don't know what's more embarrassing," Suzi continued, finally taking a sip of her latte. "Not realizing that Janitor Joe is Joe Smith or wrongly blaming the curse on Fiona."

"You're absolutely certain that Fiona isn't the one behind the curse?" Jett asked, leaning back in her chair. "After the Black Jack gum and everything."

"I'm sure," Suzi complained, putting her head back down on the table. "She has a rock-solid alibi. Joe said that Fiona has been taking lessons from him every day after school for the past week. She wasn't anywhere near the Kick Wars," she continued. "Or the orca uniform."

"Fiona plays guitar," Jett said, staring thoughtfully out the window. "That's hot."

Suzi shot her friend a disgusted look, but she was more disgusted with herself than with Jett's comment.

"I just don't get it," Suzi huffed, reaching into her messenger bag and pulling out the tube of Prom Queen Pink lipstick that

Janitor Joe, or Joe Smith rather, had given her, the paper with T@UU written on it, and the piece of gold body jewelry. Suzi put all three pieces of evidence neatly on the table and studied them for a long moment.

"All these clues, and I still have no idea who's behind the curse," Suzi said, defeated. "I suck."

Jett had just opened her mouth to rebut her friend, when suddenly, their other friend Uma Ashti, came rushing toward the table. Uma was wearing a strapless, sapphire blue dress with an apricot scarf loosely wrapped around her chocolaty shoulders. She wore almost no makeup save for a little red lip gloss, and Suzi thought she looked drop-dead gorgeous. Apparently so did Uma's main squeeze, Li Jung, because he couldn't keep his hands off her.

"Hey, ladies," Uma said, beaming from ear to ear. "How goes it this evening?" she asked, looking from Suzi to Jett and then back to Suzi again.

"You okay?" Uma asked Suzi, with genuine concern lining her voice.

"You guys on your way to the prom?" Suzi asked, quickly changing the subject. The last thing Suzi wanted to do was bring Uma down with her sob stories. Not tonight.

"You know it," Uma said, giggling as she slapped Li Jung's paws off her shoulders. "I made Li Jung bring me here for a triple caramel mocha first. I want to get all amped up on sugar and caffeine. It's an evil mix." She laughed, flipping her thick mop of dark hair.

"Awesome," Suzi said, laughing along with her friend. She had been so busy for the past week, she hadn't seen much of Uma, and she realized that she'd missed her.

"And it makes me horny," Uma added, looking coyly at Li Jung. "Darling, would you mind?" Li Jung couldn't get his butt to the barista counter fast enough. Suzi thought she actually saw a little puff of smoke where he had just been standing.

"Lipstick and fancy jewelry, are you holding out on me?" Uma teased, eyeing the silver tube of lipstick and earring still splayed out on the table.

"I'm not going to the prom, if that's what you mean," Suzi answered quickly. "This is all the evidence I collected on the case."

"Oh, yes! Congratulations!" Uma sang out, bending down to give Suzi a hug. "I've barely seen you, but you, my friend, are the bomb. May I say that I never doubted you for a single second." She gave Suzi a kiss and an amazing smile.

Suzi felt her cheeks flush with embarrassment. Uma obviously still thought Suzi had solved the case. Little did she know that Coach Katie was actually innocent and the real culprit was on the loose.

Just then, Li Jung returned to the table holding a huge caramel mocha with two straws sticking out of the top. "Darling, you know how I like it," Uma purred, grabbing the mocha and licking the cream off the straw. Li Jung looked as if he were going to lose his mind, and not surprisingly, he grabbed Uma by the hand and started to gently pull her toward the door.

"Are you sure you don't want to come with us?" Uma asked Suzi, giggling as she licked whipped cream off her lips.

"I'm sure," Suzi answered, laughing at Li Jung's lovesick antics. "Have a great time," she finished.

"We will. Thanks to you," Uma said as Li Jung started nibbling on her neck. Uma let out a squeal of delight. "Suz, you're my heroine!" she yelled on her way out the door.

"Kids," Jett said once Uma and Li Jung had left. Stumptown was eerily quiet. After all, the whole school was busy getting ready for the prom.

Well, the whole school, minus two.

"You want to hang out later?" Jett finally asked, slurping down the last of her cappuccino and slamming the empty cup down on the table. "How about if we work on some stuff at your place. I'll bring my guitar."

"Sounds great," Suzi said, playing with her cup and managing a weak smile.

"C'mon, Suz," Jett said, reaching out to put her hand on Suzi's forearm. "You did your best, and you've got guts, which is more than I can say about most people. Myself included," she continued, smiling gently.

"Thanks," Suzi said, feeling her smile strengthen.

"Ah, there's my girl," Jett said slyly. "There's my brave, bitchin' detective."

Still smiling, Jett stood up and threw her messenger bag over her shoulders. She then flashed Suzi the rock on sign before turning on her heavy boots and walking toward the door. Suzi watched Jett as she walked, thinking how lucky she was to have such a good friend, when suddenly, Jett whipped around, her mouth open and ready to say something.

"Look on the bright side," Jett yelled out across the almost-empty room. "At least you don't have the burden of being prom queen anymore," she laughed, before grabbing the door and pushing through it.

Suzi stared at the door long after her friend had left. Jett had a point. At least she didn't have to get up onstage tonight and receive the crown. But why had Jett chosen to use the word "burden?" That's the same word that Coach Katie had used to describe the crown, the crown of thorns, in Suzi's nightmare the other night. Strange.

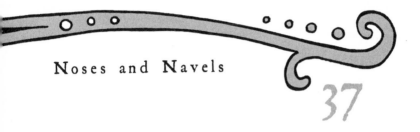

Noses and Navels

37

The sky was thundering angrily, and Suzi sat at Stumptown and stared out at the pouring rain for a good twenty minutes after Jett had left. She was just so dang tired. And hungry. And cold from her stakeout at Janitor Joe's place. It had been one helluva week, and the worst part of it all, was how everything had ended. After all of Suzi's hard work, the questioning, the following, the ducking of paint bullets, everything—the prom was just going to go on, as planned, without any closure whatsoever. The weight of this sad realization was enough to send Suzi into an exhausted stupor.

She had been so sure that it was Fiona. All of the clues had pointed right at her: the gum, the body-piercing ring, the hate for prom queens. But the janitor was a solid alibi, so clearly Suzi had missed something. Like the point, apparently.

Still looking out the window, Suzi watched sleepily as a glistening white stretch limo cruised by outside. She was sure it was full of festive prom goers on their way to the school. Gag me, Suzi thought, feeling her eyelids grow heavier as her head

slowly nodded down toward her chest. And then suddenly . . .
before she even knew what was happening . . .

Suzi was sitting in the passing white limo, with her vintage pink-lace, Betsey Johnson dress softly fluttering around her ankles. Her skin was softly scented with her favorite ginger lotion, and the sexy sounds of Marvin Gaye were pouring out from the surround speakers like perfectly aged scotch. Suzi inhaled deeply and smelled the sharp scent of real leather seats.

Suddenly, somebody's fingers are touching Suzi's shoulders, admiring their softness and pure porcelain perfection. The fingers belong to Xavier, and he's sitting only inches from Suzi, wearing a black tux with a crisp, powdery violet shirt that matches his eyes perfectly. His hair is messed, balmed, and supersexy. He looks at Suzi as if nobody else exists in the entire world, and Suzi feels her whole body succumb to his touch.

"Yee-haw! Prom, baby, yeah!" a boy's voice suddenly screamed out, right next to Suzi's ear. Apparently a group of taffeta-clad prom goers had come into Stumptown for a little preprom jolt, and they were being totally obnoxious. Suzi jerked awake, blinked her eyes sleepily, and then looked at her watch. It was almost six o'clock. She better get home before her mom started to worry, plus Jett would be coming over soon. Suzi picked her messenger bag up off the floor and was just about to collect her clues off the table, when suddenly, she saw it.

Or rather, Suzi saw her.

It was Pearl, Janitor's Joe's green-haired daughter, standing in line at the coffee counter. Pearl flicked the silver stud in her pierced tongue against her teeth and shifted her weight from one scuffed boot to another, as if she were in a big hurry to be somewhere.

Suzi studied Pearl from a distance, her choppy-chic haircut, her ripped, black Honeypot tee (that she probably stole from her dad's closet), and the thick, silver chain hanging from the back pocket of her jeans. Pearl must have felt Suzi's eyes on her, because suddenly, she shot a look over in Suzi's direction. Suzi tried to avert her gaze, but she wasn't fast enough. Pearl and Suzi's eyes had locked. And to make matters even worse, Pearl had cut out of the coffee line and was now making a beeline straight over to where Suzi was sitting.

"'Sup," Pearl asked Suzi, jutting her chin out as her way of saying hello.

"Hey," was all Suzi could say. She had to fight the inherent urge to crawl under the table and just disappear. After all, she had made a total ass of herself in front of this girl not even two hours ago.

"My dad says you play the drums," Pearl said, putting a hand in her front pocket and cocking her hip casually. As she moved, Suzi heard the sounds of her jean chains clinging and clanging.

"Uh, yeah," Suzi said, looking up at Pearl. "I love your dad's band," Suzi finished, trying to smile through her nervousness.

"My dad said that you were really nice to him, that's cool," Pearl continued, flicking her tongue stud against her top teeth. "Most of the kids at that school treat him like crap."

Suzi was almost at a loss for words. Why was Pearl being so nice to her? She must have been like, twenty, and Suzi was just a freshman in high school. Not to mention she had barged into Pearl's home and started raving like a madwoman earlier.

"About what happened at your dad's place . . ." Suzi started to say, taking a deep breath.

"I don't need to hear it," Pearl said, holding out her hand as if she were stopping traffic. "My dad filled me in; it's cool. Besides, I know that school is crazy. I went to an alternative school, thank God," she snorted, rolling her eyes.

Suzi just nodded her head. She was clearly impressed by this girl.

"Anyway, my dad said you like The Runaways." Pearl shrugged. "I have a band, The Sweets, and one of our influences is The Runaways. We're losing our drummer, so if you ever want to play with us," Pearl was saying, when suddenly, her cell phone rang out. Suzi couldn't help but notice that the ring tone was a Honeypot hit.

Pinch me, Suzi thought.

"Let me grab this," Pearl said, and Suzi just nodded. She needed the moment to peel herself off the ceiling anyway.

"Yo," Pearl answered. "I'm on my way to the show. I don't have time for this now. Schedule the nose for noon and the navel for one. Chill, Mack, chill," Pearl said firmly before slipping her phone back into her jeans pocket. "A little scheduling problem with the office," she said.

Mack? Nose and navel? Show tonight? Could this be? Suzi thought, her mind going a million miles a minute.

"Anyway, let me know, but I gotta go . . ." Pearl started to say.

"What do you do, Pearl, besides play guitar for The Sweets, that is?" Suzi quickly asked, before Pearl could slip away.

"I'm a piercing artist at this new studio on Pike Street. It's called Tattoo You," Pearl said. "The name was my idea," she finished proudly.

Pearl was just about the coolest thing since sliced bread, Suzi thought, as she sat and admired Pearl's confident body language, her competent demeanor, and her strong, yet graceful, style. It seemed as if Pearl were completely at ease with herself. She was an artist, a musician, and she was nice, and according to Suzi, it just didn't get any better than that.

Plus, once Suzi had mentioned that she had been to Pearl's studio earlier that day and had talked to Mack, Pearl had casually kicked a boot up on the chair next to Suzi's and listened intently.

"I know you're in a hurry," Suzi said, looking up at Pearl respectfully. "But I'm looking for the owner of this piece of body jewelry," she finished, picking the gold hoop off the table and holding it up for Pearl to see. Pearl took it and gave it a look.

"Sorry, but thousands of people wear these. It's a standard body ring, navel, nose, brow, whatever," Pearl said, shaking her head and handing the ring back.

"Well, can you tell me if any of your clients go to or teach at Mountain High?" Suzi asked, still hopeful.

"Except for Fiona, not off the top of my head." Pearl shrugged. "Come by the studio tomorrow and we'll talk," she finished, zipping up her leather jacket and getting ready to leave.

Suzi nodded her head and leaned back in her chair. She was disappointed that Pearl couldn't give her the answers that she wanted, but she tried not to show it. After all, Pearl had been so nice to her, and the girl did have a gig to get to.

"Hey, I have that same lipstick," Pearl suddenly said, motioning with her eyes to the silver tube lying on its side on the table. Suzi looked from Pearl to the lipstick and then back to Pearl again.

"What did you say?" Suzi asked.

"I can see the label. Crazy name, right? Prom Queen Pink." Pearl snorted, wrapping a black scarf around her neck.

Suzi felt her insides jolt. Pearl was pierced; she worked at the tattoo studio; she had access to the entire school through her dad's keys, plus Prom Queen Pink . . .

"I didn't buy the stuff, of course," Pearl added, and Suzi felt her suspicions shift. "Personally, I think the color is a little Tammy Faye." She shrugged.

"Where did you get it?" Suzi asked, giving Pearl her full attention.

"A client gave it to me. She said she didn't want it anymore, so I took it." Pearl shrugged. "I hate to waste," she finished, grabbing a hat out of her bag.

"Wait a second," Suzi interrupted. She knew she couldn't let Pearl slip away just yet. "Do you remember which one of your clients gave you this lipstick?" she asked, very slowly and very carefully.

Pearl looked up at the ceiling for a moment, flicking her tongue stud against her teeth in thought.

"I can't remember the girl's name," Pearl finally said. "But I do remember she was totally freaked out about her dad finding out she had a pierced nose. She actually asked me to pierce it so that nobody would notice. I mean, what's the point?" Pearl snorted, adjusting her scarf. "Come to think of it, the girl also bought a gold nose ring, the same type as you have there," she finished, motioning to the ring on the table.

"You can't remember her name?" Suzi asked, totally exasperated. Couldn't Pearl see that she was killing her here?

Pearl shot another quick look up at the ceiling, but then shook her head quickly.

"I'm in at noon tomorrow. We'll look at the books," Pearl said again, turning around toward the door.

Suzi slouched down in her chair. So close, yet so far away.

"Wait a minute," Pearl suddenly said, looking over Suzi's head and out the front window. "There she is right there," Pearl continued, almost laughing. "That's the person whose nose I pierced, the one that gave me the lipstick."

Suzi whipped around to see what, or who, Pearl was looking at.

Outside on the street, another white stretch limo was slowly rolling by. This one had the sunroof open, and standing up through the sunroof, laughing and dancing in the rain with their hands over their heads, were none other than Gigi Greene, Kitty Sui, Parker Peets, and Trixie Topp.

"Which one?" Suzi asked, jumping out of her chair and nearly out of her skin. "Whose nose did you pierce? Who gave you the lipstick?" she yelled breathlessly, looking back at Pearl.

"That one," Pearl said, jutting her chin toward the window. "The one in the red dress."

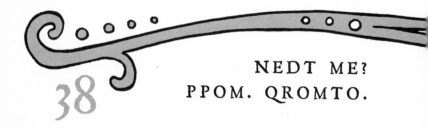

NEDT ME?
PPOM. QROMTO.

38

The wind was wicked and the rain relentless.

Suzi pedaled ferociously over the slick Seattle streets, her balloon tires slicing and hissing through the water pooling on the pavement. Her pink sneakers were soaked and slipping off the wet pedals, her black jeans were wet and heavy on her thighs, and her handlebar headlight was no match for the dark night and blinding rain, but she forged ahead. She could care less about her wet hair, her cold feet, her numb fingers, and the stripe of mucky street sludge she could feel forming up her back.

All Suzi cared about was getting to Mountain High as quickly as possible.

It was all starting to make sense, or at least as much sense as it could, considering what Suzi knew so far. It was still difficult for her to understand the why, but with Pearl's help, she believed she was finally beginning to understand the how.

The keys. The knowledge. The easy access to the inner circle. Not to mention the convenient disappearance during the Kick War game.

But the why?

No matter how much she thought about it, Suzi just couldn't nail down a good answer to that question, and she knew the only way she was going to get that answer was by confronting the culprit at the prom tonight, face to face. The thought made Suzi both nervous and excited at the same time.

Swiiissshhh!

Suzi was so in her head, she didn't notice the car that was approaching her from behind. But suddenly it rocketed past her left side, missing her bike by a hair and spitting a wall of dirty water right into her face. Suzi's eyes filled with puddles and her tires started to hydroplane. Right off the road.

Suzi landed head over heels and inside a huge bush. The bush broke her fall, as did the padding of wet, muddy earth, but she was still a little shaken. She sat up, took off her helmet, and looked down at her hands, her jeans, and her jacket. She was completely covered in mud and wet leaves. Wonderful. Suzi then looked about two feet in front of her and at her bike. Her front rim was totally bent.

It looked as if she'd be walking the last few blocks.

NEDT ME? PPOM. QROMTO.

Suzi's fingers were stiff as sticks as she stabbed at the tiny buttons on her cell phone.

MEDT ME; PPOM. PROMTO.

MEET ME @ PROM PROMTO.

Good enough, she thought, leaving a big, muddy fingerprint on the send button as she sent Jett the urgent text message. She then shoved her cell back into her soaking jeans pocket and tried to focus on keeping her legs moving as quickly as possible.

As she scurried down the halls of Mountain High on none other than the biggest, most festive night of the year, she had no choice but to parade past all the gorgeous girls in their perfect dresses and past their dapper dates in handsome black tuxes. She had no choice but to notice that while the entire school had arrived polished, perfumed, and prom-ready, Suzi had shown up soaked to the bone, messed up, leafy, and muddy.

She tried to swallow her pride as she swerved around the scrutinizing eyes and toward the main event in the gym. Suzi knew she wasn't there to impress anyone. She had a job to do, and nothing was going to stop her from doing it right this time.

Not even her apparent resemblance to the swamp thing.

Putting one wet, squeaky sneaker in front of the other, Suzi made her way around the corners and toward the gym. She stopped just short of the main entrance, gazing up at the thick, red and black streamers hanging from one corner of the doors to the other and the big poster that read, PLEASE REMOVE SHOES UPON ENTERING. ARIGATO!

Here goes nothing, Suzi thought, as she took one last breath and then dived in.

Oh. My. Gosh.

Sam had taken the boring, stuffy gym, the place where the school held its assemblies, basketball games, cheerleading try-outs, and school carnivals, and as promised, he had transformed it into a totally far out, Far East experience.

Black and red streamers bowed gracefully across every inch of the ceilings. Delicate paper lanterns hung down from the light fixtures, casting the entire gym in a soft, diffused light, and little origami rabbits and stars were dangling in each of the doorways and from the basketball hoops. Japanese paintings of clouds and mountains enlightened the drab concrete walls, and beautiful tatami mats covered the old gym floors. Knee-high tables were neatly arranged in the corners, and students sat drinking punch out of Japanese teacups while seated on bright red floor cushions. In the center of the gym, students were dancing barefoot to the amazing Asian fusion music that the DJ was playing, and everyone was staring up at the huge flat screens flashing alternating images of supercute Tokyo street fashions, painted geishas, ancient Buddhist temples, Sumo wrestlers, and delicate pink cherry blossoms.

Whoa, Suzi thought to herself, as she slowly looked around and soaked up the scene. She couldn't help but be caught up in the grandeur of it all—the decor, the music, the video show—but then, Suzi spotted the BGs standing in the far corner of the gym. Gigi, Kitty, Parker, and a few other A-list girls were huddled together in the back of the gym, next to the sushi spread, and darting their eyes around as they nibbled sushi from their chopsticks.

With a sobering jolt, Suzi remembered why she was there and what she needed to do. She started forging her way over toward the sushi table.

"Ouch!"

Suzi had been so focused on keeping her eyes on the BGs, she had accidentally sideswiped a dancing Trixie Topp.

"Oh, I'm sorry," Suzi said, grabbing for Trixie's elbow. "Are you okay?"

"Ouch," Trixie yelped again, rubbing her arm where Suzi had just grabbed her. Suzi winced at the realization that Trixie's skin still looked painfully red.

"Look what you did," Trixie whined, looking down at a wet,

brown spot on her icing-pink dress. Suzi looked down at her muddy hands. Man, she just couldn't catch a break.

"I'm sorry," Suzi said again, stepping away and trying to make her graceful exit.

"What are you even doing here?" Trixie asked as she angrily brushed at the brown spot with her hands. "No offense, but you're not exactly dressed for the occasion."

Suzi ignored Trixie as she turned and looked back toward the sushi table. Back toward where the BGs were standing and, of course, her main suspect.

But Suzi's suspect was nowhere to be seen.

Suzi quickly looked right and then left, but her suspect had somehow disappeared into thin air. Except, wait a minute. The door to the girls' locker room, right behind where the BGs were standing, was wide open.

"At least take off your shoes!" Suzi heard Trixie yell after her, as she quickly navigated her way through the dancing couples, around the shoulder-high punch fountain, over the floor pillows, and toward the back of the gym.

Suzi was heading back to where it all began. The girls' locker room.

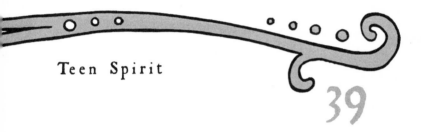

Teen Spirit

39

"Hello?" Suzi called out, taking a couple of cautious steps. The soggy squeak of her sneakers was annoying in an otherwise quiet room, so just as Trixie had asked, Suzi unlaced and continued in her wet, but silent, socks.

A dim, yellowish glow was creeping out from the showers, but other than that, every light in the place was turned off. The room was dark and riddled with shadows, offering a million different places for someone to hide. Suzi gulped nervously, but still managed to put one sock in front of the other.

She weaved around the lockers, the wooden benches, and past the utility closet. Suzi then walked past the toilets, opening each door to make sure nobody was crouched on top of the bowl, like she had been Monday in the bathroom, when she had first learned about the curse by eavesdropping on the BGs.

This time, nobody was there. The stalls were empty.

Suzi then crept down to the showers, and except for the flickering of one dirty bulb and the dripping of a wet showerhead, the showers were exempt of any signs of life. Suzi was stumped. The locker room seemed empty, but she was sure that her suspect had come in here when she was talking to Trixie.

Suzi bit her lower lip as she swept the rest of the room with her eyes. The benches were cleared, the mirrors wiped, the floors mopped, and the lockers shut tight for the weekend. Wait a minute, Suzi thought. The lockers. Maybe the person was hiding in one of the lockers, as she herself had done that day in the boys' locker room. Suzi walked over to the nearest row and started pulling.

Every single locker was tightly closed.

Suzi had just turned around to start walking back out to the gym, when suddenly, she thought she heard something. Yes, she definitely heard something. High-pitched screams, drums, and guitar riffs coming from the opposite end of the locker room.

Suzi followed the noise past the case of dusty soccer trophies, past the notice board, and past the spotless, full-length mirror. Before she knew it, she was standing with her ear pressed to the door of the gym equipment basement.

The music was grunge. Nirvana, *Smells Like Teen Spirit*. Suzi slowly opened the door and looked down the damp, dark webby stairs. She recognized those stairs, as well as the old sneaker smell, all too well.

"Hello?" Suzi yelled. Again, no answer.

Suzi slowly walked down one step at a time, stepping over the broken stair where she had found the nose ring and scissors. The music was getting louder the farther down she went, and she could see a dim light coming from somewhere.

Somebody was definitely down there.

"Hello?" Suzi yelled out again, trying to raise her voice over the music. She reached the bottom of the stairs and took a quick look around. Except for the broken parallel bars, the balance beam, and the pom-pom bag slouched against the far wall, it seemed that Suzi was alone.

But then she heard the voice again. It was a terrible singing voice, screaming over the music.

Suzi followed the screams to the back of the stairs. She cautiously peeked around the corner, afraid of what she was going to find but she also wanted to find it so badly she could taste it.

And there it was. Or rather, there she was, and it was as if everything clicked into place in that one single moment.

Under the stairs, playing a mean air guitar, whipping her long, blond hair and totally oblivious to the fact Suzi was watching her every move, danced a headbanging version of the school's most pristine player. The queen of mean, the A+ of the A-list girls, and none other than Mountain High's prom queen in waiting.

Gigi Greene.

When Gigi finally took a break to stuff a stray boob back into her strapless, she noticed Suzi standing there and froze solid and wide-eyed, like a doe in the headlights.

"What are you doing here? You're not supposed to be here . . ." Gigi spat out, her body stiff and eyes frenzied.

"Relax," Suzi said, holding her palms out to try and talk Gigi down. "It's okay," she continued.

"Get out of here or I'll tell Peasey and you'll . . ." Gigi rambled, nervously smoothing her hair and taking a step back.

"Gigi, I know everything," Suzi said, getting right to the point. She was trying to keep her voice calm and steady, but she had to yell over the music, so she ended up sounding more forceful than she intended.

"I don't know what you're talking about," Gigi said, whipping around and slapping at the boom box on the basement floor. The sounds of Kurt Cobain's wails came to an abrupt stop. "I'm just dancing," she explained unconvincingly. "Letting off some steam."

Suzi kept quiet and just stared at Gigi for a long moment. She knew she had to tread lightly here. After all, Suzi had answers (read: a confession), she needed to lure out of the Queen Bee before she could take her case to Peasey, and so far, Gigi was acting stone cold.

"Gigi," Suzi started in again, forcing a little smile. "It's okay. I know everything."

"You know nothing," Gigi snapped angrily, still smoothing her hair.

"I know you own that gold hoop I found under the stairs," Suzi said gently. "I know it's a nose ring and that you were scared of your dad finding out you had your nose pierced," Suzi explained.

The news obviously jolted Gigi for a moment, but she quickly recovered and huffed her defiance.

"I know you owned the pink lipstick that was used to write the curse notes, and I know you were in the orca uniform that attacked Kitty Sui, and that's why you locked me in the basement," Suzi continued softly. "I have proof," she finished.

A long, uncomfortable moment passed between them. Gigi nervously darted her eyes around the room, looking for a distraction, an excuse, or maybe even a quick escape.

"How dare you," Gigi suddenly said, clearly taking the intimidation route. "I'm Gigi Greene. Head cheerleader," she snorted, cocking her hip out and tossing Suzi her best ice princess glare.

Suzi just stood her ground. For the first time all week, Suzi knew for certain that she was right. Besides what Pearl had told her, Suzi could smell the foul stench of Gigi's guilt from where she was standing. Even over the smell of old sneakers.

"Gigi, it's over," Suzi said again, taking a cautious step forward.

Gigi jumped back as if she had been slapped. Her hands started shaking, the corners of her lips started twitching, and Suzi had never seen anybody's eyes look so big and scared. Suzi shifted her weight to her toes, just in case Gigi decided to make a dash for the door.

But then Gigi truly did the unexpected. Instead of lashing out or sprinting up the stairs or denying her guilt further, Gigi's entire body suddenly went limp. Like a deflating balloon, Suzi watched in awe as the Queen Bee's fight slowly leaked out of her and Gigi melted down onto the floor, her red dress pooling in the dust around her.

Gigi Greene, the most gorgeous, powerful girl in school, was suddenly splayed out and crying on the cold, damp basement floor. Looking down at Gigi's red spaghetti straps slipping off her sulking shoulders and her blond hair falling out of her perfect 'do and into her face, Suzi couldn't help but feel sympathetic.

Suzi walked over and sat down on the basement floor, too.

"The only thing I can't figure out is why," Suzi said gently.

"I tried to tell you," Gigi sobbed, and when she looked up, Suzi saw genuine tears in her eyes.

"Tried to tell me what?" Suzi asked, confused.

Gigi stared at Suzi for a long, serious moment.

"After all of your poking around, you still have no idea how hard it is to be me. To live up to everybody's expectations," Gigi said matter-of-factly. "Don't you see? Nobody cares what I want. All they care about is that they have a trophy girlfriend to brag about, a best friend to get them into all the best parties, a perfect prom queen to worship," she finished, wiping an angry tear off her face.

"But you're the most popular girl in school," Suzi said, still confused. "You can do whatever you want."

"No, you can do whatever you want," Gigi said angrily. "Everybody in school isn't scrutinizing your every move, everything you eat, everyone you hang out with, and my family?" She snorted. "All my mom talks about is 'my daughter the head cheerleader, my daughter and her boyfriend the quarterback, my daughter the prom queen," Gigi said, rolling her eyes. "You should see the party she's throwing in my honor tonight. It's sick."

The girls sat in silence for a long, heavy moment. Gigi just stared blankly in front of her as tears slowly rolled down her cheeks, and for the first time, Suzi noticed just how incredibly tired the Queen Bee really looked.

"All I want to do after graduation is throw on a backpack and take off to Italy. Do you have any idea how that went over in my family?" Gigi finally said, wiping at her wet eyes. "About as good as my pierced nose did," she sniffled, rolling her eyes at the ceiling.

"It's like I see my whole life in front of me, but it's not me living it," Gigi continued, looking at Suzi for a long, serious moment before bowing her head and breaking down again.

Suzi reached out and lightly placed her hand on Gigi's shaking shoulders. She had no idea that Gigi was so unhappy with her life. Gigi had always seemed to be so sure of herself, so beautiful, happy, and confident, but then again, so did all the young celebrities right before they checked into rehab, shaved their heads, or starved themselves skinny.

It seemed the burden of being famous, popular, or even prom queen really was too much to bear sometimes. Maybe the reign of perfection really was a crown of thorns.

"I'm sorry that you're hurting. I really am," Suzi finally said, her hand still on Gigi's back. "But I still don't understand. Why would you curse yourself and your friends?"

"I was sick and tired of being everyone's perfect little prom puppet," Gigi said, her voice squeaking. "The curse was my way out," she finished.

"You didn't want to be prom queen? Why not just drop out?" Suzi asked.

"You mean quit," Gigi said, looking at Suzi expectantly. "Not an option in the Greene family," she finished angrily.

Suzi just shrugged her shoulders.

"I thought the curse would let me back out without ruffling any feathers, you know?" Gigi explained, wiping at her eyes. "I faked my bites, wrote that note on my locker, and even cut a hole in the team's pom-pom bag so it would look like someone was out to get me. I thought people would be scared for me and just back off. But of course, that didn't happen," she said angrily.

"I had to take it a step further," Gigi continued, sniffling and shrugging her shoulders. "Give myself a bigger reason to back out."

"Parker," Suzi said, slowly nodding her head.

"Parker." Gigi shrugged again. "I feel bad, but I knew her colorist could fix it."

"But what about Kitty? And Trixie?" Suzi asked, furrowing her brow.

"I feel bad about Kitty, too. Even though she is trying to steal my boyfriend," Gigi continued, narrowing her eyes. "But Trixie? I swear, I didn't touch a hair on that girl's head. She was fried by her own means, and when she blamed the curse and everybody believed her? I thought I was finally in the clear." Gigi trailed off, shaking her head.

"But then Coach Katie was blamed . . ." Suzi started to say.

"Everything just fell apart," Gigi said, looking up at the ceiling. "Suddenly, the curse was over, and I had no excuse not to be queen. My friends were all over me, my mom called the caterer . . . the florist . . . the news stations . . ." Gigi stopped mid-sentence and started crying again.

Suzi just sat in silence and mulled over everything Gigi was telling her. It was finally making sense: Gigi didn't want to be prom queen but she felt trapped, so she cursed herself so that she could have an excuse to back out, but it hadn't been enough, so . . . Parker's blue hair, Kitty's bare butt. All the facts were falling neatly into place.

But at the same time, Gigi Greene was falling apart.

Suzi looked over at Gigi. She looked so sad and vulnerable, and while Suzi realized she finally had the answers she had been searching for all week, she also realized that solving the case didn't feel nearly as victorious as she had thought it would. Now that Suzi knew the truth, the whole truth, it was just pathetic and well, sad.

"I know what you're thinking," Gigi suddenly said, brushing

her hair out of her face and blinking the last of her tears away. "You're thinking, poor little prom queen, poor little miss popular . . ." she sniffed.

"That's not what I was thinking at all," Suzi interrupted, meeting Gigi's gaze. "I was thinking, what happened to this girl to make her think she had no way out?"

Gigi smiled and the waterworks started again, and for a moment Suzi thought she might start crying, too. But then suddenly, Suzi remembered something, and it shattered the perfect moment.

"Hey, what about me?" Suzi yelled out, furrowing her brows and standing up. "Why did you shoot at me with that paint gun and try to douse me in fish guts?" she asked, feeling her face redden.

"Believe me, I'm especially sorry about what I did to you," Gigi said quietly, staring down at the floor. "I admire you. You do whatever you want and don't care what people think," she continued. "But I'm not like you, don't you see?" Gigi asked, looking up at Suzi for a long, heavy moment. "You left me no choice."

"No choice?" Suzi fired back.

"You were on me like white on rice!" Gigi suddenly yelled out, standing up so that she was eye to eye with Suzi. The moment was tense.

"The only thing worse than lying is being caught in a lie," Gigi explained. "I was only trying to scare you. I couldn't let you find me out; my family would freak," she finished.

"But I did find you out," Suzi said.

"Yes, you did," Gigi agreed, looking at Suzi and nodding her head slowly. "Which is why I hope you forgive me for what I have to do next."

Superninja Sock Kicks

40

"Gigi, don't you dare do this again! Don't you dare leave me down here!" Suzi yelled, pounding with her fists on the basement door. Suzi was standing on one side of the door and Gigi Greene on the other.

And once again, Gigi was the only one with the key.

"Dammit, Gigi! I mean it! I'll tell Peasey everything!" Suzi yelled out again, still pounding.

"I know," Gigi said on the other side of the door. "That's why you have to stay put. I can't have you embarrassing me in front of the entire school tonight. As if being prom queen isn't bad enough, if everyone finds out what I did, I'll be ruined," Gigi whispered.

"But I'm going to tell everybody anyway," Suzi argued.

"Why? Why do you need to ruin me? You know the truth, isn't that enough?" Gigi asked.

Suzi didn't answer, but she did give the door an angry whack.

"Listen, all I need is a little more time to cover my tracks. I won't leave you down there. I promise," Gigi said.

"You said that before, Gigi! You said that before!" Suzi yelled out, but this time, Gigi didn't answer. "Gigi, are you there?" Suzi asked, pounding on the door again. Silence.

Suzi turned around and looked down the old, damp wooden stairs. The familiar feeling of being cold, scared, and locked in the spider-infested basement crept over her once again. She felt like a jerk for letting this happen a second time.

Suzi wanted to cry but she fought back the urge. She didn't have time to feel sorry for herself. She had to find a way out of there.

Tonight was the big night. Most of Mountain High, the preps, the jocks, the BGs, and the wannabes had all shown to dress up, dish out, get down, and ogle the night away at the Go Geisha! prom. Some of the geeks had even shown up to partake in the most ominous prom festivities, one of these geeks being Drexler Penn.

Drex's mom had helped him dress in a vintage black suit and a cobalt blue bow tie. Drex didn't have any shoes except for his brown loafers (which clearly didn't match, even he could tell that) and a pair of black high-top sneakers, so the sneakers had won out.

Drex was actually feeling pretty good about himself on this night. Everyone was dancing, socializing, and laughing, and he had to admit, the decorations were pretty impressive. Plus, Drex had seen Suzi. It was no big secret that Suzi was the only reason he had gelled his hair, polished his glasses, and dragged himself out from behind the computer and into this raging social scene. He had been hoping, praying even, that Suzi would be there. And she was there.

Somewhere.

Drex had seen Suzi, but only for a moment. His heart had practically skipped a beat when he saw her walk in and realized that she had come alone. But then, Drex had noticed that Suzi was covered head to toe in mud, as if for some reason, she had walked all the way in the rain. Drex had been on his way to the back of the gym to talk to Suzi and see if she was okay, when Suzi had suddenly slipped into the girls' locker room. That had been fifty-seven minutes ago, and that was the last Drex had seen of her.

He didn't know what Suzi was doing in that locker room, but he sure hoped she was okay.

One hour later, and Suzi was sitting on the top step of the stairs. She was still locked in the gym basement, and just like the first time, she was starting to get cold, really cold.

Suzi had tried everything she could think of to set herself free. She had tried to call Jett or her mom for help, but since her cell had been in her soaking wet jeans pocket, it had shorted out or something. Her phone was dead. Strike one.

Suzi had then found a stray nail on the basement floor and tried to pick at the door lock, but the nail was too thick and the lock too intricate. Suzi just couldn't finagle it. Strike two.

As a last resort, Suzi had tried kicking at the door as hard as she could, thinking maybe she could just bust it down. But since Suzi had taken off her shoes and was kicking in her socks, all that got her was an aching, throbbing foot. Strike three.

Defeated, Suzi had finally slumped over on the top step and wrapped her arms around herself for warmth.

Suzi could hear the sounds of the prom going on full-force in the gym above. She could hear the heavy bass line of the music the DJ was spinning, she could hear people cheering and screaming, and every once in a while, she could hear footsteps as someone ran across the wooden gym floor.

Some prom night this turned out to be, Suzi thought, her teeth chattering.

Suzi thought of Gigi, warm, dry, and upstairs in the gym, mingling with friends, eating sushi, and daintily sipping punch. Suzi felt her cheeks redden again, but her anger was short lived. True, Suzi was locked in the basement, but Gigi was the one that was locked in a lie.

Suddenly, Suzi heard the DJ music come to an abrupt stop and someone started talking into a microphone. It must be time to announce the prom queen court, Suzi thought. And then, the reigning prom queen.

"Yo! Suz! You in there?" a voice suddenly called out on the other side of the door. Suzi jolted in her socks and jumped up. She'd know that voice anywhere. It was Jett.

"Yes! Yes! I'm in here!" she yelled, banging on the door with her fist.

"What are you doing in there?" she heard Jett ask.

"Just get me out!" Suzi yelled back, still pounding.

"Stand back," Suzi heard someone say. It was a boy's voice. Was it . . .

"Drex? Is that you?" Suzi asked.

"Yes, and I think I can open the door, but I'm going to kick it, so stand back," Drex said firmly.

Suzi walked down a couple of steps and watched the back side of the door. She jumped as she heard one kick, two kicks, three. Suddenly the door flew open, and all Suzi could see was a shadow of Drexler Penn, all crouched down and tight like a superninja.

Suzi was most definitely impressed.

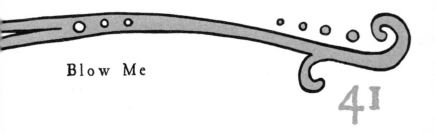

Blow Me

41

"How did you find me?" Suzi asked breathlessly, jumping up and down for warmth. She was finally on the other side of the basement door, the warm side, and standing safely in the girls' locker room with Jett and Drex.

"You texted me, remember?" Jett said, looking Suzi over from head to toe. "What happened to you? How did you get locked in the basement again? What's with the mud?" Jett fired off the questions, furrowing her brows and picking leaves out of Suzi's hair.

"I saw you come in here," Drex said, suddenly stepping up and putting his black tux jacket over Suzi's shoulders. Suzi smiled her thanks and felt herself melt into the jacket's warmth. She looked at Drex's messed up hair, his bright blue bow tie, and black high-tops. Once again, she was impressed.

"I thought you weren't going to the prom," Drex added with a shy, teasing glance.

"Yeah, well, %$#! happened," Suzi said, giving Drex a little smile.

"What happened?" Jett demanded. "Will somebody please tell me what's going on?"

"I can't get into it right now," Suzi answered, grabbing Jett by the shoulder and pushing her toward the locker room door. Out in the gym, Suzi could hear Peasey announcing the prom queen nominees and the crowd cheering and applauding. The moment was most definitely at hand. "C'mon, we don't have time!" Suzi yelled.

"Where are you going?" Drex asked, walking briskly to keep up.

"To stop this prom!" Suzi yelled, making a run for the door.

Suzi busted out of the dark, stuffy locker room and ran straight into the lights, glitz, and glamour of the Go Geisha! prom. She had to stop for a moment and blink back the brightness, but once her eyes adjusted, she noticed that all four prom queen nominees—Trixie, Parker, Kitty, and Gigi—were standing in a line up on the stage. Peasey was also onstage, standing proudly in front of the microphone and rambling on about something to do with school spirit. A spotlight shined down on all of them, and Suzi could see the nominees squirming and squinting like bugs under a microscope.

Suzi looked at Trixie in her icing-pink dress and noticed that she had a wet spot on her front where she had tried to clean off the mud that Suzi had brushed on her. Suzi then looked at Parker. In a short white dress and with her blond wig pulled back in a loose ponytail, Suzi thought Parker looked as if she had a tennis match planned after the prom. Kitty was wearing a long, silky, butter yellow dress with a dangerous slit up the side, and then Suzi zeroed in on Gigi. The Queen Bee had managed to clean herself up immaculately, and she was looking out at the crowd and smiling from ear to ear, as if the whole basement scene had never happened.

"I have to stop this," Suzi said, looking over at Jett and Drex standing next to her.

"How?" Jett asked, and Suzi watched as two students dressed in kimonos suddenly waddled out and handed Peasey a bright red pillow on which sat the pink prom queen tiara. Peasey plucked it off the pillow and held it into the light. The rhinestones sparkled and created a kaleidoscope of shimmery light.

"And now, the moment everybody's been waiting for," Peasey suddenly said into the microphone, holding the tiara for the crowd to see. Suzi felt the entire gym suck in its breath.

"This is it, "Jett said, looking over at Suzi.

"What can I do to help?" Drex asked, stepping up to the occasion.

Suzi looked at the sea of students standing between her and the stage. All she could see were rows upon rows of backless dresses and black tux jackets, but she knew what she had to do next.

"Watch Gigi," Suzi said to Drex, looking him straight in the eye. "She might make a run for it," she finished, and with that, she took off in a quick sprint.

"And Mountain High's next prom queen is . . ." Suzi could hear Peasey say, as she shoved her way through the thick crowd that separated her from the stage. People gasped and yelled and even pushed back as Suzi forged through, but she stayed on course.

"Did we have any doubt it would be anybody but . . ." Peasey continued, feeding the tension in the room.

Suzi could see the stage now, just a few more layers of prom dresses to push through and she'd be there . . .

"I give you . . . the illustrious . . . miss . . . Gigi Greene!" Peasey announced, and the crowd erupted in a frenzy of cheers. "Everybody say hello to your new queen!"

The music kicked in at a deafening level, and the spotlights and camera flashes started dancing all over the crowd. The sudden rush of moving bodies and waving limbs made it even harder for Suzi to push her way to the front, but she kept going . . . she could see the stage steps now . . . she took them two at a time . . .

"Stop the prom!" Suzi yelled out as she stumbled onto the stage.

With the loud music and cheers, nobody could hear her. Suzi could barely even hear herself.

Suzi looked around frantically, trying to get everybody's attention, but the entire crowd, everyone up onstage included, had their eyes stuck like superglue on their newly crowned queen. A swarm of crazed admirers had jumped onto the stage and quickly swarmed around Gigi, swallowing her whole. Flashes were going off everywhere, and people were jumping up and down, screaming Gigi's name and trying to get a picture or just a fleeting glance.

Amidst all the chaos, Suzi saw that the microphone was open, and she made a run for it.

"I said stop the prom!" Suzi yelled out again, and this time, everyone did hear her. The entire gym was suddenly flooded with the sounds of Suzi's voice and shrill microphone feedback. Everybody whipped their heads around and shot an angry look in her direction.

Suzi stood behind the microphone and blinked into the

blinding lights. The gym was suddenly so quiet, so still, she felt as if she were the only person in the room.

"I have something I have to tell you," Suzi continued, swallowing her nervousness. "I have some important news about Gigi," she said, doing her best to keep her voice steady.

Suzi looked into the crowd and nervously scanned the sea of expectant faces. She saw Chet glaring up at her, the football team staring at her blankly, Xavier actually winked at her, and Sam just looked at her, absolutely horrified.

"Blow me, freshman!" she heard a student yell out, and the crowd laughed.

Suzi's hands were shaking, but she tried to ignore the laughter and opened her mouth to speak. She was so ready to reveal the truth, to show the entire school she was a good detective and that she had solved the curse. She was ready to prove herself and to take Gigi down once and for all . . .

"I wanted to tell you . . ." Suzi started to say, shooting one last look over at Gigi.

But then Suzi's tongue froze in her mouth.

Gigi had been pushed to the very back of the stage and cornered by her hungry mob of fans. Everyone was hovering around her, holding a camera or a cell phone, and leaning deeply into her personal space. Some of the students even had their hands around her shoulders and on her arms, seizing the once-in-a-lifetime opportunity to have their picture taken with the queen. Suzi noticed that Gigi had shrunk as far back from the crowd as physically possible, and her tiara was slipping off her head, her red spaghetti straps were falling off her shoulders, and her hands were practically strangling the red bouquet of victory roses.

Gigi looked so scared and helpless, she reminded Suzi of a

fox that had been trapped for nothing more than its fur.

"Get off the stage!" somebody shouted again from the throes of the audience. Suzi quickly cleared her throat and leaned back into the microphone.

"I wanted to say . . ." Suzi said again, looking across the stage and straight into Gigi's wide, frightened eyes.

"Congratulations, Gigi," Suzi continued, swallowing hard and looking over at the new queen. "After everything that's happened in the last week, nobody deserves the crown more than you," she finished.

Suzi stepped away from the microphone and the crowd exploded around her. She then weaved her way across the stage, around the jumping students and the ferociously clapping principal.

"Show the girl some respect!" Suzi yelled angrily, as she pushed through the mob that encircled Gigi. Suzi shoved the frenzied students aside one by one, until she stood face to face with the prom queen.

Gigi looked at Suzi with nervous, frightened eyes, and Suzi smiled to show her it was okay. Suzi wasn't there for a confrontation, an apology, or even a picture. She just reached into her bra and pulled out the single, gold nose ring.

"I think this belongs to you," Suzi said, looking at Gigi genuinely. "I really hope you can wear it someday," she finished, and with that, Suzi turned, walked off the stage and back to her friends waiting for her in the corner of the gym.

As far as Suzi was concerned, this case was closed.

And that night at the prom, up onstage and under the spotlights, as Gigi held her victorious bouquet of red roses, her sparkly tiara glistening like a halo atop her perfect blond

locks, Mountain High's newest prom queen gave her acceptance speech as rivers of black mascara ran down her flushed
cheeks. But unlike all the other prom queens crowned across
America on that same night, Gigi's tears weren't out of joy,
excitement, or unbelated happiness.

Gigi cried out of deep and genuine sadness.

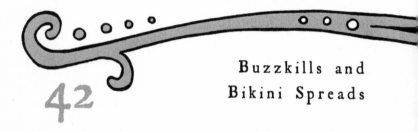

Buzzkills and Bikini Spreads

42

"Oh, man, you should have seen the look on his face. I thought he was going to pass out on the spot," Jett said, grabbing a handful of wasabi peas from the bag on Suzi's bed and picking up her guitar. Jett's Flying V wasn't plugged in, she was just playing acoustically, practicing some songs.

"I know, he looked so nervous when you asked him to dance. It was so cute," Uma chimed in while flipping through the latest Victoria's Secret catalog. "You know, I bet Drex looks good without glasses. He should totally get contacts," she finished, turning to look at Suzi. Uma was lying on Suzi's bed with her head propped on a big, fat pillow.

"Feeling any better?" Suzi asked, straining her head up and over the edge of the bed to look at Uma. Suzi was sitting cross-legged on the floor, hitting her drumsticks against her thighs to the fast beat of The Ramones' "Rock 'n Roll High School."

"I feel like a pickled mango," Uma answered, turning the page of the catalog.

"Five caramel mochas?" Suzi teased, bugging out her eyes

but staying focused on the beat of the song. "You said it your-self. Evil mix."

"Don't be such a buzzkill," Uma said, sticking out her tongue.

"Speaking of evil," Jett said, suddenly lunging at Uma and grabbing the catalog out of her hands. Uma shrieked in anger as Jett held up a page of red thong underwear for Suzi to see.

"You're evil," Uma hissed, flashing Jett an icy glare. Jett just giggled menacingly, swung her guitar off her shoulder, and started studying all the latest innovations in intimate apparel.

Suzi looked up at her friends, rolled her eyes, and went back to her drumming.

"So what's going to happen to Coach Katie?" Uma asked, propping herself up on one elbow and looking at Suzi tiredly.

"I'll show Peasey the pictures tomorrow at school. They prove she's innocent, so I imagine she'll be back and barking orders soon enough," Suzi shrugged, still drumming away.

"Just what our school needs. Another crazy person obsessed with cheerleaders or prom queens or whatever," Jett said drily, flipping a page.

"At least it keeps things interesting," Suzi said, throwing a drumstick up at Jett.

"Like how when Rider came out wearing that gold prom dress?" Uma asked, arching a perfectly waxed, black brow.

"The man has no taste in women's clothes," Jett added.

"He looked better than I did," Suzi piped in.

"What are you talking about?" Jett said sarcastically. "You looked marvelous, like Jane of the Jungle," she finished, and on cue, the three girls busted up in laughter.

Just then, there was a knock on Suzi's door.

"Hey, girls," Suzi's mom said, peeking her mop of black hair in through the crack of Suzi's door. "I made some tea. Anybody want some?"

"Heck, yeah. Thanks, Mom," Suzi answered for all of them.

"I thought you could use a little something after the week you all just had," her mom continued, walking in and placing the hot teapot on top of a paperback mystery sitting on Suzi's nightstand.

"You mean, after the week Suzi had," Jett corrected, and Suzi's mom rolled her eyes in agreement.

"C'mon. It was hard for all of us," Suzi said, looking around at her friends. "I couldn't have done it without you guys."

The entire room looked at Suzi skeptically.

"Hello?! The nose ring that I thought was an earring?" Suzi said, looking at Uma slyly. Uma sat up and beamed.

"And who saved me from the jaws of the rabid BGs like a thousand times, not to mention the basement?" Suzi continued, shooting a look in Jett's direction. Jett bowed her head, and Suzi swore she saw her friend blush.

"You guys rock," Suzi finished, giving her mom a smile and picking up her mug. The side of it read, GOOD GIRLS GO TO HEAVEN. BAD GIRLS GO TO AMSTERDAM.

"Well, I'm just glad that our little detective is back home and the prom is done and over," her mom said, giving her daughter a long, knowing glance before walking back to the door. "Enjoy the tea." She smiled, shutting the door quietly behind her.

"Done and over," Jett repeated firmly, looking at Suzi and holding up her WKPR mug for a toast.

"Here, here," Uma added, holding up her mug, which featured a picture of a mohawked Mr. T. and the words, I PITY THE FOOL! The three girls clicked their cups together and took a quick sip.

The tea was jasmine green, Suzi's favorite, and Suzi smiled as she plopped down onto her back, picked a mystery book up off her floor and started flipping through it. Uma reached for her hairbrush, and Jett put on a Joan Jett CD and resumed her bikini browsing. The girls enjoyed a deliciously amiable silence on the overwhelmingly drizzly, sulky, Sunday Seattle afternoon.

"It still sucks that the person behind this whole thing is going to walk away unpunished," Uma suddenly said, smoothing down her glossy, black hair.

"Oh, they're being punished," Suzi responded, taking a long, thoughtful sip of tea. "They're definitely being punished," she said again, nodding her head. Suzi thought of Gigi, living her life trapped inside a lie. If that wasn't due punishment, Suzi didn't know what was.

Suzi could only hope that Gigi would someday learn to like herself for who she really was, and not who she thought everybody else expected her to be.

"No way!" Jett suddenly yelled out, breaking Suzi's thoughts.

"What?" Uma asked, flipping her mop of hair over her shoulder.

"No way!" Jett said again, smiling from ear to ear.

"What is it?" Suzi asked, perking up. She couldn't help but smile along with Jett, although she had no idea what she was smiling about.

"Look!" Jett said, turning the catalog around so that Suzi and Uma could see.

Jett was looking at a full-page spread of animal-print bras

and underwear. The models were playing in the turquoise surf, somewhere tropical, Hawaii maybe.

"Ooh, I like those leopard French cuts," Uma purred, grabbing for the catalog.

"No, look," Jett huffed, pointing at one of the models and batting Uma's paws away.

"What?" Suzi asked, crawling across the floor.

Oh. My. Gosh. Suzi's jaw practically landed in her pink shag carpet.

"Is that?" Uma asked, her brown eyes bugging out of her head.

Jett nodded, and not being able to hold it in a moment longer, she exploded in laughter, spit flying out of her mouth and onto Suzi's pink bedspread.

"Watch it!" Uma screamed, leaning back.

"It's Kitty!" Jett blurted out, shoving the catalog in Suzi's face.

Suzi nodded, but she really wasn't looking at the picture of Kitty doing her best come hither in nothing but foamy surf and a leopard string bikini.

Suzi was looking at the model on the opposite page, the zebra-themed page. She was studying the beautiful, dark-haired model playing in the waves and wearing a zebra-print bikini. The model was laughing and looking straight at the camera.

The picture was the exact same one that Suzi had seen framed and sitting on top of Peasey's desk. The photo that Suzi had accidentally knocked over. The photo that Suzi had thought was of Peasey's beautiful wife.

That sly dog, Suzi thought. Peasey, along with everybody else at school, sure was full of surprises.

"I can't believe Kitty is modeling for Victoria's Secret," Uma said, grabbing the catalog out of Jett's hands and eyeing the picture hungrily. "How do you think she got that gig?" she asked.

"Don't ask me," Suzi said slowly. "The only thing I know for sure is that I have a lot to learn about people," she finished, pouncing onto the bed. Jett scooted over, Uma patted the space beside her, and Suzi snuggled right in.

"Now where is Kitty's bikini spread?" Suzi asked, eyeballing the catalog.

"Pun intended?" Jett asked, slowly raising one red brow.

At first, Suzi didn't get it. She had no idea what Jett was talking about. But slowly, a smile spread across her face. A smile that proved as contagious as it was clever.

Once again, and definitely not for the last time on that dark, cold afternoon, the three girls looked at one another and then simultaneously erupted in laughter.

For no other reason than they could.